Trust
in the
Fallen

Forbidden Pleasures series

Montana Fyre

Trust
in the
Fallen

A Dark MFM *Age Gap* Romance

Forbidden Pleasures

Montana Fyre

ISBN (Paperback) : 978-0-6459052-1-2

First edition, 2023.

Front cover design by Montana Fyre

Book design by Montana Fyre.

Edited by My Brother's Editor.

www.montanafyre.com

Acknowledgments

It's no secret that I love a why choose book, and for a long time I've wanted to take the plunge and write one. The problem? Being both author Montana and personal Montana, plus whatever two characters I'm writing at any one time... that's a lot of minds to be swapping between.

So I decided to test the waters. I decided to write a MFM romance, thinking it would be a quick smutty read and a break from writing super dark romance. Let's just say that is not what this turned out to be.

This book is angsty and heartbreaking, the story of three people who think they've fallen too far to ever trust again. Their characters evolved so naturally on the page, they became exactly what the others needed, and their ending is one of my favorites that I've ever written.

Thank you to my wonderful husband who supports me, loves me, and puts up with my crazy ass. You're some kind of wonderful and I'm grateful to have you by my side through this crazy journey.

Thank you to my incredible editor who takes such good care of my book babies even when there's so much going on in her own life. You're a star, Ellie.

Thank you to every single reader who has ever picked up one of my books. To those who take the time to reach out to talk about the characters you've fallen in love with, and to everyone who has been along this journey with me. I've forever grateful and in awe of you.

To my friends and family who have always believed in me, thank you for your constant love and support. I couldn't do this without you.

And to the Montana of the past, thanks for believing in us enough to put yourself out there. Without you, there's no way we'd be publishing our tenth book in 3 years and I certainly wouldn't have been able to follow my dreams and become a full time author.

Trigger Warning

This book contains dark themes that some readers may find distressing, including, but not limited to:

Violence

Elements of BDSM

Domestic Violence

Kidnapping

Attempted SA

Other themes which readers may find distressing.

Reader's discretion should be applied.

For the girls who think they might need two morally grey men to keep up with them. Here's all the proof you need.

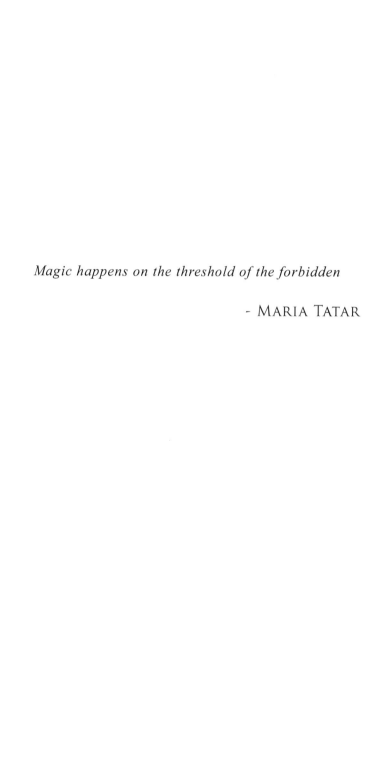

Magic happens on the threshold of the forbidden

- MARIA TATAR

PROLOGUE

WYATT

I tear my bloody shirt over my head and throw it on the couch in the middle of the office I share with my best friend.

What a fucking night.

Bishop collapses into the seat next to my shirt and runs a hand through his messy blonde hair restlessly. His green eyes that normally sparkle with mischief are cold and devoid of their normal character. This shit is starting to weigh on all of us.

Our partnership was only ever meant to be in extreme circumstances, but we didn't expect shit to start getting as messy as it has the last few months, and now they need our help more often than not.

It's not easy being the mediator for the five families, and while they managed it on their own for a long time, the day we came to an agreement and started helping them in the shadows, I swear Crew immediately started sleeping better.

That man leads the underbelly of this city with ease, but I'm pretty sure he started breathing a little easier when he and his men had more help and some neutral territory to meet on.

"Well, that was fucked." Kaos leans against the wall, his hands covered in cuts and bruises. The scars littering his skin are on display despite his usual efforts to cover them. He towers over the rest of us even when he's not standing up straight. I don't know that I've ever seen his dark eyes as dejected as they are right now. Flecks of blood and God knows what else are speckled through his dark hair. Tonight was messy.

"I've never seen anything like that." Elias, my best friend, falls into the seat behind his desk, shoving his dark hair from his eyes. "Who the fuck brought those girls into the city? And how did you not have any idea it was happening?" He turns his dark eyes to Crew as he strolls into the room, the only one of us with his suit still pristine.

His mismatched eyes turn to each of us as if we hold the answers, but we're all just as stumped as one another. He runs his fingers through his copper hair just the way his son had when he came in. They may not look alike, but their mannerisms are almost identical if you watch them closely enough.

"Fuck if I know." He sighs. "But we'll get to the bottom of it. If any of the five families think they're going to start trafficking in our city, they have another thing coming, and they will quickly be removed from their roles."

"And this earth," Kaos mutters.

The Legion has kept the skin trade out of New York since they took over ten years ago, but it seems there's someone new on the scene who has other plans.

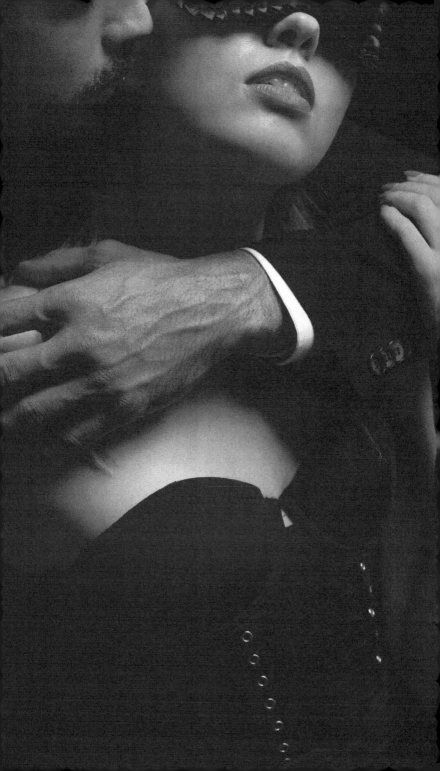

ONE

ELIAS

Halloween has always been a big night at The Scarlet Lounge. It's just another excuse for the subs to attract a Dom for the night, and the Doms to find a nice little subbie to enjoy. It's always been one of my favorite nights of the year.

The costumes, the palpable tension in the air, the extra kinky scenes. It all culminates into one big, irresistible package, but this year feels different. Almost as if something is missing.

Even as Wyatt and I put the final touches on the event, making sure our members get the exclusive experience they pay big money for, the anticipation I've felt for the last ten Halloweens, since we bought the place, just isn't there.

It's one of the rare nights we allow the outside world in, but the only way you know this place exists is by knowing a member, so we don't tend to see too many unfamiliar faces. It's also one of the rare nights we have all our members in, almost all of them making themselves available for their favorite event of the year.

Wyatt eyes me curiously as I approach him, probably sensing my mood. We've been friends, brothers even, for so many years we may as well be the same person. We live together, eat together, work together, and for the most part, fuck together.

That's our thing, our kink some may say. We love to share. There's nothing better than dealing out double the pleasure, and if the mood strikes us, double the pain, to a willing sub.

But it's been a while since someone has piqued our interest. Perhaps that's why I'm feeling so bored on my favorite night of the year.

"You look like you'd rather be anywhere but here," Wyatt comments, his blue eyes watching me closely. His lean body is covered by a superhero costume, a character I vaguely remember from a movie he made me see with him last year. I barely stop myself from rolling my eyes. He's the carefree one, the one who laughs off every problem we come across. It seems fitting that he dresses like this for Halloween.

I shrug, leaning against the bar beside him. Abigail, the waitress on duty tonight, saunters toward us, her hips swaying suggestively. All the staff here are members. When we first opened, it was hard to find staff when so many people find the kinds of things that happen here taboo. This policy ensures everyone here knows exactly what's happening, and there are no misunderstandings about the parameters of their job. Of course no one has a right to touch the staff without their permission, but the subs here are required to show the Dominants a certain level of respect.

"Sirs," she greets, her eyes lowered respectfully. "Would you like something to drink?"

I take a moment to survey the woman in front of me. She's worked for us for a few years, and Wyatt and I have scened with her in the past, but it's as if I'm seeing her for the first time.

Her dark hair is slicked back into a sleek ponytail. Her makeup is dark, and her eyeliner makes her eyes look sharp, like a cat's. A skintight black spandex suit clings to her shapely frame, and the ensemble is completed with a pair of knee-high leather boots and cat ears perfectly positioned on her head.

"Whiskey please, Abigail." Wyatt smiles before looking at me. "Make that two."

She nods once before turning on her heel and heading behind the bar.

"Okay, what's going on?" he asks, leaning his elbow on the bar and turning his body to face me.

I've never lied to my best friend before, and I don't intend to start, but the problem is, I don't know what's going on with me, and I don't know how to tell him it feels like something is missing. We've been in the same routine for so many years, it feels monotonous, and the shit with the Legion certainly isn't helping my mood.

"I don't know." It's as honest as I can be without hurting him. Wyatt is the sensitive one. He takes things personally, and if I tell him I'm bored, he'll think it's him I'm bored with. His ex-wife, like my own, fucked him up, but he wears his heart on his sleeve, and I have to be conscious of his feelings.

His brows knit together, and his lips tip into a frown. "You've never lied to me before, brother."

I sigh and rub my hand down my face. "Do you ever feel like there's something missing?"

He watches me closely for a moment, but where I expect to see hurt, I see interest. "Something like what?" he asks carefully.

"That's what I don't know," I tell him, my eyes flicking around the lounge area, as if it may present me with the answers to all my questions, but the black and crimson setting leaves me with nothing.

"Your drinks, Sirs," Abigail says softly, and a tray appears in front of us.

Wyatt smiles softly at her and reaches into his pocket, drawing out a few bills and placing them on the tray before taking both drinks. "Thank you, Abigail."

A soft blush appears on her pale cheeks before she disappears across the room to serve the other members, and Wyatt hands me my drink.

"I do," he says.

"You do what?" I turn my attention back to him, and he gives me a knowing look.

"I know what our lives are missing."

TWO

WYATT

My best friend stares at me through deep-brown eyes expectantly, as if I hold all the answers. I can't offer him the answers to all the world's questions, but I can tell Elias what the gaping hole in our lives is. He's not going to like what I'm about to say, and there's every possibility he's going to deny it, but that's only because he's the stubborn one.

I've often likened us to yin and yang. He's hard and stoic, while I prefer to live my life with a smile on my face. Even when we scene, I'm the soft one. I comfort the sub and give aftercare while Elias dishes out the punishments.

"We need a woman," I tell him.

He sighs and rolls his eyes. "You think we need to scene? That's your answer?"

"No." I shake my head. "We need a girlfriend, someone for us to love and nurture and who will complete us." It's been weighing on me for the last few months, the need to add the missing piece to our puzzle growing with each day that passes.

Elias and I have lived as bachelors almost the entire time we've known one another. It worked for us when we were fresh out of marriages we were miserable in, but we've healed. We're not the same men we were back then. We've moved on from the women in our past, and it's time we stopped letting the sins of two people dictate our futures. Not just to fuck a sub every once in a while, but to fall in love again.

Elias laughs, the sound strong and confident as it erupts from his chest. "You've lost your fucking mind."

"No, I haven't. You think there's something missing, and I can tell you exactly what it is. Whether you want to believe me now, or you want to figure it out on your own, I can guarantee you that you will come to the same conclusion." I've found that sometimes it's better to allow my stubborn best friend to realize things himself, but I'm not patient enough for that right now. Not when I realized what our missing piece was months ago, and each day we don't find them is a day too long. He may not have realized it, but we've both been getting progressively more miserable, and I don't know how much more of it I can handle.

"We agreed a long time ago that we didn't want a permanent woman in our lives, that they cause more trouble than they're worth. And even if I was willing to entertain your absurd idea, it's not safe while we're working with the Legion."

I nod. "I did say that, you're right. But it's been ten years, Elias. We can't allow Beck and Casey to ruin our lives anymore. We need to move on with our lives, and it's time we consider what our futures are going to look like. Do you want to get old and gray with only me?" I scoff. "Wouldn't you rather have a woman in our lives? One who we can take care of? Maybe even have a kid or two? Doesn't that sound better than a lonely eternity?" I know which life I prefer the sound of. But the reality is, I won't abandon my best friend. If he decides this isn't something he wants, if he decides he wants to remain an eligible bachelor for the rest of his life, then I'll be right there beside him.

Elias opens his mouth to respond when Alexander, one of our dungeon supervisors, approaches us with worry etched into his brow. "I think we may have a problem," he says.

"What is it?" I ask, placing my drink down on the counter so I'm ready to jump into whatever situation requires my attention. As I'm sure you can imagine, owning a sex club can be a lot of fun, but despite all the safeguards we put into place, there are always issues. Doms who don't listen to the rules, subs who get too deep into sub space and can't be pulled back out by whoever they've scened with. If I'm honest, it's the issues that brighten my day. They give me purpose in a life that has become mundane.

"There's a bit of an issue in the front bar." His eyes flick over his shoulder, and I'm jumping into action before I'm conscious of it.

I give a few polite smiles and hellos on my way past, but don't slow down enough to hear anyone's response. Elias is on my heels, his need to protect kicking in. It's an old habit from when we were SEALs. He feels the need to protect and serve despite having been out of the service for such a long time.

Raised voices catch my attention as we step foot into the front bar. If I had to hazard a guess, this is where a lot of the guests will stay tonight. Most people don't like to venture into the club on their first time here because it's overwhelming. There are subs tied to the Saint Andrews Cross being whipped, and women on their knees for their Doms. It's a lot to take in if you're not familiar with the lifestyle or if you're just looking to dip your toes in.

"I wish I could say I'm surprised you would do this, Jason," a feminine voice snaps. "But honestly, I'm not."

"Please, Leighton, you don't understand."

"Which bit don't I understand? The bit where you're the member of a sex club I've never visited with you? Or the part where you were dry humping another woman in a public place? Because honestly, both bits look pretty damning for you."

The moment the woman comes into my line of sight, the air is sucked from my lungs. A short white dress clings to her luscious curves, and white stockings reach the middle of her thigh. Sparkly silver pumps adorn her feet, and a full pair of angel wings complete her costume. But it's not her barely there outfit that catches my attention.

No. There's something about the angel that holds me captive from the first glance. Perhaps it's her thick brown curls, or the amber eyes I caught a quick glimpse of, or maybe it's how she holds herself with poise despite being in an unfamiliar place where she's just found who I can only assume is her boyfriend with another woman.

I can't put my finger on it, but from the moment I lay eyes on her, I know she's the missing piece of our puzzle.

Our angel.

Trust in the Fallen

THREE

LEIGHTON

I don't know what I expected when I found the invitation in Jason's pocket last week while organizing his washing to go to the dry cleaner, but this certainly wasn't it.

Of course, I could have just asked him what it was when I found it, but he would have lied to me. After all, that's what cheaters do. They lie and cheat, anything to get ahead in this world, and I always suspected that was Jason's only interest in being with me.

I am the police commissioner's daughter, and he's always wanted to go to Washington. Ever since we were kids, all he's been able to talk about is following in his father's footsteps, and I've been the poor sucker who was tagged to help him get there.

I wouldn't quite call our relationship an arranged marriage, but it's as close as one can be without crossing that line. Our parents made a deal a long time ago, an agreement that followed a mistake I'll never be able to forget. Two kids from well-respected families coming together to unite into an unbreakable force. I've put off actually marrying him for the last three years, always using the excuse of college to push the date back, but on graduation day I finally had to say yes. Not that we'll be getting married now.

I stare at my now ex-fiancé with distaste, barely able to spare the poor woman he was basically mauling. She's dressed as a nurse I think, something equally as tacky as I am, but she's pretty. I can see why Jason would go for her. She's much thinner than I am, and just generally more attractive I suppose. Her bleach-blonde hair and piercing blue eyes almost make her seem like a doll. Like I said, I get it.

Jason is objectively attractive. High cheekbones and a perfectly chiseled jawline. Dark eyes and hair that put him in the tall, dark and handsome category that women find so desirable. It helps that he spends an hour in the gym every day and takes care of himself. He also doesn't let me forget that fact and reminds me every chance he gets that I could stand to lose a few pounds.

"Leighton, can we go somewhere to talk? You're making a scene."

"I'm making a scene?" I laugh, allowing my head to drop back as the vibrations make their way through my body. He's always been a little delusional, but Jesus, this is bad even for him. "You don't think that dry humping a nurse in a bar is making a scene? Were you going to fuck her out here in the open, too?"

His gaze darkens. "You know I don't like it when you swear."

"I don't like it when you fuck other women, but here we are."

18

I shrug. I'm fully aware of the audience we're gathering, and I'm quietly smug at the negative attention he's going to get because of this little ordeal.

A gentle hand brushes across my bare shoulder, and I startle. I didn't expect anyone to touch me here, not in the open like this. If I'm honest, I don't like physical touch. Perhaps it's because I was starved of it as a child, or maybe it's because Jason is the only one to have touched me in years, and even then it's been sparse.

"It's okay, Angel. I won't hurt you," a velvety voice says from beside me. "Why don't you step into my office to take a breath and calm down? It's better to have these conversations with a clear head."

I turn around, ready to tell this guy to fuck off. I've never been one to swear. My parents would kill me if they could hear me now. But when the man comes into my field of vision, my words die before they can roll off my tongue.

I have to crane my neck to look him in the eye, and each inch of hard muscle I take in is more defined than the last. When I think I can't find this perfect stranger any more attractive, I meet his kind blue eyes. The breath I was about to take catches in my throat.

Holy hell.

He's older than Jason and me, probably by abiyt fifteen years, but that doesn't make him any less attractive. His dirty-blonde hair is carefully styled, and he's dressed as a superhero I can't identify. I've never watched much TV. My mother used to call it a waste of brain cells and would reprimand me anytime she caught me watching it as a child. Jason wouldn't even allow us to get one when we moved in together after college, so all the nights he spends at the office, or at clubs like this, are spent in a silent house, alone.

"Get your hands off my fiancée!" Jason pushes the nurse from his lap and stands, but his lean muscle is nothing compared to my hero, and just to rub salt in the wound, he's several inches shorter.

My hero raises a brow and glances behind him, shining a look of disbelief at whoever stands there. "Your fiancée? I don't want to put words in the lady's mouth, but I have a feeling you'll be adding ex to that title."

Jason glares at him and reaches for me. He grasps my wrist in a punishing hold and tugs me toward him. The sudden move causes me to lose my footing, and my ankle slips in my heel, snapping to the side and sending excruciating pain through my leg.

"Leighton, you're embarrassing me," Jason snaps, pulling me upright, and when my weight settles on my foot, I let out a pained yelp.

My hero steps forward and reaches for me, worry etched into his brow. "Are you okay, angel?" he asks, his gaze flicking between me and Jason like he's trying to anticipate our next move.

Tears spring to my eyes as Jason's fingers dig further into my wrist. He's always been controlling, but he never laid a hand on me until a few months ago. I shake my head, keeping my eyes on Hero to make sure he sees my answer.

Just as he opens his mouth to respond, a large man in a tight black t-shirt that stretches impossibly over his biceps steps up to us. "Hands off the lady," he rumbles.

Jason's eyes widen as they move toward the monster of a man in front of us. "She's my fiancée," he defends.

"I don't care. You're hurting her."

Jason looks down at where he's holding my wrist and the way I can't put any weight on my foot before he surveys the crowd who have gathered around us, taking stock of how much damage he's done to his precious reputation. Maybe he should have thought about that before he cheated on me.

His hand loosens around my wrist, and I immediately step out from his reach. Somewhere among the chaos, I forgot about the excruciating pain in my ankle, and the moment my foot hits the ground, my leg buckles beneath me.

Like my night couldn't get any worse. Like my fiancé coming to a sex club behind my back and dry humping a naughty nurse where the world could see wasn't bad enough. Now I'm going to fall flat on my face in front of all these people, who have already watched my life fall apart.

The red and black patterned carpet races toward me, but before my body hits it, strong arms wrap around me, and warmth surrounds me a moment later.

FOUR

WYATT

This guy is a fucking asshole.

First, he has the audacity to tell my angel she's embarrassing him when he's the one caught with his pants down. Then, when I'm sure I can't hate him any more than I already do, he lays his hands on her.

If Brodie wasn't handling it, I would have already stepped between them and removed his hands from my angel, but if there's one person in this building who can diffuse a situation, it's our head of security. Plus, he's intimidating as hell, and I would be lying if I said I wasn't enjoying watching this idiot squirm.

The moment he releases her wrist she takes a step toward me, but I can't allow myself to hope she feels it, too. That's a bridge I will cross when I come to it, which will be right around the time I convince Elias that she's the one. When her foot hits the floor, agony crosses her face, and she stumbles.

I step forward and catch her, and the moment her weight

settles in my arms, something slips into place that I hadn't realized I was missing. She fits right into the empty place I realized I had all those months ago, and I'm not sure how I'm ever going to let her out of my arms again.

Carefully, I slip an arm under the back of her knees and hold her against my chest, allowing myself to breathe in her sweet scent. She smells like strawberries and vanilla, an intoxicating combination I could very easily find myself addicted to.

Her eyes clash with mine and the moment takes my breath away. I can barely breathe through the emotions that slam into me.

A small gasp catches in her throat, but she doesn't take her eyes off me, as if she's as entranced by our connection as I am. "You should put me down. I'm too heavy to hold like this."

"Who told you that?" A low growl hangs between us as the last word leaves my mouth. She's anything but heavy in my arms. In fact, her weight settles the part of me that has always been adrift.

She glances over her shoulder at her asshole fiancé, or ex-fiancé now I assume. It takes every bit of strength I have not to tighten my hold on her luscious body, to keep my hold on her gentle despite the anger raging through my veins.

"Get your hands off my fiancée," Jason shouts, taking quick steps toward us and reaching for my angel, but I quickly turn my body as Brodie grabs a hold of him.

"It's time for you to go," the guard says calmly.

"Not without Leighton," he snaps.

Leighton. My angel's name is Leighton.

I meet Elias's intrigued gaze right before his eyes flick to the angel in my arms. There's something in the depths that tells me he sees what I do when he looks at her. He sees who she is to us despite only having just met her. It's not rational, and because of that, he's going to fight it. I've known him long enough to know that if something doesn't make perfect sense, he rebels against it with everything he has. But I won't let him this time. Not when the stakes are so high.

Brodie turns his attention to Leighton and me, his brows furrow as I turn her slightly. I've never felt so protective over anyone before. Not even when I was a SEAL did I feel this kind of raw sense of duty. "Do you want to go with him, Leighton?" he asks softly. He's the perfect guard for this place. Soft with the subs, hard with the Doms when they need it.

She shakes her head against my chest, allowing herself to relax into my hold, and fuck me if it's not the most wonderful feeling in the world to be needed. "No. I don't want to go with him," she whispers. She wiggles the huge diamond from her finger and throws it in the asshole's general direction.

"You fucking bitch," Jason growls, surging toward us, but Elias steps in front of me, his huge stance blocking the path.

"I suggest you get out of my club before I remove you myself." His voice is low and menacing, and I've only ever heard that kind of anger in his tone once before, when his ex-wife left him for his cousin.

"You'll be back, Leighton. You need me. You're too fucking useless to live on your own. That's why your parents basically handed you to me on a silver fucking platter. They knew no one else would want you." His words are vicious, and she trembles in my arms at the anger in his tone. He's scaring her.

"Get out!" Elias roars, repositioning his body so she's completely protected from Jason's view.

I wonder if he knows he's doing it, or if his body is moving of its own accord the way mine has been.

"She has nowhere else to go, she'll come crawling back to me once she realizes that," Jason hisses before storming across the bar and slamming the doors open on his way out.

That's where he's wrong.

My angel has just found exactly where she belongs. With us.

FIVE

ELIAS

Barely-contained rage crackles through my veins, begging to be set free.

I thought I knew anger. I've felt it enough times, but all those moments were nothing compared to right now. The way that asshole spoke to his fiancée, to the woman who looks almost too at home in my best friend's arms, it's incomprehensible.

I watch as he leaves before allowing my eyes to brush over the crowd gathered around us. It's not the first time our members have seen us throw someone out for their piss poor behavior, but it's the first time Wyatt and I have been so…protective.

The instinct is as foreign as it is natural. I wasn't like this with my ex-wife. Hell, it might just be the reason she left me. But with her, with this perfect stranger, I'd throw my body on the line to keep her safe.

The feeling is unexpected, and if I were a man who believed in fate, perhaps this is what it would look like. How else can I explain how right my best friend looks with her in his arms?

We've shared a lot over the years, but never have we felt complete.

Not like right now.

"Let's take you to my office and check on your ankle," Wyatt murmurs, his voice soft so as not to spook her.

Her amber eyes are still wild and unsure from her altercation with her fiancé...ex-fiancé, if we have anything to say about it.

Wyatt's entire being changed the moment he caught sight of her. He's never been overly possessive. After all, he's shared every woman he's been with over the last decade, but by the look in his eyes, he needs to get her out of here, get her away from the prying eyes of members. His new possessive instincts are too much for him to handle.

"Nothing more to see here," I bark and don't miss the way Leighton flinches. I take a breath, trying to calm my erratic heartbeat as I turn to Brodie. "I want his membership revoked. If he ever steps foot in this club again, I want to be notified, and I want the police called immediately."

"Yes, boss."

My eyes find the naughty nurse who was caught red-handed playing the role of the other woman and a fresh wave of anger crashes down on me. I vaguely recognize the leggy blonde from around the club, but she hasn't been around for long, and I have a feeling her time as a member is short-lived.

"Did you know he was engaged?" I rumble.

She gives me a small nod, her eyes flicking from me to

Leighton and back again.

It takes every ounce of willpower not to step in front of Wyatt and protect her from the woman who has just played a part in tearing her entire life apart. "You can leave, too."

I turn before she can respond, briefly meeting Brodie's eyes to ensure he understands what he needs to do, but I don't stick around for long. I have other things to take care of. A woman who has sparked the part of me that I thought would always lay dormant.

My heart.

SIX

LEIGHTON

The more time I spend in this stranger's arms, the more it feels like home.

I know that sounds insane, and if you told me this was possible even a few hours ago, I would have laughed in your face. Because this kind of connection is the kind you read about in books and see in rom coms. They're not real.

And yet the way I feel in his arms feels suspiciously like that.

The other man, the one who kicked Jason out of the club and looked like he was one breath away from tearing my fiancé apart, trails behind us, but I can feel him, too. The distance between us and the fact we've never so much as touched doesn't seem to matter. He's still set my body alight regardless.

On any other day, I wouldn't allow strangers to touch me, let alone carry me through what I am quickly realizing is some kind of sex club, but I suppose it's not every day your fiancé cheats on you with a naughty nurse on Halloween and proceeds to assault you in front of a group of strangers.

There's a first time for everything.

I bury my face in the man's chest, unable to look at the depraved things happening around me. The moment my eyes lock with a woman tied to what looks like a cross, her body completely bare and red marks covering her creamy skin... that's the first and last thing I see before I squeeze my eyes shut and will the images away.

I've only ever read about places like this, and I certainly never thought they actually existed. Except now I'm in one, and I'm only being carried further into the belly of the beast. And yet, I can't find it in me to ask the man to put me down, or to turn around and take me back to the safety of the bar where at the very least everyone was clothed.

The man whose arms I've found myself in draws gentle circles on the bare flesh of my thigh, and each pass of his thumb sends another shiver through my body. I hope he thinks I'm cold, because him knowing how he affects me is a bad idea.

It's not until one of his hands disappear from my skin and I hear a door open that I finally look around again. I take in the space around us, the same red and black color scheme that runs through the bar and club continues through what appears to be an office.

Two large mahogany desks are set up at each end of space, and in the center is a large, leather couch. I wonder what happens in here. Is it used purely for business purposes? Or do other things happen in here? Is this where these men bring women when they want to be alone? Is that what they expect of me?

Panic flares to life in my chest. How could I be so stupid to allow these men to take me to a locked office where they could take advantage of me? And who would come to my rescue?

"It's okay, angel," the man holding me murmurs against my cheek, his breath whispering across my face. "You're safe here."

"I'm sure serial killers say that all the time."

The other man chuckles as the door clicks shut behind us. "Have you met many serial killers, Leighton?" he asks.

"That depends on how many people the two of you have killed."

The man holding me shakes his head, a broad smile spread across his handsome face. My hero looks like just that. Even without the costume, he gives off those vibes, and I find myself wanting to know more about him.

"Sit her on the couch," the other man says gruffly, crossing the room and squatting down behind one of the desks.

Part of me is disappointed at the thought of my hero putting me down, of losing the warmth and comfort he offers, but it's probably for the best. He's clouding my judgment. His scent, his smile, his good looks, it's all working against me, and the smart thing to do would be to get as far away from these men as I can manage. But when my hero lowers us both onto the couch, sitting me on his lap and repositioning me so my feet are resting on the pillow beside us, I don't have a chance to miss him. This position is more intimate somehow, and I'm not entirely sure I like it.

The other man reappears carrying an ice pack and a first aid kit, settling some of the panic coursing through my veins. Maybe they are just being nice guys and looking after me. He squats down in front of us, his eyes brushing over my outfit. When I found the invitation in Jason's jacket the other day, I suspected something was amiss. In fact, I've suspected it for a while. He gets home late, leaves early in the morning, and he's been more distant than usual. Not that he's ever been particularly warm.

But I wanted to give him the benefit of the doubt. After all, I have no choice but to make our relationship work. If my parents get word of me leaving Jason, all hell will break loose, and that's a storm I don't want to weather. So I got all dressed up in this too-short costume, that hugs all the curves Jason and my mother insist I try to lose before the wedding. At first I thought maybe it was a work event, but the moment I stepped foot inside the bar that reeked of sin, I knew I wasn't going to like whatever I was about to see.

"You don't need to be frightened," my hero says softly. "We're just going to have a look at your ankle and see if you need to go to the hospital."

"I don't need to—" I start to argue.

"That will be my call to make, pretty girl," the gruff one interrupts.

"I don't even know your names," I snap.

My hero chuckles. "Would it make you more comfortable if you knew a bit more about us before he starts poking and prodding?" Fire flashes through his eyes at his own words, but I can't quite work out why.

Perhaps it's because I've lived such a sheltered life, but I find myself nodding anyway.

"Very well." He smiles. "I'm Wyatt, and this is my best friend and business partner, Elias. We own this club."

My eyes widen. Lord. I really am in the lion's den. Because surely if you own a club such as this, marketed to people's most base instincts, you have to have some of your own.

"This place isn't that scary," he assures me. "Now, Elias here has some medical training from when he was a SEAL. Can he please have a look at it?"

I look between them, the sincere look on Wyatt's face and the fierce determination on Elias's as his eyes flicker from my face to my rapidly swelling ankle. Since I was lifted in Wyatt's arms, I hadn't paid much attention to the screaming agony radiating down into my foot and up through my leg, but I'm feeling it now.

I give a small nod, and he gets to work immediately. First he carefully unclasps the buckle around my ankle, his large fingers working delicately to ensure he doesn't hurt me. I can't tear my eyes from his movements, because they seem so unnatural for a man of his size. Even squatting beside the couch, he towers over me, and an image of him moving over me flickers into my mind. His hard body brushing against my soft one. His huge hands gripping on to my hips and leaving marks on my creamy skin.

Where the heck did that come from? A deep blush spreads across my cheeks, and when I look up at Wyatt he gives me a knowing look that makes my core heat.

I'm in so much trouble.

SEVEN

WYATT

I readjust Leighton in my lap as my cock grows harder against her perky ass.

Jesus, I can't remember the last time my body reacted to a member of the opposite sex like this. I've fucked so many women, especially in recent years, and I've enjoyed every single one. But I haven't felt a pull like I am right now.

When I brought her into our office and the idea of no longer having her in my arms settled over me, I panicked. Because this woman doesn't know us, and there's every possibility in the world that she's going to leave at the end of the night, and we're never going to see her again.

The horror on her face when we passed Hannah on the St Andrew's Cross and the way she buried her face into my chest for the rest of the way tells me she isn't cut out for this life, and can Elias and I live without it? We've been in the scene for so long it's become part of us, and I have a feeling my best friend wouldn't be willing to give it up for anything.

"I'm sorry, I must be hurting you." Leighton pushes against my chest, trying to slide from my lap and onto the cool leather.

I wrap my arms tighter around her middle, not willing to put even an inch of space between us. "Stay where you are, angel," I rumble.

"But I'm obviously hurting you," she argues.

"Not in the way you think," I murmur, pressing a kiss into her bare shoulder. As soon as I do it, I know I shouldn't have, but there's something so natural about holding Leighton. Having her in my arms is like finding the missing piece of our puzzle, and I'm willing to do just about anything to keep her exactly where she is.

Elias's eyes flash to mine, an amused smirk playing on his lips as he tugs the ridiculous heel from her foot. When she's ours, she won't be risking herself with such high heels. Not unless we're around to carry her so there's no chance of her hurting herself.

His fingers brush down her calf, and she stills in my arms. She's like a deer in headlights. She doesn't quite know what to do, and more often than not her reaction is to freeze. "You might want to hold on to Wyatt, pretty girl. I need to test your movement, and it's going to hurt like a motherfucker."

Fear crosses her eyes, and the protective side of me I've only ever known during my time in service flares to life again. The thought of her being hurt or scared makes the caveman inside me start beating his chest, demanding to be set free.

I move one of my hands from around her waist, making sure I still have a good grip on her with the other and carefully pull her face around to meet mine. We're so close her breath whispers across my cheek, and the air stills in my lungs. She's perfect. So fucking perfect it hurts. How am I going to allow my angel to walk out the door when this feels so right?

"Should I distract you, angel?" I ask, my eyes flicking to her lips for the slightest moment, but she notices, and her cheeks burn brighter. Fuck. The pink of her cheeks makes me think of how her ass would look after a hard spanking. Rosy and delicious. The thought has my cock hardening even further.

"What do you—"

Before she can finish her question, I pull her face forward and crash our lips together, unable to take another moment without knowing what she tastes like.

A deep groan tears from my throat the moment her sweetness touches my tongue, and I'm addicted from the very first taste. There isn't a drug on this earth more intoxicating than my angel.

I don't give her a chance to go into her head because while I've only known her for a short time, I already know she's a thinker, and the last thing Elias and I need is her overthinking all the things that are going to happen between the three of us.

Because the things we're going to show her, that we're going to ask of her, they defy the normal, and they're a far cry from anything she would have experienced with that pissant, Jason.

Her lips move against mine tentatively, like she's never been kissed by a man as hungry for her as I am.

My tongue probes her lips, demanding entry, and the moment she relents is like all my dreams coming true. She tastes like

41

strawberries and cream, the sweetness dancing on my taste buds and tearing another groan from my throat.

"Jesus," Elias mutters, but I can't pull myself away from my angel to look at my best friend.

Leighton flinches, but she doesn't break our connection as he tests her ankle. Or at least that's what I assume he's doing considering the small movements of her leg. I don't think it's broken, but I'm also not willing to make an assumption like that about the health and safety of the woman who has taken my breath away.

It's not until Elias clears his throat that I finally find the will to pull away, but I hold her against me. Leighton is a flight risk, and the more we push her, the more likely she is to take off, and seeing as I've just tasted every inch of her sweet mouth, I'd say the pushing has started.

Her cheeks are deep pink when our eyes lock, and I can't quite tell if she's blushing because she's nervous and uncomfortable, or if our kiss has her little pussy hot and ready for us.

"I told you to distract her," Elias grumbles.

"That's what I did, isn't it, angel?" I smirk.

She opens her mouth to respond but immediately snaps it closed as her blush grows deeper, spreading down her neck and chest.

I don't allow my eyes to linger on her barely-contained cleavage because I'm already hard enough my cock is about to tear straight through my costume. I don't need to make a fool out of myself by also coming without her so much as touching me.

"What's the prognosis, doc?"

Elias rolls his eyes, but there's a hint of a smile tugging at the corners of his lips. It's been too long since I've seen my best friend happy, and I wonder if it's too much wishful thinking that my angel might be the one to give him that moving forward. The way his eyes fall on the woman in my arms is like he's seeing the sun for the first time.

It's everything.

EIGHT

ELIAS

I can't take my eyes off her.

No matter how much I should, how much I try to convince
myself Wyatt was wrong, and I don't want this, I know I'm
only lying to myself.

From the moment I caught sight of her I haven't been able to
drag my eyes from her silky skin and sinful curves. I want to run
my tongue over every inch of her body and drag unimaginable
amounts of pleasure from her over and over again until she
can't possibly give me more, and then I'll demand exactly
that. I want to see her ass covered in my marks and hear her
cries of pleasure and pain as I force her to walk the blurry line
between the two. I want it all.

I clear my throat, realizing how long it's been since my best
friend asked me a question, and I tear my eyes from her to
meet Wyatt's amused ones. He sees it. He sees how completely
obsessed I am with Leighton despite knowing her for less than
an hour, and there's no sense trying to pretend that isn't the

case with the man who knows me better than I know myself.

"It's not broken. It is a nasty sprain though. I want to ice it for the next few hours and then wrap it tight to keep the swelling down."

"Hours?" she squeaks, her body tugging forward from Wyatt's chest for a moment before he drags her back down against him. He looks so comfortable with her in his lap. More so than I've seen in…ever. He's never looked so settled.

I give her a small nod and carefully lower the ice pack to her heated skin.

She hisses out a breath and tries to pull her foot away from the cold, but I grip her knee, holding her leg where I need it. Being this close to her short skirt is making me heady. Knowing that I could be feasting on her sweet cunt in a matter of seconds makes it hard to focus on anything else, but caring for her is enough. For now.

"I can't sit here for hours. I have to go home," she argues, trying and failing to push against Wyatt again. It's pointless. She's small and wounded, and my best friend is an ex-Navy SEAL and more than capable of restraining her to stop her from hurting herself more.

I blow out a breath, trying to calm my racing heart. She can't leave. She can't ever leave. But I can't say that to her, because she'll think I'm a fucking lunatic. Hell, I wouldn't disagree with her. But all I know is if she walks away from us tonight, Wyatt and I will have a hole in our hearts that only she can fill, and I'm not ready to go back to that emptiness. I've lived that life for so long, I don't want to go back, and I don't want Wyatt to either.

"Do you live with Jason?" I ask.

Leighton draws in a pained breath and a look of horror crosses her face.

"That's what I thought."

"I…I have to go back," she whispers.

"You don't have to do anything you don't want to, angel," Wyatt says softly.

"I don't have a choice. We live together. I don't work. He and my parents made sure of that." Her voice shakes with each word that falls from her lips, and my chest cracks at the sound. I already hate her being in pain, would already burn the fucking world to the ground to make sure she's never scared or alone again.

"You have choices, pretty girl. You just have to be brave enough to take them."

She shakes her head, but doesn't try to get away again. "My mother won't allow me to leave him. She's been planning our wedding since we were in high school. She'll never let me break up with him."

Wyatt's eyes flare with the same anger that rages to life in my chest. What the fuck kind of mother would allow their child to stay with a lying, cheating piece of shit, let alone actively force it upon them? "I'm sure she would understand, angel," Wyatt says. "I'm sure she wouldn't want someone who isn't faithful to marry her daughter."

"She doesn't care about my happiness. All she cares about is me marrying a respectable man from a good family, and popping out two point four children to carry on Jason's family name. She's lived in a loveless marriage for the last twenty-five years. Why wouldn't she expect the same of me?"

Wyatt and I stare at her, but there are no words. What kind of mother does she have that she's been made to believe that her happiness isn't worth anything? I can't comprehend that, and by the look on my best friend's face, it seems he can't either.

"Listen, I really appreciate you both taking care of me, but I should go." Leighton pushes against Wyatt's chest, but he holds her securely in place.

"Stay where you are, angel. You can't walk on your foot right now, and you're only going to hurt yourself more if you try."

"I have to go. Jason is already going to be angry I didn't leave with him. I just want to get into a taxi and go home to bed so I can pretend tonight never happened."

I blow out a breath, trying to settle the anger bubbling in my chest. This isn't her fault, and I don't want to snap at her when she's already dealing with all of this, but fuck, every word out of her mouth only makes me want to fucking kill Jason and her parents more.

I drag my eyes from Leighton and look at Wyatt whose gaze meets mine. The same fire running through my veins is evident in his eyes. "A word," I rumble, pushing myself up from the ground and storming out into the hallway. I've always been known for my anger, but I never want Leighton to see that side of me.

She deserves the world, and that's exactly what I intend to give her.

NINE

WYATT

"I'll be right back, angel," I murmur as I place Leighton down on the couch. There isn't a cell in my body that wants to be away from her, but Elias and I need to come up with a plan of attack because I don't know about him, but there's no way in hell I'm letting her walk out of this club and back to that asshole. He doesn't deserve to breathe the same air as my angel, let alone marry her, and it will not be happening.

I latch the door closed behind me and turn to see Elias pacing up and down the hallway like a caged animal. I've never seen him like this, so uncontrolled. He's had his fair share of anger issues over the years, but nothing compared to the rage burning bright in his eyes. He looks about ready to kill someone, and hell, after what Leighton just confessed to us, I'm right there with him.

"She's not going back to him," he growls.

"I know."

"He doesn't deserve her."

"I know."

"He hurt her."

"I know."

"Can you say something other than 'I know'?" he snaps, finally standing still for long enough to glare at me.

"You need to get a handle on your anger, man. So I'm just letting you go until we can get to the part where we work out what we're going to do from here." I shrug. Elias and I have been friends for a long time, and after so many years, I've learned he's not ready for a solution until he's worked through what's in his head.

"What the fuck are we going to do?" he asks, slumping against the wall and running his hand through his perfectly gelled hair.

"I'm not entirely sure," I admit. I usually have the answers, or at the very least an idea, but not right now. Because we both heard the resignation in her voice as she told us her mother would never let her leave Jason. She's already admitted defeat and getting her to change her mind will be near impossible, but we have to try.

"I'm...I..." Elias leans his head back against the wall and blows out a frustrated breath. "You were right."

I scoff. "I'm always right. But please enlighten me as to what I was right about this time?"

He rolls his eyes but lets out a sigh a second later. "We need a woman. We need her."

"When will you start believing that I always know what I'm talking about?" I smirk.

"It's not the time for your bullshit ego, Wyatt," he snaps. "What the hell are we going to do? Because I can't let her walk out the door. I can't do it." His words are full of conviction, but behind that is something else, something I'm not used to hearing in my best friend's voice.

Fear.

He's scared of losing Leighton. And he's not the only one.

Ten

Leighton

The moment Wyatt's arms are no longer wrapped around me, I start to panic. What the heck am I doing? How the hell could I allow myself to get comfortable inside a *sex club* of all places. If my mother, or any of the women from the country club, get wind of my whereabouts, I'll be shamed for the rest of my life.

It won't matter that the only reason I'm here is because Jason came here to cheat on me, or that he basically assaulted me in an attempt to get me away from the people who were trying to defuse the situation. All that matters to Margaret Chalmers is her reputation. And a daughter who steps foot in a place like this will make her look bad. We can't have that.

I lean forward and slip the ice pack from my ankle, hissing at the agony that follows. Holy Mother of God, I did a number on it.

Once I breathe through the pain, I locate my missing heel and cringe at the thought of putting it back on my sore foot. But then the thought of walking through this place barefooted makes bile pool in my throat. God knows what these carpets have seen.

I suppose that saying about the devil you know being better than the one you don't is true. Sometimes it scares me how many of my mother's opinions have rubbed off on me over the years, but then again, I didn't have much choice but to fall into line.

As carefully as I can manage, I slip my foot into the ridiculous shoe and barely hold in the yelp that claws at my throat. Is Elias sure it's not broken? Because this is what I imagine having a broken bone feels like. I've never had one because my mother didn't believe in her daughter playing sports or having fun with my friends. All she ever cared about was marrying me off to a high-class family so she can stay relevant. Eventually my father will have to retire, and she'll hold onto her social standing by having her hooks in my husband and me.

The moment I stand I fall straight back down with a cry. Holy hell that hurts. Maybe the carpets are the safer choice...

Before I can think better of it, I slip both stilettos from my feet and pick them up in one hand. When I stand it still hurts like hell, but not to the point I can't take a step forward. Progress I suppose. I take a quick look around for another door, hoping I won't have to go out the same way Wyatt and Elias did, but there's only the one exit.

For some reason, the thought of them knowing I snuck out without saying goodbye strikes a cord in my chest. Emotion isn't something I was raised to feel. In fact, it was openly discouraged in my household. But there's something new, something unfamiliar that has been filling my chest since the moment my hero caught me.

I limp across the room, hissing out a breath every time I place any pressure on my sore ankle. How undignified would it be to crawl out of here? God. If my mother even knew that thought crossed my mind, she would have a fit.

I lean my ear against the door, listening for any voices, but the bass from the music down the hall prevents me from hearing anything. Nerves crawl up my throat, leaving heat in their path. What if they catch me? They don't strike me as the kind of men who would allow me to just up and leave after causing a commotion in their club.

Once I let out one final nervous breath, I pull the door open slightly and immediately slam it shut when I catch sight of the men who have lit a fire in my body standing beside the door. I'd really hoped they would have gone further away to have a discussion about me, but with how my night has gone, perhaps I should have expected this to be the outcome. Of course not even this could go in my favor.

I barely make it two steps before the door swings open, and both men fill the doorway. Their eyes are mirror images of the other, thunder filling both pairs. "What the fuck are you doing standing on your ankle?" Elias snaps, immediately closing the gap between us, and I flinch out of instinct. Usually when someone comes toward me with anger in their eyes, their intentions are to harm me, but the moment confusion followed by a new type of anger crosses his eyes, I realize he would never harm me. Not in the way my mother and Jason have in the past at least.

I know enough about BDSM to know there are elements of pain within the practice, and I'm sure a man like Elias enjoys inflicting his fair share of blissful agony.

"Sorry, pretty girl, I didn't mean to startle you," he says softly, bringing his hands up in front of his chest in a sign of surrender. "You need to stay off your ankle to avoid doing any further damage."

"I need to leave," I whisper.

"No you don't, angel. You can stay here for as long as you need." Wyatt approaches me as if he's approaching a frightened deer, at risk of taking off any second.

"No, I can't. You don't understand," my voice wavers, and I curse the emotions bubbling in my chest. I'm not used to them, so I'm not sure how to make them go away.

Elias glances at his best friend who gives him a small nod. "Sit down, pretty girl," he demands, but this time, the command in his voice doesn't elicit fear. It brings something else entirely to the surface. He doesn't wait for my response before sweeping me into his arms and depositing me on the plush leather couch.

"We can't allow you to go back to him, angel. Not after what we saw tonight." Wyatt kneels down beside the couch and takes one of my hands in his while Elias takes the other. It's strange drawing comfort from a man, let alone two of them.

"It's fine." I force a smile to my face, although I'm certain it looks as insincere as it feels. "He didn't mean to hurt me. He was just angry."

Wyatt closes his eyes and blows out a strained breath but keeps his hand soft in mine. "Angel, I'm sure you know that's the excuse every woman uses when their significant other harms them."

"He doesn't hurt me," I argue. "Not really." I don't know why I'm bothering to defend a man I have no attachment to, but the words escape from between my lips before I can swallow them down.

"You're not going back there. Not tonight at least," Elias says, squeezing my hand as if he's preparing for me to make a run for it. "He'll be angry tonight, and I don't trust him to not lay a hand on you."

"You're going to come home with us tonight, angel. You're going to come home with us, and we're going to show you a world you've never dreamed of. One so full of pleasure that you will forget these fucked up notions that you have to marry a man who hurts you, and in the morning, if you still want to go back to him, we'll…" He pauses to swallow. "We'll drive you back to him, and you'll never hear from us again." There's something in the way he says the words that makes me think he doesn't mean them, or that somehow he'll find a loophole around it, but for some reason I don't care. All I care about is opening Pandora's box and exploring all the things I've been missing because Jason is a two-pump chump.

I drag in an unsteady breath and squeeze each of their hands, pulling strength from them to utter a word I never thought would fall from my lips in a situation like this one.

"Okay."

Eleven

Elias

I thought she would put up more of a fight than this. In fact, I expected to have a clawing kitten on our hands. But when she agrees to spend the night with us, the breath I've been holding since the moment I locked eyes on her releases.

She's coming home with us.

She's not going back to that asshole tonight. And that's a start. It's more than we had when we walked out of the room, and maybe, just maybe, we can show her how much better her life could be if she was with us. We would worship her, show her all the things she's been missing out on in this life, and we would *never* lay a hand on her in anger. While she hasn't said as much, I get the distinct impression that tonight's little show wasn't the first time he's hurt her, and if I have a say in the matter, it will be the last time he ever gets the chance.

Wyatt and I look at one another before jumping into action before she can change her mind. He gathers her up in his arms, handing me her heels and bag before heading back toward the door. I quickly turn off the lights and trail after them down the hallway toward the back door the staff use. If her initial reaction to the club was anything to go by, walking her back the way we came would only set her off again.

By the time we reach Wyatt's Land Rover, excitement bleeds into my veins at the prospect of having Leighton in our space. We've never had a woman in our home, only ever playing in hotels or at the club, and that's always worked for us. But when an image of Leighton spread out on my bed, in my room, fills my mind, I can't think of a single thing I want more.

Wyatt opens the back door and carefully positions her in the seat before wrapping the seat belt around her and securing it.

"I could have done that," she murmurs.

"I know, but I like doing it for you." He shrugs, leaning forward and placing a gentle kiss on her cheek.

The car is silent as Wyatt drives us the short distance to our house. We bought it a few years ago because it was so close to the club, but it quickly became a home after we moved out of the apartment we had lived in since our divorces.

When the car stops, I chance a look over my shoulder at the angel in the back seat. Wyatt's nickname for her would be perfect with or without the costume. There's an innocence that surrounds her, one that I want to dirty up and watch Wyatt rebuild, just so I can destroy it all over again.

Just the thought has my cock hardening in my pants to the point of pain, and I have a feeling if we manage to convince Leighton to stick around, this will likely be my permanent state. Hard as a fucking rock.

"I'll grab Leighton, you go open up," I say quietly, quickly opening the door before he can argue. We've never fought over a woman's attention before, but I have a feeling navigating a real relationship in a dynamic like this might be a little different. But we have to get there first. We have to convince Leighton that this is what she needs, just the way it's what the two of us need.

By the time I reach her door, she's already got her seat belt undone, and she's turned in her seat ready to slip from the car.

"What do you think you're doing, pretty girl?" I rumble, sliding one arm beneath her legs and the other behind her back before lifting her from the car and kicking the door closed behind us.

"You guys shouldn't be carrying me around like this. You're going to hurt your backs."

I raise a brow at her, my palm twitching behind her back to turn her ass a pretty shade of pink for that comment, but she's not ready yet. We haven't discussed limits or safe words, or any of the other things we need to say before we jump into a scene with someone who is not only new to the scene, but who has also likely never been with more than one partner at a time.

What we're asking of her is a lot, but I know she'll love every single moment she's with us. I just hope it's enough to make her stay for more than just one night.

"Are you trying to imply Wyatt and I are weak?"

Her eyes widen, and a smile tugs at the corners of her plump lips. Fuck I want to taste her the way Wyatt did in our office.

But not here. Not on the street outside our home. I want her to be comfortable, and I want to know where her limits are because I have a feeling the moment I get a taste of Leighton, not even the devil himself could stop me from taking what I need from her.

"No," she breathes.

"Well that would mean you're saying something negative about yourself, and that's something we will not tolerate."

A shiver makes its way through her body at my tone, and I barely manage to stop the smirk that tugs at the corners of my lips. She may not realize it, but she likes the idea of being punished. We'll have to tread carefully with her, because although we've got her this far, she is still a flight risk. By the sounds of it, she grew up in a conservative household, and the things Wyatt and I like in the bedroom are exactly the opposite, but she's going to love every single second of what we give her.

I meet Wyatt's gaze over her shoulder, and he looks almost uncertain, which is an emotion I've rarely seen cross my best friend's face. He's the most confident, sure of himself guy I've ever met, but when the stakes are this high, not even he is immune to the gravity of the situation.

Without uttering a word, I walk us through the house and straight into the kitchen. I kick the chair at the end of the dining room table until it's pulled out enough for me to take a seat and then position Leighton in my lap the same way Wyatt had done earlier. The moment her weight settles on me, it's like I'm breathing for the first time.

How is it possible to have only known this woman for an hour, but already know we have our entire future in our reach, and all we have to do is make her see the same thing in us that we saw in her from the moment we glimpsed her.

TWELVE

LEIGHTON

I don't know what I was expecting when they said they were going to bring me back to their home, but this wasn't it.

When we pulled up outside a beautiful brownstone a few blocks from the club, I had to do a double take. The house is stunning. All original features but modernized to have all the most recent appliances. The color scheme is warm and neutral, and the original wooden floors are to die for.

The further we get into the house, the more questions swarm my mind. Do they live here together? Or is this just one of their homes? How many women have they brought home to share? Is that what they intend to do to me? Is that what I want?

By the time Elias sits me in his lap at the dining room table and Wyatt sits beside us, quickly pulling my swollen ankle into his lap, I'm a bundle of nervous energy ready to explode. I didn't think this through. I'm engaged. Or at least I was a few hours ago. What the heck was I thinking allowing two random men who I barely know bring me back to their home to do God only knows what to me?

I've never done something this reckless in my life, and I don't know why on earth I would start now.

Because your mother has dictated every move you've made in the last twenty-two years. It's time for you to make a choice for yourself. Even if it's a mistake.

The voice in the back of my head pipes up, and I allow my body to relax. Soon enough, I'll be married to Jason. I won't have a choice in the matter, and he'll spend the rest of our lives using me as his good little wife to bear his children and stand by his side at events, while behind closed doors he'll use any excuse to stray. I'll live my life sad, alone, and unsatisfied. So why not make the memory of a wild night with two sinfully attractive older men to reminisce on when I'm lonely?

Wyatt's fingers move gently over my foot and ankle, his touch sending goose bumps up my bare legs and shooting into my aching core. God. They set my body on fire in a way Jason never has. "You're trembling, angel," he murmurs, allowing his fingers to trail further up my calf.

I suck in a breath, the sensation makes it impossible to think past his touch, but I need more. I need everything they can give me.

Lips trail down my neck and drag a gasp from my throat. Elias chuckles and continues his path to where my neck and shoulder meet where he sinks his teeth into the sensitive flesh.

I cry out, my hips shifting with the need for relief, and my ass collides with a very hard length beneath me. Oh my god, he's huge.

Elias chuckles against my neck, his breath whispering across the bare skin and making me shiver with desire. I've never been this wound up. Hell, I don't think Jason has ever actually got me even slightly wound up, let alone ready to combust from innocent touches.

"I think she's just felt how hard you are for her, brother," Wyatt muses.

"Do you like what you feel, pretty girl?" He murmurs against my ear, sending shockwaves straight to my aching clit. I didn't know it was possible to be this turned on.

"I...I..." But the words catch in my throat and refuse to go any further.

"I think she does," Wyatt says, putting me out of my misery. "Are you nervous, angel?"

"Yes."

"Would it make you feel better if we told you a little more about ourselves and what we would like to happen here tonight?" His gentle fingers brush along the inside of my knee, and I barely swallow down the responding moan.

I nod, unable to think past their hands on me, their presence and scent wafting around me like an endless air of intoxication.

Wyatt smiles over my shoulder at Elias who continues his gentle assault on my senses with his lips. "Tell me, angel. What do you know about BDSM?"

My heart stalls in my chest, and the breath whooshes from my lungs to the point I almost choke on the question, only making them both chuckle.

"I'll take that as not a lot then?"

"I think that's fair to say," I squeak.

"It's not as scary as you may think, angel. I suppose the parts that are most...important to Elias and me are around control. Have you ever heard of the terms Dominant and submissive?"

I nod. "Only in a couple of books that I've read," I whisper. If Jason or my mother knew I was reading such things during my days at home, they would both be appalled. My mother would probably go as far as to invite our pastor over for dinner to reinforce that the devil lives in literature like that.

"That's good, pretty girl." Elias brushes his lips against the shell of my ear, and a small groan escapes my throat.

"I think she likes that, brother." Wyatt smirks. "Well, angel. Those are the types of dynamics that Elias and I need. We crave control. We crave submission."

"Do you...are you...together?" I force myself to ask. At this point it doesn't matter to me, but I would rather know what I'm in for than be surprised halfway through whatever we're about to do here.

"No. Wyatt and I are both straight. We just like to share."

I suck in a harsh breath, and the edge of panic begins to whittle away at me. I've been calm up until this point, and it's not even the first time they've alluded to the possibility, but hearing the explanation from the horse's mouth so to speak is another story altogether.

"Does that intrigue you, pretty girl?" Elias asks against my ear. "Do you want to find out what it's like to submit to two men at the same time?"

"I don't know what I'm doing," I admit, my eyes dropping to the hardwood floors to avoid Wyatt's piercing gaze. Heck. The longer I spend in the presence of these men, the more I struggle to remember a reason I need to return to my boring, mundane life tomorrow. There's nothing but loneliness waiting for me, but for tonight I can pretend that isn't my future. I can allow myself to live in a fantasy land where these two men bring me unimaginable pleasure and none of the pain Jason does.

"We'll teach you everything you need to know, angel." Wyatt carefully stands, placing my foot on the chair he was sitting on and kneeling beside us. "We're going to ask a lot of you tonight, Leighton, but we won't push you any further than your limits. We're going to give you a safe word. If you say it, we stop no questions asked. It's as simple as that."

I nod, looking over my shoulder at Elias who is watching me curiously. "What's my safe word?"

"Red," Wyatt says. "And if you want to slow down, I want you to say yellow. Elias and I will stop what we're doing, and we'll talk about what you're feeling, and if you want to continue or change directions."

"Okay," I whisper, burying my face in Elias's chest. The comfort these two men give me is unlike anything anyone has ever given me before, and I don't hesitate to lean into the feeling.

Elias tips my chin up until I'm looking into his intense gaze. The two of them are like night and day in so many ways. Wyatt is soft and reassuring, and Elias has an intensity that should scare me, but all it does is send shockwaves to my core. "Have you ever had a partner spank you, pretty girl?"

I shake my head. The heat that rises to my cheeks makes me want to tear my eyes away from him, but his grip on my chin doesn't allow me to.

"You don't have to be embarrassed, Leighton. I'm more than happy to pop your pleasure and pain cherry." He winks.

"I don't...I haven't..." I squeeze my eyes shut as I force myself to get my words under control. Just spit it out, Leighton. What's the worst that can happen?

They decide you're more trouble that you're worth and send you back to Jason to a lifetime of boring sex and an unhappy marriage.

"I've only ever been with Jason," I admit. "And he's not really into trying new things...with me at least." Anger fills my belly at the memory of the nurse all over him. How many other women have there been? And is it strictly missionary with the lights off with them? Or is that just for his slightly chubby fiancée? Am I so undesirable that's all he can offer me a couple of times per month?

Self doubt washes over me. I can't do this. In what universe do I think I can sleep with not one but two men who are so out of my league it's unbelievable? Things like this don't happen to women like me? Maybe if I was twenty pounds lighter and had been with more than just my asshole high school sweetheart, but not as I am.

THIRTEEN

WYATT

O ne moment she's clinging on to Elias as if he holds all the answers, and the next doubt flashes through her eyes, and she's looking for the closest exit.

If I'm honest, I'm not entirely surprised that she's only ever been with that asshole, or that he's not adventurous in the bedroom. Those kinds of guys are all the same. Sons of rich assholes, their whole future planned for them before they even leave the womb, and then they think they're too good for everyone else.

Elias must feel the change in her body language because one second he's holding her against his chest, and the next he's laying her face down in the middle of our dining table and swatting her ass with his huge hand before I can stand from where I'm kneeling beside them.

"Hey!" Leighton screeches as Elias flips her skirt up, and his palm cracks across her bare ass for a second time. She's wearing the skimpiest pair of panties I've ever seen in my life, a string of lace and a small triangle barely covering her pretty pussy.

"I don't need to hear the words come out of your mouth to know where your mind just went, pretty girl, and I won't stand for it." Another loud slap lands on her ass, and a red handprint immediately blossoms on the perfect globe.

Fuck me.

I've watched my best friend punish a lot of subs, and I've punished my fair share as well, but I've never been as close to losing my mind as I am right now. She's perfect. So fucking perfect I don't know how I'm going to allow her to walk out the door tomorrow morning if that's what she chooses to do.

"That asshole doesn't deserve to breathe the same air as you, Leighton." *Slap*. "He certainly doesn't deserve to put his tiny cock in your pussy." *Slap*. "And he absolutely does not deserve to have his ring on your finger." *Slap*. "Men don't cheat because they can't get what they need at home, pretty girl." *Slap*. "They cheat because they don't realize what they have is better than anything they could ever find elsewhere." *Slap*. "They cheat because their ego thrives off knowing they've still got it." *Slap*. "But I'll let you in on a little secret, Leighton. Men who cheat aren't men at all. They're little boys who want to hoard all the toys in the playground for themselves. They're children who have never grown up and who take everything they have for granted until one day it's all gone." *Slap*. "Wyatt and I are not little boys. We are men, and we will always treat you exactly how you deserve to be treated. You deserve to be worshipped, and that's exactly what we're going to do. We're going to show you exactly what you're worth so you won't ever allow that asshole to disrespect you again."

Each time his palm connects with her ass, she lets out a little squeal, but after the first few she's rubbing her thighs together desperately seeking some kind of relief.

I step forward and grip her good ankle, tugging it until her legs are spread wide. "None of that, angel. You'll get relief when we see fit, and not a moment sooner."

She groans in frustration but doesn't argue. Instead, she rests her cheek against the wooden table and lets out a shuddering breath. She's been through so much tonight and we're about to put her through so much more, but she can take it. And once we're done with her, she'll know her worth, and it's a hell of a lot more than that asshole can afford.

"Now, angel." I move to stand beside her head and brush locks of her hair from her eyes. "There are some rules for you to follow tonight and if you break them, you'll find yourself in a very similar position to the one you're in right now, do you understand?" I ask, brushing my fingers across her bare shoulder until goose bumps appear in their wake.

"I understand," she whimpers. Her eyes are wide and full of arousal and bliss. She may never have been on the receiving end of a spanking before, but my angel needs it. She needs to find that place where there's only her and her Dom, or in this case, Doms, and the rest of the world is quiet. And that's exactly where we're going to take her tonight.

Elias and I look to one another, communicating silently the way we've learned to do over the years. Normally our roles are clear. He's the one who enforces punishment, the harsh one so to speak, and I'm the nice guy. I coddle and comfort. I'm all about encouragement and pleasure. But it's not as clear cut with Leighton because our roles are already becoming blurred. It's not a bad thing by any means, but it is different, and that means we're wading into uncharted territory. The roles we've played with women in the past were only for the night, but if we have anything to say in the matter, Leighton will become a permanent fixture in our lives.

"If one of us directs you to do something, it is expected you will do it without hesitation. The only exception to this is if you need to say yellow or red. Do you understand?" Elias says.

"Yes."

"Yes, Sir," he corrects. "That's your next rule. You are to address Wyatt and me appropriately at all times."

"Yes, Sir," she whispers, and my cock jumps in my pants.

I'll need to free it soon, or I'm at risk of it tearing straight through my pants. The words on her lips are downright sinful, and by the lust swirling around in my best friend's eyes, I can tell he's struggling just as much as I am to keep the beast inside caged.

"Good girl," he rumbles, and a shiver vibrates through her body.

"She likes that, brother," I muse. "I bet her pretty pussy will pulse on your cock if you call her that while you fuck her."

Leighton's cheeks turn a deeper shade of pink. She isn't used to men talking to her like this, but she had better get used to it. There are a million dirty things I want to whisper in her ear as we bring her unimaginable pleasure.

"Do you want to be a good girl for us, angel?"

"Yes, Sir."

Fuck. This woman is going to be the end of us, and I don't know about Elias, but I'm more than happy to watch my own demise if I'm doing it balls deep inside my angel.

FOURTEEN

LEIGHTON

Oh my god. I can't believe I'm doing this. I can't believe I'm allowing two men to touch me, and I'm calling them Sir while they do it. Who am I, and what have I done with Leighton Grace Chalmers? The woman I was when I walked into the bar tonight is worlds away from the one laying face down in the middle of a dining room table with two sinfully attractive older men staring at her like they're starved for her. I've never felt so powerful.

The rapture in their eyes is so intense I almost look away, but I force myself to look between them, to be brave. Tonight I don't want to be the meek woman who lives her life by the country club's standard of normal. I want to be the goddess these two gods need.

"Let's move this party to my bedroom," Wyatt says, stepping forward and bundling me against his hard chest.

"I can walk. You're going to hurt you—" But I don't get through my sentence before two harsh slaps meet my already tender ass.

"Enough," Elias growls. "Another rule, pretty girl. No putting yourself down. We will not stand for it, and if you want to come tonight, that's the last time you will even think such a thing."

My mouth drops open, but all arguments die on my tongue when he gives me a pointed look.

"That's another rule, angel. You're not to come without permission," Wyatt says against my ear, dragging a soft moan from my throat. Every touch makes it harder to think through what's going to happen next, and maybe that's the point. "I need your words, angel. Nodding isn't going to fly tonight because we don't want to risk missing a head movement, and it forces you to use your safe word, okay?"

"Okay, Sir," I murmur.

"For now, there are only two other rules for you to follow. You will only speak when spoken to, and you are not to lie to us. That last one goes for both in and out of the bedroom," Elias brushes his fingers down my cheek softly.

Wyatt carries me into a dark room, and the moment the lights go on I suck in a breath. A huge California King four-poster bed sits in the center of the room with a half wall behind it. Black sheets match the black curtains and styling with timber accents. The room smells like Wyatt, making me wonder how on earth I'm going to survive a night of being surrounded by not only their heat, but their masculine scents as well.

"I don't want you putting any pressure on this ankle tonight, Leighton," Wyatt says as he sits me on the edge of the bed, the mattress dipping under my weight. "Elias and I will help you move into any position we order you into, and we will be as careful as we can of your ankle, but if it starts to hurt or if we knock it by accident, I want you to tell us immediately, okay?"

"Yes, Sir."

"I'm never going to get enough of hearing those words on your pretty lips, angel," he groans. His fingers slip beneath the short skirt of my costume and inches up my thigh. His movements are slow and unhurried despite the fire burning in his eyes.

The moment he tugs the costume over my head and I'm left in nothing but a pair of skimpy panties and a lacy bra that does nothing to hide my hardening nipples, I automatically wrap my arms around my stomach protectively. I'm not used to men looking at me with the lights on. That's something that Jason has always been very set on. He doesn't like to have sex until the lights are off, and I've always been very self-conscious about that.

But Wyatt's not having a bit of it. He carefully unwinds my arms and presses me back onto the mattress with my arms pinned above my head.

"There will be none of that, angel," he tuts, his lips pressing a gentle kiss to the swell of my breast, quickly followed by sinking his teeth into the soft flesh and dragging a startled scream from my throat. A blush climbs up my cheeks, and if my hands were free, I would cover my face from embarrassment. I've never made a noise like that. In fact, Jason tends to adopt more of a less is more philosophy.

Elias and Wyatt groan in unison, the sound making my

stomach sink. Oh no, they want me to be quiet, too. I can do quiet. I've been doing quiet for years.

"Jesus, that was the sexiest fucking sound I've ever heard in my life." Wyatt laps at the angry red mark his teeth left.

My eyes widen at his words, words so different from any a man has ever spoken to me before. Jason is the only person I've ever been intimate with, but I'm certainly not his. Despite the big deal he and his family made about my virginity and the need for it to be intact, the same could not be said for him. Before our families came to an arrangement, he slept his way through almost our entire year level, including my best friend, or ex-best friend I guess.

"She's thinking again," Elias notes as he drags a single finger down my sternum, the light brush of his calloused skin on mine causes a shiver of need to vibrate through my body.

"We can't have that, now can we?" Wyatt's smile is wicked as it tugs at the corners of his lips, and then he sinks his teeth into the other breast the same way he did the first.

And once again I scream, except this time I don't bother to censor myself despite the nagging voice in the back of my head telling me I should be ashamed of the sounds I'm making.

I'm never going to see these men again after tonight, so what does it matter?

FIFTEEN

ELIAS

E very inch of Leighton is intoxicating.

Her smooth skin. The way her eyes roll into the back of her head each time one of us touches her. How her full, pouty lips part with silent cries as she tries desperately to train her reactions to us.

But more than any of that, it's her submission that brings me to my knees. She's fucking beautiful in the way she succumbs to us, how she follows every order we give her, even when her mind tells her not to. I have no idea what that asshole has done to her and why she thinks she shouldn't make a sound, but I'm going to kill him for it.

I'd all but decided I'd be ending his life by the way he grabbed her wrist, but this just settles it. He can't be allowed to walk the earth after committing such a travesty as telling this beautiful creature not to show her pleasure.

I meet Wyatt's gaze as he releases the abused flesh of her breast. It's been a long fucking time since I've seen him like this. Content. Barely holding on to his control. Obsessed. Everything I see in his eyes, I feel deep in my chest, and for a moment it's fucking terrifying.

There's a reason we haven't cared about anyone else in such a long time. A really good reason. But right now it's all gone out the window, and all that matters is the beautiful woman laid out for us like a feast.

I drag my finger further down her body, and her eyes widen as I brush over her stomach. She has reservations about her body clearly, but there won't be any confusion after tonight. After tonight she'll know just how fucking beautiful she is because we're about to worship her like the goddess she is.

Her lust-filled eyes flick between the two of us, but she isn't sure which one to look at. I'm still shocked to my core she agreed to this if I'm honest. She's a good girl. She probably goes to church on Sundays and prays at night. But the only prayers she'll be saying tonight will be to beg us to fuck her harder.

I tease the edge of her panties, the flimsy lace giving way easily as I slip my hand beneath it. She's warm and bare under my fingers, and a guttural moan drags up my throat. But it's when I slide between her soaking folds that I almost come in my pants like a fucking teenager.

"Is she wet?" Wyatt asks between pressing kisses to her neck.

"She's fucking soaked," I groan as I flick the tight bud of nerves at her crest, causing her to cry out.

We both smirk down at her, her eyes heavy lidded as she watches my hand disappear beneath the lace.

"Does that feel good, angel?" Wyatt asks as he trails his fingers around the bite marks scattered across her tits. He's always had a thing for marking his women, but I have a feeling Leighton is going to bring that out in him tenfold.

She nods as she sinks her teeth into her bottom lip. Fuck, I want to be the one to bite that soft pillow.

"Words, angel," he reminds her with a pinch of her nipple through her lacy bra, eliciting a squeak from her throat. His other hand flexes around her wrists, ensuring she's secure against the mattress.

"Yes, it feels good, Sir." Her words are rushed and quiet, but that only serves to make my cock pulse harder. I need to be inside her. I need to feel her hot little pussy clench around me until she's mindless. But there's so much to do before then.

"There's our good girl." I smile down at her.

Her eyes dilate at the praise as she arches her back. Oh she most definitely likes that.

I slip my fingers through her folds, testing her wetness before pulling my fingers free from her panties. She watches my every move as I bring my fingers to my mouth and suck her juices from them.

Her mouth pops open, probably about to object, but Wyatt quickly presses his lips to hers and cuts her off before she can voice it.

We've shared a lot of women over the years, but this is different. It's not just for a bit of fun. It's not just to get our dicks wet. It's more, and that scares the shit out of me while simultaneously lighting a fire inside me that was extinguished years ago.

She tastes like heaven. Even sweeter than I thought she would, and I couldn't trap the guttural moan even if I wanted to.

I watch as Wyatt kisses her with rough swipes of his tongue. He's not going easy on her, and she doesn't seem to have any objections. Her arms flex against his hand, trying desperately to break free, but he doesn't even look like he's trying to restrain her.

I never believed in fate, or love at first sight, or any of that fairy tale crap women like to make a big deal about. But that all changed tonight. Because watching our angel and my brother brings me peace. It reminds me what it feels like to feel at home.

Men like us have no right coveting someone as sweet as Leighton, have no right putting our dirty hands all over her soft skin, but I don't think even the devil himself could keep us away from her.

Wyatt leans back slightly, his eyes flicking from the angel laid out below him to me where I'm kneeling on the other side of her. He doesn't need to say a word for me to know exactly what he's thinking.

Leighton is the missing piece we didn't know we needed.

SIXTEEN

LEIGHTON

I 'd say this moment is a dream come true, but not even my mind could conjure this image.

Two dominant men worshipping me, my body overwhelmed with sensations, my brain completely useless through the pleasure they're giving me.

My skin burns everywhere their hands touch, and each breath is more labored than the last. Coming into this I thought it would be a memory I would hold on to in my cold, loveless marriage when I can no longer put it off, but I realize it's more than that. As soon as I had both of their hands on me, it became so much more than that.

Tonight will be stained onto my very soul.

Wyatt's fingers tighten around my wrists and drag me back to him. His face only a breath from mine, his eyes dark with lust. "I can see we have our work cut out for us keeping you out of your head, little angel."

I open my mouth to respond, but he slowly shakes his head telling me I don't have permission to speak right now. I thought with having so many rules I would struggle to remember them all, but they come naturally to me, and I don't allow myself to think about what that means.

"What are you thinking, Wyatt?" Elias asks as his large hand moves up the inside of my thigh toward my aching core.

If there's anything I'm certain of, it's that I've never been this turned on in my life, and I doubt anything that comes after tonight will compare.

"I'm thinking she might need something to help keep her in the moment." The corners of his lips lift into a smirk.

Elias chuckles and bends both my knees toward my chest, taking extra care with my swollen ankle. If I'm honest, I've all but forgotten about the sprain, and while I'm certain it will hurt in the morning, right now, it's the last thing on my mind. "How many?"

I lift my head to look at him, but he's not talking to me. His eyes are locked on Wyatt's as they have a silent conversation. Anxiety bubbles in my belly. I'm spread open for them. They can see everything, and I've never felt so vulnerable in my life. If it weren't for the strong hand around my wrist, I would reach for the nearest blanket to cover myself, but alas, that's not an option right now.

The bed shifts as Elias moves lower, giving him an even better view of my bare pussy and ass. No one has ever been this close with the lights on. Heck, Jason has only gone down on me a handful of times in the dark. Mostly I'm just a warm body for him to slide into when he feels the need. He's never had any care for my pleasure, instead taking what he needs from me and leaving me unsatisfied.

My eyes must give away my discomfort because Wyatt's free hand moves to brush down my cheeks, his thumb lingering across my bottom lip. "No need to be nervous, angel."

I open my mouth to respond but quickly close it again, and he gives me a wide smile that makes my heart flutter in my chest.

Before I have a chance to bask in the silent praise, a heavy hand comes down on my bare ass and drags a scream from my throat. I don't get a chance to ask what the heck he thinks he's doing before Elias peppers another three spanks down on the soft globes.

He groans. "Fuck, you're pretty in pink, Leighton."

Heat moves over my cheeks and down my chest, I'm sure matching whatever color he's bringing out on the battered flesh of my ass.

Wyatt's pupils are blown wide as he stares down at me like a starved man. Every time I think I may be able to handle whatever they throw at me tonight, I'm reminded of the limited experience I have with the opposite sex. "Still thinking."

Elias lets out a satisfied chuckle before his hand strikes me four more times in rapid succession, each time pulling a squeal from my throat. It hurts. More than I expected it to in fact. But it's not the pain that catches me off guard. It's the warmth that moves over every inch of my body. It's the heady feeling that tears away conscious thought and leaves behind the pliant doll they want me to be. Every muscle in my body is relaxed despite the searing pain, and the tears that prick at the corners of my eyes aren't those of sadness. They're of peace.

It takes me long seconds to realize he's stopped, and that Wyatt's hand has finally released my hands. In fact, neither of them are touching me and for the briefest of moments I panic that I've done something wrong. They couldn't keep their hands off me a few seconds ago, and now they're nowhere to be found.

The haze begins to clear, and I notice them both staring down at me. Their corded muscles tight, their eyes wild with lust, and they're both down to just boxer briefs. Their bulges are huge, far bigger than Jason, and I can't help but stare at them. How the hell am I going to take one of those things? Let alone both?

Elias and Wyatt have matching smirks as they watch me with hunger. "You took your punishment so well, angel," Wyatt praises as his fingers trail down my cheek. "Remind me of your safe word?"

"Red, Sir," I reply softly.

"Good girl," they say in unison, and if it were possible to die from praise, I would be six feet under.

Jason never spoke much in bed other than to tell me when he wanted to change between the two positions he liked, but clearly I had no idea how much I was missing.

"How's your ankle feeling, pretty girl?" Elias asks, his eyes moving to where my legs are still pushed back against my chest. "The swelling seems to be settling a little."

"It's fine, Sir."

He groans and squeezes his hardness through his briefs. "That word sounds too fucking pretty coming from your lips, Leighton."

Wyatt climbs onto the bed and sits against the headboard before dragging me across the soft sheets as if I weigh nothing at all. The way these two have thrown me around tonight I might almost believe the narrative my mother has been feeding me about my weight all these years is false. But sadly one night can't change a lifetime of belief.

He positions me carefully between his muscular thighs and lifts each of my legs over his, leaving me spread wide and on display for Elias. He gathers my hands in his and carefully wraps something around them, but I realize too late that it's a silk scarf.

"Wyatt—" I start but quickly stop myself. Not quick enough, though.

Elias lands a sharp smack to my aching core, the blow sending shocks of pain and pleasure through my whole body. "What are the rules, Leighton?" His fingers linger on my clit, unmoving. Maddening.

"I...I'm to address you both as Sir." I gasp for air. How is it possible for two men to be so completely overwhelming that I can barely breathe?

"That's right." He nods. "And if you're uncomfortable or concerned about something, what are you meant to say?"

"Red, Sir."

"So are you uncomfortable or concerned and need to stop?"

I look down to where a red scarf is wrapped around my wrists. The knot isn't tight by any means and I'm almost certain I could get out of the binds if I really wanted to. "No, Sir."

He smiles down at me and finally moves his fingers through my soaking folds.

Wyatt lifts my bound hands behind his head, leaving my entire body exposed and helpless. His hands trail down my body slowly, stopping to tweak each of my nipples. Elias's eyes track each of his movements as he drinks me in.

The further we get into this, the more I begin to doubt whether I'll survive it. But there are worse ways to go than overwhelmed by the most attractive men I've ever met.

Trust in the Fallen

SEVENTEEN

WYATT

E lias has never looked at a woman like this. Not his ex-wife, or any of the women we've shared over the years. No one.

The reverence in his eyes as they move over every inch of our angel's bare skin is like nothing I've ever seen from my best friend in all the years we've known one another.

After our wives left us, and we bought the club, the things we got involved in, the ways we were able to use our talents from the SEALs, we didn't want to get a woman involved in any of it. Hell, up until tonight Elias still didn't want to. But we're going to have to make it work.

We can keep her away from our darkness. She never has to know about the dark parts of our lives. She doesn't need to know the people we're involved with or the things we do under the cover of night.

She never has to know.

Elias's eyes flick up to mine, and his brow furrows. We've known each other for so long we can almost read one another's minds, and he doesn't like whatever he's seeing in mine right now.

Leighton's oblivious to the silent exchange, too focused on the way my fingers pinch her nipples to the brink of pain and then bring her back with gentle circles, and Elias continues to tease her pretty pussy. She's so receptive to our touch despite her obvious hesitation. For her this is a night of debauchery before she thinks she'll go back to that asshole and live a life with a white picket fence and a bunch of kids. For obvious reasons that won't be happening, and that piece of shit will be lucky if he's breathing past tomorrow after the way he hurt our angel.

There's the shrill ringing of a phone, dragging all our attention from one another. "That's mine," she says quietly, her body instinctively trying to coil in on itself.

"Ignore it, angel," I whisper against the shell of her ear, nipping at the lobe to pull her back to us. I look up to Elias to get him on board with distracting her, but his shoulders are tense.

"I can't." She tugs at the scarf around her wrists, but there's no way I'm letting her out of this bed. If we give her the time to think about the life she lived up until she walked into the club tonight, it'll all be over. We won't be able to coax her back into this position, and I haven't had nearly enough of her yet. I'm not sure I ever will.

I glare at my best friend, and he finally drags his attention back to the two of us. The tension is still evident in his body, but his fingers are moving gently again, trying to distract

Leighton the same way I am.

"I'm sure it's nothing you can't deal with in the morning, pretty girl," Elias murmurs and shifts his fingers further down until they're teasing her entrance.

She opens her mouth to respond, but he shakes his head.

"Your job is to focus on us. Not on your phone. Not on the outside world. On Wyatt and myself. Now I'm sure I can give you a reminder of that in the form of a punishment, and Wyatt would be more than happy to hold you still for me, but I'd prefer we don't go backward." He presses a finger into her tight channel, and she hisses out a breath. "What do you say?"

The phone finally stops ringing, and she nods against my bare chest. "Okay, Sir."

"There's our good girl." He flicks his attention to me and nods his head toward the couch. "I don't want any more interruptions."

I smirk and carefully disentangle myself from Leighton's bound arms. "I'll be right back, angel." I kiss her cheek gently and pad out into the living room. I've known Elias for long enough to know he wasn't asking me to just come out here and put her phone on silent, and I have to move quickly despite the fact he'll have her well distracted in my absence.

I spot her bag on the dining table and slip my hand inside to fish out her phone. What I'm about to do is morally gray at best, but I'm quickly realizing there's nothing I won't do for my angel, including violating her personal property to put a tracker on her phone.

I make quick work of the passcode lock from the fingerprints on the screen and find six missed calls from that asshole Jason, as well as two from her mother and one from her father. We need to get Bishop to do a full background check, just to be sure we're not running into any surprises, but that can wait until the morning.

I go through the motions of installing the tracking app and hiding it within a folder in a folder so she's not likely to stumble across it before putting the phone on silent and slipping it back into her clutch. I should feel guilty, but I don't. I've done a lot worse shit in my life than this, and I'm sure it won't be the worst thing I do when it comes to Leighton.

By the time I make it back to the bedroom, Elias has two fingers buried inside her, and his pupils are blown wide with lust. Leighton's moans are like a symphony, each one making my cock pulse in my briefs. Jesus, I have no idea how either of us are going to last more than one pump when she's making sounds like that.

I push my boxer briefs off and I climb back onto the bed and take my spot back behind her. There's something about having her body wrapped within mine that settles the demons that usually run rampant through my mind. She calms me in a way that's so foreign I wouldn't believe it was possible if someone had told me twelve hours ago.

Her breathy moans make my cock ache so badly I'm certain I'm going to die if I don't get inside her soon, if I can't feel her tightness wrap around me. By the way Elias is looking down at her, his hand fisting his own cock, it's evident that he's right there with me.

She bites her pouty bottom lip and squeezes her eyes shut. She's trying not to speak, to beg for the release Elias is teasing her with. The man's a master of control. He's always been the disciplined one while I'm the indulgent one. If I were in his position I'd be overwhelming her with orgasm after orgasm until she was begging me to stop, until her pretty pussy was so sensitive it was painful, and then I'd probably make her come a time or two more.

"You're so pretty when you're chasing your pleasure, angel," I whisper against the shell of her ear. "I bet your greedy cunt is soaking his fingers, isn't that right, baby?"

She gasps out a moan and nods against my chest.

"Words, Leighton," Elias reminds her. He withdraws his fingers from her pussy, and before she can let out the breath of disappointment, a hard slap hits her wet folds, causing her to scream.

"Yes, Sir. I'm sorry," she rushes out.

I brush my finger up her sides gently, soothing some of the sting as goose bumps spread across her milky skin. Jesus, she's perfect. Every inch of her is soft and unblemished, a direct contrast to the darkness Elias and I carry around with us.

"I think she's ready." He looks up at me, the lust burning in his eyes brighter than I've ever seen.

I smile down at my angel, her eyes darting between us like she can't quite work out what we're talking about. "Come here, baby." I lift her and carefully turn her until she's facing me, her knees trapped between mine.

Her gaze darts from me to Elias over her shoulder, but I quickly capture her chin between my fingers and bring her lips down to mine, desperate to taste her. "One day we'll both take that pretty pussy together, Elias will fuck your pussy while I fuck your ass, we'll have you in every single way we can think of." Her eyes widen until her brows are almost in her hairline, and I can't catch the chuckle before it leaves my throat. "But not yet."

I slip my fingers into her hair, fisting the soft strands and pulling her until her lips clash with mine. My tongue demands entrance immediately, needing to taste her, to claim her, to take the air right from her lungs so she can't breathe without me. Because I have a feeling after tonight, I won't be able to suck in a breath without her.

Eighteen

Leighton

T hey're too good at this. It shouldn't be possible for two men to be able to constantly render me speechless while simultaneously reading my body better than even I can. And yet here we are.

Wyatt takes my lips hungrily, his tongue demanding entrance, and I'm powerless to deny him.

I can't breathe.

I've never been this wired, this in need, in my life. I thought romance novels were lying when they said you could feel so consumed by another human being, or in my case, two. But they weren't lies, or even exaggerations. If anything, they played down just how much fire someone else can ignite in you.

I'm on my knees between Wyatt's legs, his hands holding me steady, but I feel anything but. Giving control over to someone should come naturally seeing as I've been doing it my whole life. First my parents, every move dictated, every after school activity organized, and then Jason. Heck, Jason was decided by my parents, too. They decided I would marry him. They told me I would live my life as nothing more than arm candy for a man set for greatness. I had no choice in the matter.

But I have a choice in this. And I hand the control over willingly. I was taught never to trust easily, except where my parents were concerned of course, but this comes as easily as breathing. Submitting to these men, handing my decisions and body to them is the easiest thing I've ever done.

"You okay, Angel?" Wyatt asks me quietly. His palm presses against my cheek, the warmth of his calloused hand giving me something to cling to.

I nod. "Yes, Sir."

He smiles at me, his eyes showing a vulnerability I don't remember ever seeing in Jason. "Good girl. You tell me if that changes, yeah?"

I give him a small nod but decide words aren't necessary in this instance. I don't know that I'd ever get the hang of this, but for one night I can feel my way through.

A satisfied smile tugs at the corners of his lips, and he fists a hand in my hair as he looks up at whatever Elias is doing behind me.

Part of me wants to look, to see his dark eyes and see firsthand what he's doing, but Wyatt's grip on my hair holds me in place, keeping me from doing something that would almost definitely lead to more punishment. Not that I'd be altogether upset about that. There's something freeing about the pain. Which is strange because my pain tolerance has always been next to nothing. But it's different. Everything is when their hands are on me.

Fingers move between my ass cheeks and circle my puckered hole, the one Jason never would have dared to think of touching. I flinch but force my body to remain still.

"Relax, pretty girl," Elias soothes, trailing his deft fingers lower until they dip into my wetness. My entire body buzzes with barely-contained need, the evidence of my arousal dripping down my thighs. "Someone's needy."

Wyatt chuckles and tugs my hair until I'm forced to look into his eyes. They're harder than they were before, like he's trying desperately to hold on to control. The flecks of darkness make my stomach clench, something I've never been attracted to before. Safety has always been what I craved, but right now, the danger these two men emit is better than any sense of calm I can imagine. Maybe it's the way my core is pulsing that stops all rational thought, or maybe there's something that's been dormant within me, waiting for something to break it free.

"She does look desperate, doesn't she?"

I open my mouth to respond, to defend myself, but he's not wrong. I am desperate. My body has a mind of its own, like the woman I was when I walked into that club just a few hours ago is a totally different person from the one I am right now. The needy, desperate woman who would do just about anything for the men worshipping her, including doing away with everything she thought she was.

Even if I could have found the words, they would have been cut off immediately as Elias plunges two thick fingers into me. He doesn't pause to allow me to adjust, instead he curls his fingers and hits a spot inside me that has stars dancing in my vision. The sensation is overwhelming and blissful all at once, and as if he's done it a thousand times, he brings me right to the edge within seconds.

I open my mouth to scream, but I'm quickly silenced by Wyatt's cock. My jaw stretches impossibly around his impressive size, and no matter how hard I try, I can't take more than a few inches.

"Holy fucking shit," he grunts, his fists tightening in my hair.

I chance a glance up at him. Veins bulge in his neck, tension pulsing through his entire body as he fights to maintain control.

He meets my eye and smirks, the darkness in the depths only seeming to heighten the pleasure Elias is dragging out of me. "Your mouth is a fucking paradise, angel."

"She likes that," Elias comments. "Her sweet pussy is gushing. Do you want another finger, pretty girl?"

I nod around Wyatt's cock as best I can because I need more. I need everything they can give me. I need to push my body to its limits and then some, because this is probably the only chance I'll ever have. The rest of my life will be in a loveless marriage, with my husband cheating on me while I care for the children I was obligated to give him, and only having sex when he can't find someone else to stick his dick in.

Elias chuckles and withdraws his fingers from my aching pussy. I let out a keening sound I don't recognize, and Wyatt strokes my hair reminding me to keep bobbing up and down on his hard length.

A moment later, three thick fingers push their way into my pussy, and I let out a groan of relief. I'm overstimulated in the best kind of way. My body craves a release at their hands, something no man has given me before, but their rules echo in the back of my mind.

Don't come without permission.

Don't come without permission.

Don't come without permission.

I chant the words in my mind over and over again, trying desperately to hold myself from falling over the edge of oblivion. I've always been afraid of disappointing the people around me, but never more than right now.

"Our girl looks so fucking pretty stuffed with my fingers, brother."

Wyatt groans, his fist tightening as he pushes me down with a little more force than he has so far. "I bet she'll look even better stretched around our cocks."

The pressure in my core is getting to the point of no return. The pace Elias has picked up, the way his fingers massage the place inside me I was sure was a myth, and the filthy words make it almost impossible to hold myself back from the brink.

"Don't come, Leighton," Elias's voice turns hard and dominant, but it has the opposite effect to what he was hoping, because it only brings me closer. My orgasm is careening toward me, and my body is too overstimulated for me to stop it.

My scalp protests at the rough tugs Wyatt is dealing out as he takes over thrusting into my mouth. I'm almost relieved because I can't focus past the pleasure rolling through every fiber of my being, but right as I'm about to fall, the blissful pleasure of my orgasm just a breath away, they both stop.

Wyatt pulls my mouth off his hard length, my saliva coating his cock and his eyes wild with need, at the same time Elias pulls his fingers from my pussy and lands a hard smack over my clit, tearing a strangled scream from my throat.

"You need to learn to control your pleasure," Elias growls as he lands another two spanks, each harder than the last.

How am I going to survive the night with these men?

Nineteen

Elias

It's been a long time since Wyatt and I have shared someone as inexperienced as Leighton. As a rule, we only play with members of the club who have signed ironclad NDAs and waivers about bodily harm. But there's something endearing about how little she knows about the dynamic she's about to find herself in.

Wyatt wipes the tears from her cheeks, his gaze flicking from her to me and back again. Her tears aren't from the punishment I just inflicted on her. No, they're tears of frustration, of need. But she's not getting what she wants yet.

That's the first lesson she needs to learn. Patience.

She'll get everything she craves. We'll give her every fucking thing she could ever want, but in our own time.

We'll shape her into our perfect little whore.

"Okay, angel?" Wyatt murmurs as he slips his thumb between her pouty lips. Fuck she looks so good stuffed full of us.

His cock in her mouth, my fingers in her greedy cunt, and soon my aching length. The pressure in my balls is almost unbearable, and I'm starting to wonder if I'm going to have an embarrassing trip back to when I was a teenager and could come from thought alone.

She nods. "Yes, Sir."

Every time the words fall from her pretty lips, I think my heart is going to stop beating in my chest. We've been called Sir by any number of subs over the years, including all the ones who work at the club, but it's never sounded so fucking perfect.

Unable to hold myself back a second longer, I slide the head of my cock through her wetness and barely swallow the groan that claws its way up the back of my throat. Fuck. How the hell am I going to last when I slide my cock into her when I'm already so fucking close to the edge.

"Are you going to take us both, pretty girl?" I rumble.

"Yes, Sir. Please."

I brush my palm down her spine, relishing in the soft skin beneath my calloused hand. She's clean where we're filthy. She's good where we're bad. She's an angel in the company of demons. I move my hand over the globes of her ass, rubbing the red marks that still mar her pretty pale skin from her punishment.

"I like it when you beg, Leighton. I think it might just be my favorite thing that comes from those pouty lips of yours."

I line my cock up with her entrance and meet Wyatt's gaze for the briefest of seconds. His eyes shine with the same thing that radiates through my chest. This is it. Leighton is the missing

118

piece of our puzzle. The piece I didn't realize we didn't have until she walked into the club tonight.

Together we push forward and let out a guttural moan each. Holy fucking shit. Her cunt is perfection. Her muscles clamp around me at the intrusion, but I push forward until I'm buried inside her. If I thought she looked good full of my fingers, nothing could have prepared me for the sight of my cock deep inside her, her pretty pussy stretched around me and her wetness dripping down my aching balls.

Jesus fucking Christ.

This is as close to heaven as a man like me is ever going to get. I'm destined for hell, but for as long as I'm buried balls deep in this woman, I may as well be behind those pearly gates.

"Good girl," Wyatt praises as he tightens his hold on her deep-brown locks. She's trying to keep up with him, but he's taken over thrusting, fucking her mouth as gently as a man like him can. Out of the two of us, he's the soft one, but that doesn't mean much. "You take our cocks so well, angel. Look at you, our perfect little whore."

Her muscles clamp around me, and I slam into her a little harder. Fuck. She loves it. The praise. The degradation. She fucking loves it all.

I push through the burning in the base of my spine, the need to release myself in this woman, thrusting harder, forcing her to take every inch until I'm sure she's ready for her release.

"Jesus, your mouth is sin, angel," Wyatt groans. "Do you want to swallow my cum, baby? Or should I coat your pretty face with it?"

I let my head fall back, and I squeeze my eyes shut. His filthy mouth is only meant to be pushing her closer to the edge, but the idea of seeing her covered in our seed, of claiming her, is almost enough to send me barreling off the edge.

She looks up at him, but she can't speak. Her lips stretched around him, tears rolling down her cheeks, her body at our mercy. It will inevitably be his choice, but she loves the dirty talk so much, how could we deprive her of it.

"Open wide, angel." Wyatt's thrusts become stuttered, his release plummeting toward him. His fists tighten in her hair, and her pussy clenches around me. She loves the bite of pain. Just like she loves everything else we're giving her.

Beneath the good girl exterior she wears so well is a deviant who can handle anything we throw at her. And I'm more than willing to push those boundaries as far as they'll go.

He pulls back just far enough for the tip of his cock to rest on Leighton's tongue and white streams of cum coat her lips, her cheeks, her mouth. I wish I had a better view. I wish I could see the mess he's made of our pretty little whore. But there's nothing that could stop me from pounding into her tight cunt.

"She looks so fucking pretty right now, brother." Wyatt drags his fingers through the mess he's made and wipes them on her tongue. She stares up at him diligently, never breaking eye contact. "Suck."

The way her lips close around his thick fingers is what sets off a chain reaction I was hoping to hold off just a while longer. But who am I kidding? I never would have been ready for this to end, and if I play my cards right, I'll find myself buried inside her every night for the rest of our lives.

"Are you ready to come, little one?" I grind out.

Leighton tries to speak around the fingers in her mouth, but the garbled sounds that come out instead only bring me closer to my own release. I want to drag this out. I want her to beg for her release. But I don't have that kind of restraint right now.

I wrap an arm around her waist and move my fingers over the sensitive bundle of nerves that will set her off any second now. She lets out a scream around Wyatt's fingers and chokes slightly causing her pussy to tighten around me. Jesus. I'm hanging on by a fucking thread.

"Better come for me, pretty girl. I want you to soak my cock."

As if the words conjure her orgasm, her entire body shakes, the power of her release stealing her ability to hold her body steady, but we can do that for her. All she needs to worry about is doing as we say, and we'll take care of the rest. She lets out a silent scream, the pleasure stealing the sound before it can leave her throat.

Wyatt steadies his hold around her shoulders, holding her through the tremors while I grip her hips tighter. She'll have marks in the morning, and that thought only makes me press my fingers deeper into her soft flesh.

"Good girl," Wyatt praises. He repositions his hold slightly to stroke her hair. It was so perfectly curled when she walked into the club tonight. Now, there's no mistaking what she's been doing for the last hour. "Give us everything, angel."

She cries out, a sob filling the otherwise quiet room. I've never seen anything as beautiful as Leighton falling apart for us, and I can't wait to put her back together just so we can destroy her over and over again.

TWENTY

LEIGHTON

I fall forward despite the two sets of strong hands holding me in place. My body is ravaged, the power of my orgasm waning until the only thing my body is capable of is breathing, and even that's ragged and labored.

There aren't words for the out-of-body experience I just had. I can't even reconcile how sex can be so different depending who you're with, because there's no way Jason could ever elicit that kind of reaction from me, and I'm not sure he would want to even if he could.

Elias slams into me with a few final pumps, his grunts evidence of him chasing his own release while Wyatt lifts my front half and moves himself so I can rest my head on his chest. The steady *thump, thump, thump* of his heart gives me something other than exhaustion to hold on to as Elias's cock swells inside me, followed by a guttural moan that sounds almost animalistic.

I'm more spent than I can ever remember being, and yet my

body feels more alive than it ever has before. Every nerve ending is firing while my heart beats so hard in my chest I think it might try to escape.

Calloused hands rub my back, while another set gently brush my hair away from my face, but I couldn't move even if I wanted to. Which I don't. I never want to leave the cocoon of safety these two men give me.

Wyatt's eyes meet mine with a mix of worry and awe. But that doesn't make any sense. I didn't do anything other than kneel here and let them take me.

Wait a minute.

I lift my head with great effort and throw a glance back at Elias as he hesitantly withdraws his softening cock from my aching heat. It's deliciously sore from the pounding he gave me, and I almost allow myself to focus on that and lean back on the hard bare chest I was enjoying moments ago, until I notice he isn't wearing a condom.

I've never had unprotected sex. Despite Jason's constant whining about it, I've always made him wear a condom. The list of excuses has gotten longer as each year has passed, but the one that seems to work best is "what would it look like to our families if I'm pregnant before we get married?" His obsession with his own image is sometimes his biggest downfall.

"You're not wearing a condom," I whisper, as if I'm afraid of the words. I have an IUD, but all birth control can fail. That's why I've always insisted on being double protected.

He doesn't seem at all concerned as he looks down at the mess he's made and runs his fingers through my sore folds without pushing them inside me. "You're right, pretty girl. I didn't."

"We're clean, angel. We get tested regularly, and our last one was just last month," Wyatt tells me.

"What if I wasn't protected?" I push myself up and roll away from them before they can catch me, but somewhere between all the pleasure and the blinding panic of having to tell my mother I was pregnant from a one-night stand, I forgot about my ankle. As soon as I try to use it to push myself off the bed, tears spring to my eyes, and I let out a low whine. I'm still not all together convinced I don't need a hospital, but I'll deal with that once I get out of here.

A strong set of tattooed arms wind around my waist and tug me against his hard body. "Careful, angel." Wyatt presses a gentle kiss to my shoulder and settles me between his legs, forcing me to look at Elias sprawled out in front of us with an amused smirk playing on his lips. His body is a work of art. All hard lines and muscle. Intricate tattoos wind around his arms and chest as I trail my gaze downward out of instinct. I don't know what it is about these men that makes them so damn irresistible to me. I've never openly gawked at a man before, but Wyatt and Elias are the exception to that rule, making them all the more dangerous.

I glare at Elias, his uncaring attitude making me seethe with annoyance. What was I thinking coming here tonight? I was hurt. I thought being with them would be my way of getting back at Jason before accepting a life as his dutiful wife. But I was an idiot to think it would be that simple.

"Our girl has a bit of fire behind those pretty brown eyes." Elias rolls onto his knees and grasps my chin between his fingers. "It would be all the better if you weren't protected, Leighton. Because then there would be no way you could run from us."

My eyes widen, but I can't form a single word let alone a response.

Wyatt chuckles behind me, the ridge of his hardening cock pressing into my ass as he presses kisses along my shoulder. "But you are protected, aren't you baby? You wouldn't risk that asshole ex of yours putting his micro penis inside you unless you knew you were."

The way he talks about Jason should offend me. Despite all his faults, he's the one I'm meant to spend my life with, but that doesn't seem to stop the scoff that climbs up the back of my throat.

Elias presses a soft kiss to my lips, holding me in place with his grip on my chin. "Wyatt's going to wash you up while I order us some food. You'll need all the sustenance you can get for all the things we have planned for you tonight, dirty girl."

I open my mouth to protest, because there's no way my body can handle any more of what we just did, but despite how exhausted I am, I crave more. "I'll just have a salad please."

He gives me a sharp look before his dark eyes flick to Wyatt behind me. "I don't think so, Leighton."

And before I can protest, he's gone, not bothering to pull on a stitch of clothing as he strides from the room.

What the hell have I gotten myself into with these two?

TWENTY-ONE

WYATT

I know why Elias volunteers me to shower with Leighton, and while the decision had very little to do with torturing me, it doesn't make it any easier to run my soapy hands over her mouthwatering curves.

She's propped on the tiled seat of my shower, her eyes guarded but her body open to me. At first she had her arms wrapped around herself defensively, but I shook my head, and she dropped them without me having to issue a vocal command.

Such a good girl.

But she's not speaking either. She hasn't said a word since she requested a salad, and Elias immediately shut her down. I would have done the same thing. She has these preconceived notions about her weight that will take some work to break down, and the earlier we start, the sooner she'll see how beautiful she is in our eyes.

I kneel down in front of her and squeeze more body wash into my hands before working them into her shapely legs. I don't think I could ever get enough of touching her. Her softness is such a direct contrast to my rough hands, and each touch brings me closer to obsession.

Elias was right when he said we would be better off if she wasn't on birth control. If one of us could plant our seed, there's no way she could run from us, and that's exactly what she's planning to do right now. I can see it in the way her eyes dart toward the door, how her body tenses under my touch when it occurs to her she shouldn't be enjoying this as much as she is, and how resignation etches into her features each time she thinks about leaving.

I'm not sure if she's normally this open, or whether we've just fucked her walls down, but it's proving useful in understanding what she's thinking.

Aftercare has always been my thing more than Elias's. It's not that he doesn't know how to give it, or that he doesn't like to, it's just that I enjoy it more. Having a sub in my care is the most free I ever feel, and that with Leighton is only amplified.

"Are you sore?" I murmur as I massage my hands toward her swollen sex. We weren't gentle with her, and the evidence of that is how pink and puffy her cunt is.

She nods. "A little, Sir."

I smile at the use of the word. She wouldn't be in trouble if she dropped the formality while we're outside the bedroom, but I'm not going to stop her either, not when my heart lodges itself in my throat every time the word falls from those pretty pink lips.

I brush my fingers over the swollen flesh, and she flinches

ever so slightly, but just enough that I look up in question. That doesn't seem like a little.

"Okay, maybe more than a little." She blushes. "I've never had sex like that before."

The admission is hardly a surprise, but I'm pleased at how she's opening up for me, showing me the parts of herself she may have tried to hide just a few hours ago. "We should have been more gentle."

She shakes her head. "No, I...I liked it."

A slow smirk tips up the corners of my lips. "Oh I know you did, angel."

She gives me a small smile, but there's doubt behind those pretty eyes, and all I want to do is take it all away, to shield her from the darkness in the world, from whoever has put the doubts in her mind. I want to steal her away and lock her in an ivory tower where nothing and no one can ever hurt her again.

The idea has some merit, and to be honest, it's not out of the cards, but although we have very questionable morals, I'd rather not begin our lives together with kidnapping.

I grip her chin between my fingers and hold her gaze for long seconds. "What's on your mind, angel?"

"It's nothing."

I shake my head, wordlessly reminding her one of her rules is not to lie, and she sighs.

"It's just that...I had the time of my life tonight. I'll never have an experience like that again. But for you two, that's probably a regular Friday. You're both so confident and so good at it. I just can't see how I would measure up to the women you're normally with."

I'm shaking my head before she can finish her sentence. She has no idea how wrong she is. No idea that her inexperience makes her the perfect sub for us to mold into one that will fit the two of us to perfection. No idea that what we shared was beyond anything Elias and I have ever experienced. And no idea how hard the two of us are falling, despite only having met her tonight. "You've got nothing to worry about, angel. Believe me when I say Elias and I have *never* experienced anything like that. You're perfection."

Her protests are cut off when Elias pokes his head into the bathroom, his eyes falling on the two of us immediately. "Food's here."

I guess we'll just have to prove how wrong she is.

TWENTY-TWO

ELIAS

I 'm not sure what I interrupted in the bathroom, but the heaviness in Leighton's eyes when she emerges in nothing but one of Wyatt's shirts, her arm wrapped around his waist as she hobbles toward the table, tells me whatever she's thinking is far from good.

I meet Wyatt's eyes, and he shakes his head slightly. To share women the way we do, as well as all other facets of our lives, we've learned to communicate silently, but right now I wish I could read his mind.

Leighton's hair is damp around her shoulders, the natural waves framing her bare face. She was beautiful with a face full of makeup, but she's fucking incredible without it. The dusting of freckles across her nose and cheeks, the beauty mark just below her lower lip, the brightness of her eyes under her lashes. Jesus. I could fall to my knees and worship her right now. But something tells me she wouldn't believe a word I said.

She needs to trust us first, and I have a feeling trust isn't something she gives out easily.

Wyatt helps her sit on one of the chairs before taking his own seat on the other side of her, sandwiching her between us.

I drag her toward me until her knees are trapped between mine, and I can finally let out the breath I've been holding since I rolled out of bed. It doesn't come naturally to me to care. Even with my ex-wife, I struggled to see when there was something on her mind, but I don't have that problem with Leighton.

I pull a pizza box toward us and break off a piece, keeping a close eye on the way doubt creeps into her eyes as she watches me pull it apart into bite sized pieces.

"Open," I say as I bring a piece of cheesy dough to her lips.

She does as she's told and takes the piece from between my fingers, chewing slowly like she's warring with herself. Her hang-ups about her body are unacceptable, but I'm not so cocky that I think that's something we can train out of her in one night. If the snippets she's shown us are anything to go by, these issues have been rooted into her mind over years, and it's going to take some time to break them down.

As soon as she swallows that piece, I have another waiting at her lips, giving her no time to argue with me like I can see she wants to.

Wyatt takes a piece of pizza from the box and brings it to his own lips, but his gaze never leaves the two of us. He's both amused and confused by the series of events unfolding in front of him, but he doesn't question me. If anything, he seems pleased by my actions.

We continue like this until an entire piece is finished before I pull another toward me and start the process again.

"Elias?" she says quietly, and I look up from where my fingers are tearing apart the dough. "I can feed myself. And you should have some before it gets cold."

I chuckle and shake my head as I continue. "I'm well aware that you can feed yourself, pretty girl, but I happen to like taking care of you. And I also know that if I were to allow you to feed yourself, you would pick at it until it seems like you've eaten enough, thinking that we'll let you get away with it. So I think this arrangement works just fine."

Wyatt laughs behind her, his head falling back as the sound fills the space. "I have a feeling you're not going to get away with anything here, angel. Might as well roll with it."

She opens her mouth to protest again, but this time I have a piece of pizza ready, and I quickly slide it between her lips before the argument can fall from them.

She needs the two of us to take care of her. And more than that? We need her to make us complete.

Once she's made her way through two slices, she shakes her head. "I really can't eat anymore," she whispers.

"Because you're full, or because you think you shouldn't eat anymore?" I raise a brow, watching closely for any mistruths she might try to tell me.

"I'm full," she says truthfully.

I nod and take my first bite of pizza. In the past I may have been annoyed that I wasn't eating when it was hot and fresh, but the warmth that's settled in my chest is better than any hot slice of pizza could ever be. Taking care of Leighton may just have become my favorite pastime.

She tries to push her chair back to put some distance between us, but I quickly hook my foot around the leg of hers, halting her escape.

"Where do you think you're going, pretty girl?"

"I was just going to give you some space to eat."

I shake my head. "No."

She shoots a glance over her shoulder at Wyatt, but he just chuckles, finding my actions far more amusing than he should.

"Nice try, angel. You can't pit us against each other, though. If Elias says he wants to eat with you where you are, I'm not going to overrule him."

She sighs and leans back in her chair, allowing her shoulders to relax slightly.

"Good girl." I smile.

LEIGHTON

This is not how I saw the rest of the night panning out.

Heck, I thought I would be putting myself in a cab the second we were done and going back to a life I have no interest in living. But nope. Somehow I've found myself nestled between Elias and Wyatt on their obscenely large couch watching some movie I've never heard of.

Their hands have been on me in one way or another since we finished dinner. A gentle brush of my bare thigh, an arm around my shoulders, a calloused palm holding my soft hand. I've never been shown this much affection in my life, and I'm finding it a little overwhelming despite how much I'm enjoying it.

It feels like their eyes are burning into me as I watch the movie, barely taking in the storyline, but every time I chance a look at either of them, their gazes are glued to the television.

My foot is propped up on the ottoman in front of me, a bag of peas resting on it, to bring down the swelling Elias claimed.

If I didn't know better, I would think it was just to give them a reason to sandwich me between their warm bodies and keep me close.

But that's ridiculous. Isn't it?

"Do you always think this loud, angel?" Wyatt asks, a hint of teasing in his tone.

I look up at him and find him already staring down at me. "I'm not sure."

"I guess we'll have to turn that brain off again, won't we, pretty girl?" Elias tugs my body toward him, easily lifting me until my back is pressed against him while Wyatt carefully relocates my foot to rest on his bare thigh.

It was hard enough to keep my eyes off them when they were fully clothed, but since we finished in the bedroom, neither of them has bothered to pull on more than a pair of shorts, and I'm painfully aware of how hard it's been not to stare at their bare chests and defined arms.

The scorching heat at my back warms me as the bag of pea is discarded back on the ottoman, and rough hands move up my calves in a teasing motion. "There's something else we need to discuss, isn't there Leighton?" Wyatt prompts.

I stare at him, trying to work out what he could possibly be talking about, but nothing of note comes to me. Maybe it's the exhaustion that bites at the edge of my consciousness.

"Do you care to repeat what you told me in the shower so Elias can hear?"

I drop my gaze to where my hands have fallen in my lap. Oh

that. I don't want my insecurities out on show, not with these two men who so effortlessly break down the walls I've spent my entire life building.

Large hands settle on my belly and hold me tight, silently telling me I'm safe here, even if I've never felt safe anywhere else.

"I just said that I'd had the time of my life, but I couldn't understand what either of you were getting out of it," I whisper. There's no point trying to evade answering because Wyatt just would have paraphrased, and it's better coming from me. Less room for interpretation.

The room falls silent apart from the dim whisper of voices on the television. One of them must have turned the volume down as they repositioned me. Elias's body tenses behind me, his arms holding me firmly so I couldn't escape even if I wanted to, which despite the conversation we're having, I still wouldn't want to.

I can't help but fiddle with the scar on my hand, the one Jason gave me last Christmas when I accidentally broke a champagne glass. He swore up and down that he didn't mean it, that he was only placing the broken fragments into my palm when he lost his balance and applied more pressure than needed. But after tonight I'm not so sure. There's a list of injuries I've had over the last five years that just don't quite add up if you look at them past face value.

I chance a glance up at Wyatt, but he's looking right past me to Elias. If I didn't know better I would think they're communicating silently, but people don't really do that, do they?

"Why do you think we wouldn't be getting anything out of being with you, Leighton?" Elias rumbles, his deep voice startling me from my thoughts.

"Well, I guess because you're both so good at what we did, and I'm just...me." I shrug and immediately internally berate myself. Surely I could have explained that better. Surely I could have given a better reason than I'm just me. "I mean, I guess there's a reason Jason cheated on me."

That's your idea of a helpful addition? I admonish myself.

Both men stiffen, and the arms around my waist only seem to tighten, making sure there's nowhere I can go. But even with how awkward this conversation is, there's still nowhere I'd rather be.

"Just so we're clear, angel," Wyatt rumbles. "You're under the impression that you somehow deserved for that fucking piece of shit to cheat on you, *and* that also means you can't see why Elias and I are interested in you?"

I open my mouth to respond, but I guess that is what I said, and every time I speak I only seem to make it worse. My mother used to say I had a big mouth as a child. Maybe I didn't grow out of it as well as I thought I had. I give a small nod before looking away. Their scrutiny is almost more than I can handle, and staring right into Wyatt's eyes right now is just too much.

The arms around me move, and for a second I panic. He's going to leave. I've pointed out the obvious, and he's realized I'm right. Will they both go? Or I suppose I will, seeing as I'm in their house? I'm not sure where I'll stay tonight. I can hardly go home to Jason tonight after how angry he was, smelling of the two men who saved me from him.

But a second later, my fears are squashed when Elias perches me on his knee, and his palm cups my cheek, forcing me to look at him.

"We're going to get something straight right fucking now, Leighton, and the next time we have this conversation, we'll be having it with you over my knee while Wyatt holds a vibrator to that pretty pussy of yours and forces you to come over and over again, even when you beg us to stop. Do we understand each other?" His stern voice gives no invitation for argument.

"Yes Sir."

"That asshole doesn't deserve *you*, Leighton. He doesn't see what an incredible woman he's had by his side, and that's his fuck up, not yours. Men like him blame their mistakes on everyone else, never taking responsibility for their own actions. But this is not on you. Nothing he's done is your fault, no matter how many times he tells you it is," he pauses, and his thumb brushes over my bottom lip. His harsh gaze softens slightly before he continues, "Now, on to what Wyatt and I get out of having you here with us." He looks to his friend who must have moved closer as he takes my face in his hand and directs my eyes to meet his. "You're fucking beautiful, angel. The moment I saw you in that bar, I fucking knew this is where you belonged. What do we get out of it? Every fucking thing. We're selfish bastards for coveting an angel we don't deserve, but we're not going to give you up."

"You don't even know me," I whisper because I know my voice will break under the weight of how true those words are. And while my inexperience might be endearing right now, and their savior complex might flare to life because they see me as a damsel in distress, the more time they spend with me, the more they'll realize just how dull I really am.

Which is why this can only ever be tonight. Because at least then there'll be two people who were never disappointed in me, and I can cling to that for the rest of my life.

TWENTY-FOUR

WYATT

Despite his tone, Elias has handled this well. Normally if a sub were to say something negative about themselves, they'd find themselves with a bright red ass and be denied for the rest of the night.

But not Leighton.

His eyes flick to me, and I nod as I carefully pull her down off his lap until her head rests on his knee, and she's spread out for me. The shirt she's wearing has ridden up and shows off the shapely legs that will be wrapped around my neck in a few seconds.

There's an uncertainty in her eyes that I don't like, but I don't stop to ask questions. It seems as if sometimes with Leighton, the only way to get past her walls is to crash right through them until she forgets about whatever bullshit that asshole ex of hers thinks. Soon she'll learn there are only two people on the earth she needs to please, and we'll do just about anything to make her smile.

I glide my hands up the soft skin of her thighs, gathering the shirt and pushing it up until her perfect pussy is on display. Jesus fucking Christ. She's beautiful.

Her arousal fills the room, and I can almost taste her. I can't take it another second. I need to worship her. I need to show our angel that whatever lies she's been told are just that. Lies.

I dip down and drag my tongue over her soft folds, and we let out a mutual groan. She tastes fucking divine, and I don't waste another second before burying my face in her cunt.

I flick my gaze up to Elias, but he's caught up in Leighton. One of his hands is wrapped around hers, holding them above her head on his other knee, while the other wraps gently around her throat, massaging her pulse point.

"That's it, little one, grind that pretty pussy all over his face," he murmurs, his lips brushing over her cheek in an intimate gesture I don't think I've ever seen from him before. We've shared a lot of women, but I think we can both agree at this point we may have found the last.

His reassurance gives her the confidence to lift her hips and take exactly what she needs from me, and I'm more than happy to give her everything she could possibly want.

"You can come whenever you need to, pretty girl."

I shoot a look at him because he's always been stingy with giving women orgasms, always wanting to drag their pleasure out for as long as he possibly can. I don't think I've *ever* heard him give a woman free rein without the plan of overwhelming her with more orgasms than she can handle. But his gaze is stuck on her, his eyes flitting over her face, taking her in as she

152

lets out a gentle moan.

Maybe I never allowed myself to consider what it would be like if we ever found the woman that would make us whole, but I guess this is it.

We found her.

And we're never going to let her go.

Twenty-Five

Leighton

T he cold light of morning reminds me that last night was a one time only kind of deal. As nice as it's been to be worshipped by the men sleeping on either side of me, it was just a bit of fun, and now I need to get back to my real life.

Even as I think it, my body tenses involuntarily. I don't want to go back to Jason. I don't want to hear from my mother about what a lovely man he is and how a woman like me should feel lucky that he wants to marry me. And I certainly don't want to go back to the monotonous life I've grown accustomed to.

I don't want to feel alone anymore. If only I had a choice in the matter. But I learned long ago that I don't. I'm just a pawn in someone else's game, and that's all I'll ever be.

Before last night, I'd made peace with that. I'd accepted that some people just aren't destined to feel real love or to live a life that sparks joy in their souls. I'm just one of those unlucky people. But actually experiencing it, feeling what it's like to have someone, two someones in this case, care for me, it's going to make it hard to go back.

Wyatt's arm is thrown over my middle, his warmth making it even harder to make myself leave, while Elias's gentle breaths whisper across my cheek from where he's buried his face in my hair. Is this what it feels like to be wanted?

I can't remember the last time Jason held me through the night, or even when he had sex with me because he couldn't bear to not touch me for another second. Has he ever felt like that with me? I'd often wondered if he had a reminder set in his phone once a week to have sex with me, just to keep up the pretense of our relationship, but that would be ridiculous… right?

Given I found him with another woman last night, maybe not so much.

I flex my ankle, and some of the searing pain has eased with sleep and how well it was taken care of last night. Is it terrible of me that I kind of hoped it would still be bad? That I wouldn't be able to leave because I couldn't walk on it?

Disappointment floods me at the thought of walking out the door and never seeing Wyatt and Elias again. But what other option do I have?

With a sigh of acceptance, I wiggle my way from Wyatt's hold and slip down to the end of the bed, carefully testing my foot to make sure I can walk on it. I wince, but the pain is bearable.

As quietly as I can manage, I creep around the room collecting the clothes they stripped from me last night. Images of their mouths on my skin, their hands bending me in the ways they wanted, of the way every ounce of their attention focused on me, assault me with each step I take.

Even as I throw a glance over my shoulder, deciding once and for all to leave, I know I'm making a mistake. Because nothing has ever felt as good as being theirs, even if it was just for the night.

T he cab ride home feels like an eternity, and yet it's not long enough. Every mile I put between me and the brownstone feels like an entire continent and regret settles low in my belly.

I left a note on my way out, thanking them for the best night of my life as I fought the tears threatening to fall, but it's not enough. Nothing I could ever give them would be.

The New York streets pass by, bringing me closer and closer to the Upper East Side and to the home I share with Jason. A gift from my parents for our engagement. A place I wish I could walk away from and never see again.

Jason normally works on Saturday mornings. He always says only lazy people take a full weekend, that no one really needs more than a day of rest before the week starts again, but I've always thought those comments have more to do with me sitting at home all day every day than how he actually feels about the five-day work week. Not that he gave me any choice in the matter.

I *wanted* to work. I begged him, and my parents, to let me put my degree to use, but they insisted there was no point. Not when we got engaged on the day we graduated from college, and as soon as we're married there's no sense in working because we'll be starting a family. Not that I have any say in any of that. That's the plan they have for me, and one that I'm expected to follow along with blindly.

The early morning sun shines brightly on our quiet street, a rarity in the heart of such a big city, surrounded by skyscrapers and people rushing to get on with their day, but all I see is the future I don't want sitting in front of me.

I pay the cab driver and climb out. The stupid angel costume hangs from my body, my bare feet touching the ice-cold concrete of the sidewalk before I drag myself up the stairs to the front door, my ankle protesting with every step. My keys sit heavy in my palm as I raise my hand to unlock the door, but before I can reach for the lock it swings open, and I'm face to face with the man I found cheating on me last night.

"Where have you been?" He growls and pulls me into the house with a harsh tug. He glances around the street, making sure no one saw me doing the walk of shame before slamming the door behind me. "I waited up all night for you."

"No, you didn't," I say quietly, yanking my arm from his grasp with a wince. He's not normally so physical with me, but the last few months he's been changing. His anger has been escalating, and with that have come some things I probably shouldn't have overlooked.

"How would you know?" he snaps. "And you didn't answer my question."

"I don't plan to either." I start toward the stairs, dreading every step that will bring me closer to the bedroom we share on the third floor. The place is way too big for just the two of us, but as my parents always say, soon it will be filled with kids.

I only get up the first few steps before I'm pulled back down, and I don't get the chance to catch myself before I land on my ass at the bottom with a heavy thud and shooting pain spreads through my whole body.

"We're not done here," Jason forces through gritted teeth, and for the first time since I walked in the door I actually take him in. His shirt is rumpled, his eyes dark and crazed, and there's something unhinged about his demeanor that I can't remember ever seeing before.

This isn't the calm, collected, and frankly boring man I'm supposed to marry. No. This is a monster who hides behind a persona.

He crouches down to my level and grips my chin in a tight hold. "Where. Were. You. Last. Night?" He enunciates each word and sends dread spiraling through my stomach.

"At a friend's," I whisper. "I didn't want to see you after seeing you with that woman at the bar. I needed some time to cool down and collect my thoughts."

He watches me for long seconds, looking for some kind of sign that I'm lying, but I hope he won't find anything. Can he still smell the sex on my skin? Can he tell by the way my makeup is smudged and my hair rumpled that I'm not telling him the truth? Did he have me followed? Did he track my phone?

Each thought hits me like a truck, until it's not a metaphorical truck that hits me but a fist, straight to the temple. I can barely take a breath before another hit lands on my stomach, and a moment later stars burst into my vision, and there's nothing I can do to keep myself awake.

TWENTY-SIX

ELIAS

Since being discharged from the SEALs, sleep hasn't come naturally to me. At first it was the memories of what I'd seen, the horrors of watching the men I considered brothers die right in front of me. But then I guess it was just a habit. I spent so many years barely getting a few hours of sleep a night, that my body learned to live on small bursts of sleep.

But as consciousness tugs my body from what would normally only be a few hours of rest, I realize I slept the entire night and from the bright sun streaming through the open blinds, into the morning as well.

Leighton's soft floral scent surrounds me, and a small smile tugs at the corners of my lips. Is she the reason my body finally allowed itself a full night of rest? Could this be what it's like for the rest of our lives? Waking up to her, fucking her into oblivion, happiness?

I drag my eyes open and turn my head, expecting to see her

dark hair fanned across the pillow and her sleepy smile, but instead I only see Wyatt on the other side of the bed.

Where the hell is she?

I sit up with a start and look around, desperately searching for anything of hers that we discarded when we stripped her last night.

But it's all gone.

She's gone.

Emotions crash over me all at once until I can't differentiate what I'm feeling at all. Anger. Sadness. Resentment. Fear. The ache in my chest deepens, and I rub the center to try to ease some of the pain. How could she leave after all we shared last night?

But then again, everyone leaves Wyatt and I. Our families. Our ex-wives. Now Leighton.

I take a deep breath and will my body to calm down before reaching over to shake Wyatt. I don't want to have to break this to him, not when he got his hopes up so high. But we can't bury our heads in the sand. We've never been those kinds of men, and I don't plan to change that now.

His sleep-filled eyes open and meet mine, the same smile I had on my lips when I first woke up etched into his. Everything about last night felt right. Leighton felt right. But maybe we were wrong.

"She's gone," I say quietly. I'm not sure if the blow will be easier to take hearing from me, or if it would have been better for me to let him figure it out on his own.

His eyes pop open and move around the room, following the same trail mine had just a couple of minutes ago. Before I can say anything else, he jumps from the bed and tugs his shorts up his legs. He's out of the room before I can think to do the same, and by the time I make it out to the kitchen, he's bracing both hands against the edge of the counter with his head hung over what appears to be a note.

"She went back to him," he whispers. "He's going to hurt her, Elias. I know it. The way he touched her last night. He's going to really hurt her." Each word is more strained than the last.

I reach the counter and tug the note toward me, reading the elegant script several times as if the words have some kind of clue behind them.

Thank you for last night, it will always remain the best of my life.

The paper crumples in my hand, and I find myself in a similar position to my best friend. Nausea rolls through my stomach, every fiber of my being knowing Wyatt's right. That asshole has all the makings of an abuser. We've both seen plenty in our lives and can normally spot them from a mile away. But why would she go back?

"Did you install a tracker last night?" I ask.

He nods.

"Check it's operational. I'm calling Bishop. I want to know everything before we go get her." I take a few steps toward the bedroom.

"She left us, El. She doesn't want to be here."

I shake my head. "There's more to it. I'm sure of it." Leighton may be the most genuine person I've ever met. She doesn't have a bad bone in her body, and if she felt like she had to go back to that jackass, there has to be a reason behind it.

I find my phone in my discarded pants and make quick work of pulling up Jason's file from the club. I never got Leighton's last name, but that doesn't mean I can't find it.

I scan the file quickly, scoffing when I see he marked his relationship status as 'single'. Asshole. Jason Collins. A boring name for a boring motherfucker. His profile is vague at best, and I make a note of the staff member who checked this off. It's not complete enough for my liking, and from what I can tell, at least some of it is fabricated.

A quick Google search finds me a photo of him and Leighton at a charity gala last month. His arm wrapped around her waist, barely allowing himself to actually touch her, and the smile across her beautiful face is forced. None of the light I saw while she was with us in her eyes, and my chest aches to have her back with us, to see that spark I took for granted. Perhaps I would have savored her more if I knew. Or maybe knowing would have tainted the short time we had together.

I shoot off a text to Bishop asking him to gather everything he can about both Leighton and Jason, before turning my attention back to Wyatt.

He hasn't moved even though the note is no longer sitting in front of him. It's been a long time since I've seen him withdraw like this, and I don't fucking like it.

I clap my hand on his shoulder and squeeze. "We'll bring her back," I promise even though I have no right to do so.

Because there's a chance she didn't leave because she had to. There's a chance that she wanted to go, or more likely, that she didn't want to stay. But I won't believe that until she tells us that herself.

Our angel could run to the ends of the earth, but we'd never stop chasing her.

TWENTY-SEVEN

LEIGHTON

Consciousness returns to me, and the ache in my temple intensifies as soon as I open my eyes. What the heck happened?

I remember leaving Elias and Wyatt's house and getting into a cab. I remember the sadness that weighed me down all the way home. And then I remember...

Jason.

He hit me.

Hard.

He knocked me out.

I force my eyes open past the pain and nausea that rolls over me as I realize I'm in our bedroom. He must have brought me up here after I passed out.

I turn my head and wince when my neck protests. I'm alone in the room, which allows me to let out a breath of relief, but it's short lived when faint voices carry up the stairs.

With a sigh, I allow my eyes to drift closed. I couldn't move right now even if I wanted to, not with the agony that tears through my body every time I blink.

If I hadn't already realized that I made a mistake leaving the men who made me feel *everything*, this would be the moment that realization washed over me. Not only did I leave without saying goodbye, I left without getting so much as a phone number. Regardless of what they said last night, I know that soon they'll find someone else to play the part I did last night, and I'll become a distant memory, if that.

As carefully as I can manage, I roll onto my side and pull the pillow against myself. But there's something not quite right that makes my eyes pop back open despite the screaming agony behind them.

I'm not in that ridiculous costume anymore.

I'm in the pair of silk pajamas that were folded at the end of the bed last night when I left the house with no idea how my life was about to change. When I found that invitation in Jason's jacket pocket, I had no idea what to expect. But it certainly wasn't what I found.

Which means he stripped me and put me in them.

Twenty-four hours ago I wouldn't have blinked at that. But right now the urge to scrub my body clean of his touch almost overwhelms me. I don't ever want to feel his hands on me again.

I need to find a way out. But that task feels like too much right now.

168

All our bank accounts are linked. He'll know if I withdraw money from the accounts because although I have no proof, I'm almost sure he gets alerted every time I touch the accounts, even when it's just for a coffee from the local café. On top of that, there's no way my parents will let me leave him. It won't matter that he hurt me, or that he might do it again. No. All that matters to them is their image. And how would it look if their daughter left the governor's son?

And even if none of that was an issue, where would I go? There's nowhere I could run that they wouldn't find me. Not with the connections they have. The police commissioner of New York could pull the tiniest of strings, and my escape would come unraveled.

I bury my face in the pillow and fight against the tears welling in my eyes. What am I going to do?

The voices start to grow louder, and I stiffen instinctively before making the split-second decision to pretend I'm still asleep. It's not going to work forever, although I wish it would, but it might buy me just a little more time to work out what my next steps should be.

It's only when they reach the top of the stairs that I realize who it is.

My parents.

He called my parents.

He hit me, knocked me out, and called my parents. If that's not proof of how messed up my life is, I don't know what is.

"She's still asleep," Jason tells them quietly.

My mother sighs, and her heels click as she moves further into the room. "You shouldn't have hit her face."

He shouldn't have hit my...face. Good to know she's fine with my fiancé hitting me, just as long as it doesn't ruin my appearance.

"I know."

"She'll need to stay home until the bruising starts to calm down and can be covered by some carefully applied makeup." Her voice comes from near my face, and I try to keep my breathing as even as I can. "Do you have any events she was meant to accompany you to?"

"Not for another week. I'm sure by then she'll be able to hide them."

"Were you able to ascertain where she spent the night last night?" My father asks, his tone as disinterested as it always is when he talks about me. What did I do to deserve parents who are so indifferent when their child is hurt?

"No. She said she was with a friend, but something was blocking the tracker I have on her phone, and I can't see any of the women at the country club having that kind of technology in their home."

Tracker? He has a tracker on me?

"See if you can't get some more information out of her when she wakes. She should know all friends need to be vetted by myself." My father pauses, and I pray they're done here, but I'm not that lucky. "I trust you will keep your extracurricular activities more discreet from now on?"

"My membership to that club has been revoked."

"I suggest if you're going to step out, you do it in another state. It's much less likely you'll be caught that way."

I balk at his words, but manage to remain completely still. My father just gave my fiancé advice about how to cheat on me without raising any suspicion. Even for my parents that's messed up. Is he speaking from experience? Admitting in front of my mother that he's cheated on her? I'm sure it doesn't come as a surprise. I'm not sure he's been faithful a day in his life.

And yet he's one of the most highly regarded men in the city, and the one who chose my fate.

TWENTY-EIGHT

WYATT

After I got over the initial shock of waking up and Leighton being gone, we jumped into action like we never have before. The business we're in means we have to be ready for anything all the time, but I don't think I've ever seen Elias work with such purpose.

He's been on the phone with Bishop for the last half hour learning everything there is to know about Leighton, her family, and that asshole who cheated on her.

It's a hard pill to swallow that she would choose to go back to him rather than stay with us, but there has to be a reason for it, and we're going to work out what that reason is.

We were able to get some basic information pretty easily. Her full name. Address. Where she went to college and what she majored in. But everything else has been buried a little deeper than you would expect.

From that though, I've been able to track her and confirm she's at a house on the Upper East Side that appears to be in both hers and Jason's name. The confirmation that she is in fact with him stings, but at least we know where she is. Whether she's safe might be another story altogether.

"Bishop said there's a convenience store up the street from the house that might have cameras. Can you try to hack into them?" Elias asks, barely pulling the phone away from his ear to speak to me.

I nod and quickly move through the motions. This comes as naturally to me as breathing does. It's one of the reasons the SEALs have routinely begged me to come back over the last ten years, but they wouldn't be asking if they knew what I did with my skills since I was honorably discharged.

How we started working with the Legion is still a mystery to me, a marriage of convenience for both parties that just made sense, but it comes with its own set of unique challenges.

Crew and Elias went to school together, grew up together through circumstances I wouldn't wish on my worst enemy, and when we were discharged and bought the club Crew reached out with an offer we couldn't refuse. Without it we would have had to align ourselves with one of the five families, something neither of us was all that keen to do, and all we did in return was allow meetings to be held at the club, and help the Legion when they needed some extra hands.

Killing people comes almost as naturally to me as hacking does, so I have no problems helping them clean up the odd mess.

I find the cameras easily enough, making my way through the convenience store's shoddy firewall without a hitch, but the camera quality is going to be a problem. Some of these businesses needed to join us in the twenty-first century. But I guess it's a nice neighborhood, on a quiet street, there's probably not all that much crime to worry about.

I run through the tape from the last few hours, looking at anyone who came or went in the time since Leighton left, which according to our own cameras was about three hours ago now.

A cab pulls into the frame, and I move closer to the screen to get a better look, not that that's going to help the camera quality improve. But even with that, I can tell the woman in the feed is our girl. She looks up at the house, hesitating to approach the front steps.

I'm relieved to see she didn't try to put those heels back on before she left, but the idea of her walking around the city of New York in bare feet makes me want to take her to a doctor for every shot they can think of. I take a deep breath and stamp down the protective urges that flare to life when I think of Leighton and watch as she carefully pulls herself up the steps.

I can't see her facial expressions, but it's obvious each time she puts weight on her ankle that she's still in pain, and I make a note to myself to add to her punishment for hurting herself more.

The door flings open before she can reach it, and a second later she's yanked through the door so quickly she stumbles into her asshole ex.

How dare he handle her like that? Especially after how he hurt her last night. If I didn't already have plans to kill this cunt slowly, I'd be making those plans right about now.

"I got her." I force the words out and turn my laptop around for Elias to watch what I just did.

"This motherfucker needs to die," he growls, and I swear I hear Bishop laugh on the other end of the line. In the time we've known him, Crew's son has never seen either of us like this about a woman, so I'm certain he's finding it fucking hilarious.

Elias stops what he's doing and listens intently to what Bishop is telling him before rubbing his face with his free hand. "Fuck."

"What?"

"Can you send me what you've found so far?" Elias says into the phone before listening for a few seconds and continuing. "Thanks, Bishop. I appreciate your help."

He ends the call and falls into the seat beside me, his head in his hands. It's not often I've seen my best friend seem so... defeated, and I don't like the look on him at all.

"Are you going to tell me what he found?" I ask impatiently.

Elias looks up and sighs. "Leighton is Police Commissioner Chalmers's daughter. And Jason is the son of Governor Collins. From what Bishop can gather, their whole relationship has been orchestrated by their parents, and it doesn't look like she's ever been given much of a choice in the matter."

I open my mouth but snap it shut again. What the fuck am I meant to say? It won't be as easy as getting her back and away from an abusive fiancé, not when people like Chalmers and Collins are involved. As crooked as they come. People look down on the Legion, but they're the ones who keep order to the city, something the men in question should be doing instead of encouraging rebellion within the families and starting wars, and that's just the tip of the iceberg. There are rumors the two of them have been working on a side project of sorts. Legion have kept trafficking out of the city for the last ten years, but in recent times there have been moves against them. Back door deals that could see its return.

I wonder if my angel knows the sorts of things her father and almost father-in-law are involved in. And how far from the tree does the apple fall? How involved with this shit is Jason?

There is one thing I'm sure of though.

"Leighton didn't leave because she wanted to."

Elias shakes his head. "She probably doesn't think she has a choice."

TWENTY-NINE

LEIGHTON

I can't remember the last time Jason was home during the week. In fact, I don't think he's worked from home a day in his life. And yet this week he hasn't left once.

He also hasn't spoken to me.

We've been in complete silence since my parents left on Sunday, and I can't see that changing anytime soon because there's certainly nothing I have to say to him.

I glance over at his office door and sigh. Usually when he has to do anything work related he'll do so with the door closed unless he thinks I'm not around, but that door hasn't closed once, which just confirms he's keeping an eye on me.

The housewares magazine in my hands is just another thing to make me look busy while he's home. My mother has been harassing me about setting up our gift registry for the wedding we still haven't set a date for, but they're getting impatient, and so is Jason's father. I'm not sure what benefit our parents get from us marrying, or if it's purely from a social standpoint, but the longer we put it off, the more I say I want more time to make sure everything is perfect, the more they hassle us.

Eventually it will wear me down. My parents have gotten very good at that over the years. Bullying me until I agree to whatever they want. Poking and prodding until I can't possibly deny whatever they're asking of me. And this will be no different.

I touch my cheek gently and sigh. The bruising is going down and my mother was right, I'll be able to cover it with some well-placed concealer tonight when we go to the charity event Jason's father is throwing for some organization he doesn't actually believe in.

How do I know that?

Because last year when I graduated from college and it was emphatically decided for me that I wouldn't be going into paid work in data science like I spent four years studying toward, I asked if I could work at his foundation a few days a week to get out of the house and to help people.

I made the mistake of bringing it up in front of my parents and Jason, and the lot of them laughed.

"You're above that," they told me through their amusement.

I dropped it, just like I did everything else they told me wasn't worth my time, but my need to help people has always been strong. I'm painfully aware of how privileged I was growing up, even with parents who cared more about who I married than my happiness. I never wanted for anything. I never had to go hungry or miss out on field trips. I had a trust fund to pay for my Ivy League schooling, and I lived in a house with staff who did anything I asked.

And all I ever wanted to do was help the people who weren't born into a life like mine.

I need to start getting ready soon, but the thought of Jason touching me makes my skin crawl. He hasn't so much as reached for me since he changed me after knocking me out, and it's a good thing because I'm not confident about how I would react.

The phone beside me buzzes on the couch cushion, and I let out a breath when I see my mother's name flashing. Of course.

"Hi, Mum," I say, but my voice is flat. Not that I think she'll notice.

"Hello, dear. I was just calling to see how you're feeling and making sure you're up for the event tonight."

Ah yes, of course she would phrase it like I was sick. Not like my fiancé hit me, and not only were she and my father okay with that, they discussed how they could cover it up. "I'll be fine for the gala," I tell her as I flick through a few pages of the magazine. We already have a house full of appliances and housewares that I picked out when we moved in, but apparently I have to choose all over again.

"Are you sure? I'm sure Jason could find someone else to go with him if you're not up to it." If the bruising hasn't gone down enough to hide.

"No, Mother. I'm fine to go," I insist. I usually hate going to these things with him. He always holds onto me all night, introducing me to people I have no interest in meeting, and talking about how investment banking is going to boom over the next decade.

We go to one of these things at least once a month, and each one wears on me more than the last. Perhaps it would be different if the people who attended were genuinely concerned about whatever cause they're supporting, but they aren't. They just care about eating a three-course meal, drinking at the open bar, and bragging to their friends about whatever business deal they've made that week.

"If you're sure." Her voice seems hesitant, but I don't allow myself to read into it. I've disappointed her from birth, so whatever I've done that she's upset with now is really of very little consequence to me. "Do you have a dress you can wear? I know you haven't been able to get out of the house this week."

I barely swallow the urge to call her out, but I force my words to remain even and civil. "I have plenty of dresses."

"Just make sure you don't wear the red one you wore last year to the Smith's Christmas party. You looked a little…plump for it."

I roll my eyes and flick them to the clock on the wall. "I won't wear that one, mother. I better get going so I can start getting ready."

"Oh yes, of course. I'll see you tonight. Say hi to Jason for me."

I hang up the phone with another eye roll. Doing that would mean talking to him, and I have no intention of doing that.

Not for the first time in the last week I imagine what it would be like if I never left Wyatt and Elias's place. In such a short time my entire life could have changed.

If only I'd been brave enough to follow my heart.

THIRTY

ELIAS

"Are you sure this is a good idea?" Wyatt asks for the ninth time since we left the house.

"Do you have a better one?" I question, my brow raised as we walk through the ballroom. I pick up a glass of champagne for each of us and hand one to him.

"I mean, no. But ambushing her at a very public event seems like there's a lot of things that could go wrong."

He's not wrong, but we've been staking out Leighton's house all week, and there's been no sign of her. She hasn't so much as walked to the end of the street in that time, and if I don't get eyes on her soon I'm going to lose my fucking mind. Or break into her house and kidnap her. Neither option is especially good. So this is what we've got to work with.

We get invited to a lot of these things and happened to have an invitation sitting in our personal assistant's tray to politely decline, but she hadn't gotten around to it yet, which worked well for us. Wyatt and I have no problem donating money, and we do frequently, but these events are nothing more than a pissing contest for the wealthy families of New York, and there's nowhere I'd like to be less.

Except for tonight. We've been digging and digging and digging all week, finding out everything there is to know about Leighton and her family, as well as her asshole fiancé and his family, and boy, has it been enlightening. A police commissioner who all but promotes reckless policing, a shoot-first-and-ask-questions-later approach that I can't figure out how he's getting away with. And a governor who has more interest in making money on the dark side of the city than he does actually helping his constituents and doing what's in their best interests.

Both men are breaking laws left, right, and center, and yet they're getting away with it. I guess that says a lot about the country we live in. That's not to say we're good men because no one could ever accuse us of being that, but at least we're honest about it. We know what we are, and we own up to it.

I down the glass of champagne, but I barely taste the bitter bubbles as they go down. As much as I wish I was as confident about this plan as I keep making Wyatt think I am, I'm not. Through all our digging, there's been one thing we keep coming back to, and we haven't been able to uncover it no matter how deep we dive.

What are these two influential families getting out of marrying off their only children to one another? And why are they both going along with it?

It's then that I catch sight of our girl, and she's even more beautiful than I remembered. It's only been a week since we've seen her, but it might as well have been a lifetime, and by the way Wyatt relaxes beside me, he feels the same way.

It doesn't seem to matter that we only spent a night together, or that we've learned more about her from files and research than we have from anything she's told us, somehow she became our entire world that night.

Jason's hold on her arm is anything but gentle as he steers her around a group of photographers, navigating her to the opposite side when they're forced to pose for a photo.

"That's strange," Wyatt comments, his brows pulled together the same way mine are.

I nod. "It is."

They continue toward a table at the front, but there are too many people around for me to get a good look at her. She's wearing an elegant black floor-length satin gown and fits her curves like a glove. Her hair is styled in waves over her bare shoulders, and the perfect amount of her ample chest framed by the strapless sweetheart neckline.

She's a fucking wet dream, and I can't wait to devour her over and over again. But even then, I'm not sure I'd get my fill.

The smile pulled across her ruby-red lips is tight and forced, and if I'm not mistaken, there's a hint of fear dancing in her eyes. If we hadn't already decided over and over again that this dick was going to die a slow, painful death, he's just signed himself another death warrant.

"What's our plan?" Wyatt asks and drains his own glass before dropping it on a nearby high table.

"Let's go find our seat." I smirk.

THIRTY-ONE

LEIGHTON

I knew tonight was going to be bad before I even finished putting my makeup on. There wasn't any one thing that gave me that impression, but a whole bunch of little ones.

The way my fake lashes stuck to my fingers instead of my eyelashes when I was applying them, how Jason's eyes roamed over my body disapprovingly as he perused what I was wearing, and how he hadn't let go of me since we walked out the front door.

Does he think I'm going to run away from him?

The idea definitely has merit, but he and I both know I don't have that kind of choice. He and my parents have made sure I'm trapped. I didn't really think of it that way until the night I spent free, but they've done everything they could to make sure there's no way I can survive on my own, right down to only letting me intern at places they vetted, which means I have no references that aren't connected to them. And then they didn't allow me to work, which given how competitive the industry is, almost makes my degree obsolete.

The terms of my trust fund were changed around the same time our parents agreed to our marriage, meaning I won't see a cent of it until I have a ring on my finger, and I'm sure somewhere there's a clause stating I have to marry someone they see fit, not that I've bothered looking into it. Because what's the point?

Jason pulls my chair out for me and smiles down at me as I take the seat, but his gaze is anything but warm. This act isn't for my benefit, it's for all the people around us. The ballroom is crawling with politicians and potential contacts, and he wants to make them all think he's a gentleman.

And I'm sure they'll all believe he is. But they can't see the bruising under my makeup, and how swollen my ankle is already after only being in these heels for an hour. They don't know that he's been ignoring me all week, that the first words he's spoken to me since he hit me was to warn me to be on my best behavior.

I've never once done anything but exactly what I've been told my whole life.

I take a sip of champagne and relish in the bubbles filling my mouth. I don't tend to drink much, but these events always make me want to feel numb. Everyone that comes to these things does so with false pretenses. They're not here to help people—that's just a farce, an excuse for a party and an open bar, but they almost always have an ulterior motive.

Jason's hand holds my thigh in a tight grip, and I drain the glass to help me swallow down the nausea his touch brings. He's talking to his father on the other side of him, something about stocks and what they're expecting from the next twelve months of rise and falls. I'm sure I'll hear some variation of this same thing no less than twenty times tonight, which means I'll need to keep the champagne coming.

"Oh good, you made it." Jason's father, Governor James Collins, beams at the two men approaching the table, and when I follow his gaze, I choke on the bubbles, suddenly regretting drinking so much all at once.

Across the table from me stand Wyatt and Elias, each looking utterly breathtaking in their perfectly fitted suits. Is it legal to look that freaking delicious with clothes on? Surely it's not.

They make no attempt to hide their amusement at my surprise, or even to disguise that they know me. My stomach drops at that thought because if Jason can put the pieces of last weekend together, I can't imagine what will be waiting for me when we get home.

I shake my head slightly, hoping like hell they're not about to blow my entire life apart with just a few words, but that only seems to make Wyatt's smile grow.

Elias shrugs out of his jacket and slings it over the back of the chair directly across from me before rolling his sleeves up his forearms.

I can't tear my eyes off the coiled muscles flexing with each move he makes, and I realize they're not the only ones who could reveal what happened last weekend. I'm just as likely with my own reactions.

"Thank you for the invite." Elias smiles, dragging his attention off me for long enough to look at my future father-in-law. "I'm sorry our RSVP was so late. Our assistant put the invitation on my desk which I promptly buried. I'm sure you know how it is." He chuckles.

"I certainly do." James turns to his son who looks almost as surprised as I am to see the two of them, and that makes my stomach sink painfully. "Son, this is Elias Ford and Wyatt Keller. They own quite a few businesses throughout the city." He turns back to the newcomers who have now taken their seats and smiles. "This is my son, Jason, and his lovely fiancée, Leighton."

Jason opens his mouth to say something, probably to pretend he's never met the two of them in his life, but Wyatt has other ideas. "We've actually met. Jason here was a member of one of our clubs until recently."

I choke on the last sip of champagne in my glass and barely stop myself from spitting it across the table.

Why are they doing this? Are they angry I left without saying goodbye? What did they expect? That I would stick around for an awkward morning and for them to eventually tell me I'd overstayed my welcome? I don't think so.

"Oh fantastic." James claps his hands together.

Just in time, a waiter stops by the table and takes my empty glass, leaving a fresh one behind which I immediately bring to my lips. I have a feeling I'm going to need a whole lot of these tonight.

THIRTY-TWO

WYATT

I wasn't sure how I was going to react to seeing Leighton again after she snuck out on us last weekend. I'd be lying if I said I wasn't pissed that she would leave with nothing more than a note to say she had a great night, but when I saw her across the room with her asshole fiancé's hands on her, all that fell away. All that was left was the need to get her away from him and back where she belongs. With us.

I slip my jacket down my arms and rest it on the back of my seat the same way Elias did before sitting down right across from my angel.

Her eyes are wide and the edge of fear dancing in them only makes me want to kill the motherfucker next to her more. It's not us she's afraid of. She knows we would never hurt her, but I don't think the same can be said for Jason.

The footage of him yanking her into the house last weekend plays on repeat over and over again in my mind. It's all I've been able to think about. Did he hurt her? Was that as rough as he got that day? Or was there more we didn't see behind closed doors?

"How's business going, gentlemen?" James asks, his gray hair clipped shorter on the sides and deep-brown eyes almost giving the illusion of caring. But we all know he couldn't give two shits about us and our business. The only reason he bothers with us is because we are so closely linked with the Legion, and that's of benefit to him. Too bad Crew wouldn't be seen dead getting into bed with the likes of this asshole.

"Very well. We're seeing more and more traffic through our establishments and thankfully not feeling any of the hurt some are feeling," Elias answers as vaguely as he can manage. James isn't the kind of guy who asks about business unless he's fishing for something. Most wouldn't be able to see it as anything apart from him making small talk, but when you've been in this game for as long as we have, you learn a thing or two about your opponents.

"That's great news. There are many people in the city hurting." He gestures around at the ballroom, as if the show of wealth and power being exhibited tonight shows anything other than their own selfish need to appear giving.

I glance at Leighton as she finishes another glass of champagne, but she avoids looking anywhere near either of us as her gaze flits around the room. The carefully placed smile on her face is forced, but I wonder if anyone else at this table can see that, or if Elias and I got to know her better in one night than any of these assholes have in the years they've known her.

"So you mentioned your son is getting married, has a date been set?" I ask, dragging my attention back to James and Jason. Men like them won't allow a question like this to be directed at Leighton, and I don't want to put that kind of pressure on her right now when we've already bombarded her.

"We're thinking about the summer," Jason forces out begrudgingly, doing nothing to mask the loathing in his voice. I doubt his father knows he was kicked out of one of our establishments and barred for life, and if he does, I'm certain he didn't get the real reason.

Elias nods, his face completely passive as if he doesn't care that the woman we've become obsessed with thinks she's marrying this asshat. But we've already agreed there's no way in hell this is happening. "Such a nice time of year in the city." He turns to Leighton, and her eyes widen under his scrutiny. "I'm sure you'll make a beautiful bride, Leighton."

A deep blush covers her cheeks, and she looks away. "Thank you."

"She'll need to lose a few pounds before we go dress shopping, though, won't you, honey?" The middle-aged woman who has had entirely too much Botox says as she approaches, and I recognize her immediately as Leighton's mother.

Margaret Chalmers is a career socialite. She knows everyone who's worth knowing in the city, but we've never had the displeasure of meeting her. Her long blonde hair is curled down her back and her makeup a little too dark for her petite features. Where her daughter looks healthy with curves in all the right places, her mother is stick thin without an ounce of fat on her. She's closer to our ages than her daughter is, but despite her best efforts, her age is catching up with her.

I open my mouth to defend our angel, to tell her mother that she's perfect just the way she is, and any man should count his lucky fucking stars that she even looks in his direction, but Elias kicks me under the table, clearly sensing my unease about the insults that have just so easily flown from her mother's mouth.

"I don't think we've had the pleasure." Her gaze settles on me, perusing the lines of my forearms without even pretending to hide it. This woman is a fucking piranha. How could she possibly have given birth to Leighton? "I'm Margaret Chalmers. And you are?"

I open my mouth to respond, but James quickly steps in to do the introductions. Ever the gracious host. "This is Wyatt Keller and Elias Ford. They own some very successful businesses downtown."

Her eyes light up, as if our success is something she may be able to get some kind of gain from. I wonder how Elias would feel if we put Margaret on the hit list immediately after Jason. Something to consider at the very least.

THIRTY-THREE

LEIGHTON

After forty minutes of mind-numbing chatter I finally see my opportunity to excuse myself and take it without hesitation. Jason won't be pleased later, but I don't care right now.

I need to take a breath away from my condescending mother, my fiancé's vice grip on my thigh which I'm positive has bruised, and the gazes of the two men I thought would be nothing but a dream for the rest of my life burning into my flesh.

I can't work out what they're doing here. They don't seem to have any business dealings with James, and they haven't left the table once to mingle, so why the heck are they here? The hopeful part of my heart flutters to life. Are they here for me? Did they track me down? Did they orchestrate sitting at the same table so they could be close to me?

I shake my head as I walk down the corridor to the bathroom. That's ridiculous. There's no way they would go out of their way to find me, not with how I left. Tonight is just a torturous extension of our limited time together before I marry Jason.

The thought has a cold sweat breaking out on my forehead. I don't want to be Mrs. Jason Collins. I don't want to be the mother of his children. I don't want this life that's been set out for me, and each second Wyatt and Elias are nearby is another second closer I am to breaking. Because I don't have a say in the matter. I never did.

It was obviously too much to ask for the bathroom to be empty because when I push the door open, three women are touching up their lipstick in the mirror, and two of the five stalls have their doors closed.

Perfect.

I hurry into one of the free stalls and lean against the door before allowing my eyes to fall closed. I only have a short window of reprieve before Jason will come looking for me and no doubt be mad that I left at all. At the last one of these things I ended up with a UTI because he wouldn't let me leave his side to use the bathroom all night, and I think the only reason I was able to sneak off tonight is because he's so off-kilter due to the men sitting across from us. Small mercies I suppose.

By the time I do my business, touch up my makeup, and make it back to the hallway, my stomach is heavy with unease. There isn't one part of me that wants to go back to that table, not when I'm constantly reminded of everything I can never have.

The hallway is empty when I step into it, and I take a few moments to enjoy the quiet. I spend most of my life in silence, only speaking or being spoken to when Jason is home or my mother decides she has something to insult me about, and perhaps I should loathe it for that reason, but right now I crave it.

There's nothing I wouldn't do to be at home right now in dead silence, just my own demons playing on loop in my mind.

I only make it a few steps toward the ballroom when a pair of arms wrap around me and pull me into a cool, dark room. A scream gurgles at the back of my throat, but a firm hand secures over my mouth before I can let it out.

And just when I thought tonight couldn't get any worse.

It takes me a few moments to realize I'm pressed between two bodies, and what I think may be a mop. A cleaning closet. Perfect.

"It's just us, angel," Wyatt's cool voice whispers across my cheek, his hands tugging me back against his body, and I let out a breath of relief. They won't hurt me…will they? "I'm going to remove my hand, but you have to promise not to scream."

I nod before I've even made my mind up. I'm obviously not going to tell them if I'm planning on screaming anyway, so there's not much to think about.

The hand lifts from my mouth as promised, and I let out a breath as I look up Elias's body in front of me. It's too dark in here to really see him, but I'd be able to tell it was him in the pitch black.

Wyatt's hands drop to my waist and hold me tight against him, and I'm ashamed to admit I can breathe for the first time since

I climbed out of bed from between them last weekend.

"What are you doing here?" I hiss. Jason is probably already looking for me, and if he even suspects I might be with them there's no telling what he'll do. It's better for everyone involved if I just go back to my boring little life with my arranged marriage and never see them again. No harm no foul.

Fingers wrap around my chin and tug my face up until warm breath whispers across my cheeks. The small amount of light that pours in around the doorframe affords me the outline of Elias's face. His sharp jaw. The line of his nose. The curve of his lips. And it takes everything in me not to lean forward. Their scents are overwhelming, making it hard to remember all the reasons this is a bad idea.

How can something that feels so right, be so wrong?

"Wanna tell us why you ran from us, pretty girl?"

I squeeze my eyes closed and try desperately to steady my breathing. There are too many reasons, but none of them they would understand. How could they?

"This is the part where she tells us she didn't have a choice, isn't it angel?" Wyatt's voice is playful, but there's an edge to it. He's hurt that I left without a word, but can't he see I am, too? Don't they realize walking out that door was the hardest freaking thing I've ever done?

I open my mouth to respond, but Elias gets in first. "But you're wrong, Leighton. You have a choice. And you made the wrong one."

I let out a shaky breath, tears brimming at the corners of my eyes. But I can't let them fall. If I smudge my makeup, I'll be in a whole new load of trouble. Wouldn't want to embarrass the governor's son at his own event. "You don't understand," I whisper, not trusting my voice to remain even.

"What don't we understand? Tell us why you think you don't have a choice," Elias presses. If only it were that simple.

"Because I don't."

"That's where you're wrong, angel."

I sigh and squeeze my eyes tighter. It's too much being in a tight space with them. It was too much sitting across the table from them, but right now it's impossible to breathe. "I have to go. If Jason realizes I'm gone for too long…" I trail off. I can't tell them what he'll do, can I?

"Who gives a fuck about that asshole?" Elias growls. "He cheated on you. Repeatedly if the club's records are accurate. And I'm sure he has no plans on stopping, men like him never do."

"And he *hurt* you, Leighton. He put his hands on you," Wyatt adds and it takes everything in me not to laugh. They don't know the half of it. While they've never been anything but gentle with me, there's an air of danger that surrounds them. Maybe it's their time in the SEALs, or maybe it's more. And while I wish I could stick around to find out, I can't. Whatever reason God had for putting them in my path was just some kind of sick joke.

"It doesn't matter."

"Like hell it doesn't matter, Leighton." Elias's grip on my chin tightens, and his lips whisper over mine, the slightest of brushes I would almost think I imagined, but his kiss is burned into my skin, a brand I would recognize anywhere.

"I have to go."

"We could get you out of here. We could get you as far away from that asshole and your insufferable mother as physics will allow. You just have to say yes," Wyatt pleads.

It's on the tip of my tongue to say yes, to *beg* them to take me away.

But then my phone vibrates in my purse, and reality comes crashing down on me.

I allow myself one more second of being surrounded by them before slipping from their grasp and out of the tiny cleaning closet they pulled me into.

I don't bother stopping to check my phone. The message would only make the temptation to go back to them that much stronger, and I'm barely holding on as it is.

THIRTY-FOUR

WYATT

"**F**uck!" I slam my hand into the wall beside me. The plaster protests loudly until cracks form around my hand.

She left again.

Why the fuck does she keep leaving us?

Can't she see we can give her *everything*?

"She's not ready yet," Elias states, his tone cool and even. How the fuck is he so calm? I'm ready to climb out of my fucking skin.

"What if she's never ready?"

He lets out a breath and leans back against the wall behind him. "She will be. We just have to be patient."

"He could really hurt her."

He nods solemnly. "He could."

I growl and fling the door open, giving little regard for if there's anyone else in the hallway. I need to get out of here. I can't handle being here when she's with him. I can't stand the sight of his filthy hands on her after all the shit we've uncovered in the last week. He doesn't even deserve to breathe the same air as her.

I'm outside in the cool New York air before Elias can think to catch up to me. I don't want to go home because it feels fucking empty without her there. I don't want to go to the club either. Every inch of the fucking place reminds me of her, of the ways I'm going to fuck her as soon as we get her back with us.

Elias catches up just as the valet brings my Ferrari around. I don't know what made me buy the extravagant car last year, but I'm damn glad I have the kind of speed I need to work out some of my frustrations.

He slips into the car without a word, and I gun the engine toward the only place I can think of that isn't home or the club.

Neither of us speak as I push the car to its limits through the city, dodging traffic and pedestrians as I go. I wouldn't normally speed like this in the heart of the city, but I don't much care right now. I need to be in control of something. I need to feel like I'm doing something, instead of sitting around waiting for Jason to hurt Leighton.

Because that's exactly what's going to happen. He's going to hurt her, and I just hope she'll still be the same woman we fell hook, line, and sinker for on the other side.

Elias doesn't ask any questions when I slam my foot down

on the brakes outside Riot. Instead he climbs out of the car and strides inside with me by his side. This is why we work so well together. We know when to question one another. We know how to deal with the moods we each get in. And right now, I need to feel someone else's blood on my fists. I need to hold another human's life in my hands and watch as the spark dims from their eyes.

Everyone thinks I'm the happy-go-lucky one out of the two of us, that Elias is the brutal one, but they have no idea of the darkness running through my veins.

Kovu catches sight of us, and a wicked grin spreads across his face. This is his show to run, and one he runs so fucking well none of the other members of the Legion would think of taking it away from him.

His wild blue eyes are more subdued than normal tonight, and it's not until I notice the flecks of blood across his face that I realize why. He's just been in the ring, and if the blood is anything to go by, I'm willing to bet the other guy has taken his final breath.

He runs a bloody hand through his chocolate-brown hair, brushing the sweaty strands away from his face and giving the room around him a view of his tattoos. The man is covered head to toe from what I can tell and makes no attempt to cover the art etched into his skin.

"What are you two fuckers doing here?" He slaps me on the back, smearing some poor asshole's blood over my tailored suit. I'm sure Martha, our housekeeper, will appreciate that when she finds it. "Bish said you had some fancy gala tonight; otherwise I would have invited you."

"You know he hates it when you call him that." Elias chuckles.

"That's *why* I call him that." He smirks.

"I need to fight," I tell him, not bothering to beat around the bush.

He turns his intense eyes on me before looking over what I'm wearing. "We better find you something else to wear otherwise these pissants will think they've got an easy win on their hands."

Elias shakes his head. "They always think that anyway."

"And they're always wrong." I smile.

It doesn't take long to find me a pair of Bishop's shorts he keeps here and change. He may be the most together of the four of them, but that doesn't mean he's not every bit as bloodthirsty as the rest of them are.

You don't step up into the role of gatekeepers of the New York City underworld without craving blood as badly as you do your next breath.

I look around the busy club that doubles as a fighting ring and spot Elias and Kovu by the huge ring in the center of the space. I've kicked off my shoes and haven't bothered with the shirt he handed to me as I stride through the throes of people, each staring at me as I pass. The people that come here do so for the brutality of it just as much as the fighters.

"You ready?" Kovu asks.

"You found me an opponent?"

He smirks. "Of course I have."

I jump up into the ring and bounce from foot to foot, warming up my muscles. The workout I did this afternoon before the gala was more about getting the nervous energy out than preparing for a fight, but it'll do.

The man who climbs into the ring across from me is exactly what I would expect in a place like this. A guy who has more muscles than brains, angry pimples all over his chest and arms are the evidence of steroids, and his pupils are blown wide. There's no rules here to say you can't be hopped up on drugs during a fight, and I'd be willing to bet a lot of money that's exactly what I'm staring at right now.

He smirks when he sees me, thinking he's got himself an easy match up. I'm not the biggest guy in this place, but my six foot three frame is muscular without being bulky.

The bell rings, and he advances on me without hesitation, but I make quick work of blocking his first three hits before slamming my fist into his face. The crack of his nose sets the fire in my chest alight, and each hit I land only amplifies it.

It's not until he's bloody and broken on the floor in front of me that I'm finally satisfied. Crimson coats my hands and arms, but the aching in my stomach is settled for now. Leighton will come to us when she's ready, and until then, I have somewhere to come where I'm in control.

THIRTY-FIVE

LEIGHTON

J ason barely acknowledges my existence for the rest of the night. His hand is always planted somewhere on my body, but he makes no attempt to speak to me or include me in any conversations he has.

And you know what? I prefer it this way. The less I have to speak to him, the easier it is for me to get through the night without allowing the tears threatening at the edge of my vision to fall.

Walking away from Wyatt and Elias broke my heart the first time. But the second? It obliterated it to the point I'm surprised it can still beat in my chest. They showed me all the things I could have if I were just strong enough to break away, but they don't see the rest of the picture. They don't realize that the deal my father and Governor Collins have that binds Jason and I together is a matter of life and death.

I can't allow anyone to get hurt because of me, even if that means I have to give up everything I've ever wanted.

The car ride home is quiet, the chauffeur in the front quietly tapping the steering wheel in time with the beat of the music. I'm exhausted. After a week locked in the house, a whole night around people, in this uncomfortable dress and shoes that make my ankle ache to the point of tears, I'm ready for another week in bed.

If only.

I thank the driver as he helps me out of the car, and he gives me a kind smile in return, but Jason doesn't bother saying anything to the man as he climbs the steps.

He's never been especially mean to any of the staff, but I also wouldn't call him nice. For the most part he just ignores them, pretends they don't exist because he thinks they're below him. I tried to make friends with one of the cooks last year, a woman a little older than me. She saw me reading one day, and we got to talking about our favorite books, and a friendship blossomed from there. At least until Jason got wind of it and fired her. He didn't even tell me before he did it. He just let her go, told her never to contact the house again, and we've never spoken about it again.

He wanders down the hall toward his office while I make a beeline up the stairs to the bedroom. I don't hesitate in stripping the dress over my head and kicking the strappy heels from my feet.

I wince when my sore foot hits the cool floorboards, but go through the motions of hanging the designer gown on its hanger ready to go to the dry cleaner tomorrow morning and putting my shoes where they belong.

I'm just pulling a silk dressing gown around my body when

216

I step out of the walk-in and almost slam straight into Jason. Whiskey touches my nose, and I try to step away. He's always rougher when he's been drinking, and I wasn't paying close attention to just how much he was drinking throughout the night.

He catches my elbow and tugs me into his body, forcing me to look up at him. His eyes are dark and wild, a touch of danger dancing in them as he stares down at me.

"I'm tired," I say quietly and pull my arm from his grasp, but he doesn't let me get far. I only make it two steps toward the bed before his arm wraps around my waist and pulls me back against him. His grip on me is tight, too tight. Whatever this is, he's intending to inflict pain on me and that thought has panic settling in my gut. "Jason…"

"Shut up," he snaps. He brings his free hand up to cover my mouth, rendering me completely speechless. "Did you fuck them, Leighton? Hmm? Did you let those fucking criminals stick their cocks in you?"

My eyes widen in surprise, but I couldn't answer even if I wanted to, and that's by design. He doesn't care what I have to say. He's made his own mind up about what happened last weekend, and nothing that comes out of my mouth would change it.

"You did, didn't you?" He chuckles against the shell of my ear. "Did they fuck you good? I thought I smelled them on you when you came home, but then I thought there's no way goody two-shoes Leighton would have a one-night stand with not one, but two, men. You don't even fucking swear, you would never do that. But you did."

The venom in his tone slices right through me. As far as I'm concerned, I didn't cheat. At the time I'd made my mind up about leaving him, and I'd told him that. I told him it was over. I gave him the freaking ring back.

He was the one who cheated. Repeatedly if what Wyatt and Elias told me tonight is anything to go by. He's the one who didn't care about our relationship, the one who snuck around behind my back.

I shove my elbows into his stomach, trying desperately to dislodge myself from his hold, but it's useless. He's stronger than me.

"I don't think so, Leighton. Why don't you show me how you fucked those cunts? Why don't you suck my cock like the whore they made you?"

Every muscle in my body tightens to the point of pain. Jason's done a lot of things over the years, but he's never forced himself on me. He's never taken what I didn't offer, and fear grips me around the throat, making it impossible to drag in a breath.

He shoves me to my knees, and I cry out as they hit the hardwood floors. One hand fists my hair at the base of my skull while the other grips my face tightly. "Did you let them fuck you together? Did they take turns fucking your cunt? Your mouth? Did you let them in that tight little ass you've denied me all these years?"

A pained sob tears through my chest as red hot tears fall against my cheeks. Terror is a powerful emotion, potent and overwhelming in the way it seeps through your veins, rendering you completely powerless to your situation.

"Take my cock out, Leighton. I'm going to fuck your whore throat until you pass out, and then I'm going to fuck that pussy you've been offering to anyone who will take it."

My hands shake as I do as he asks. What choice do I have? He has the upper hand in every single way, and I'm just the useless girl I've always been.

"Hurry the fuck up," he snaps, immediately followed by a slap so hard my ears ring from the force of it.

I unbuckle his pants as quickly as I can, but my own trembling makes it hard to do much of anything. Every move he makes causes me to flinch, expecting the next blow to come at any second, and I don't have to wait very long before his fist comes down on the side of my face, and he shoves me away.

"I have to do everything myself with you. You're fucking useless." I try my best to creep backward toward the door, hoping by some miracle I can make a run for it. I don't really have anywhere to go. Most would say to go to my parents, but they'll bring me right back. All my friends are through Jason, he's never allowed me to have any of my own, and the reason for that has never been clearer. Friends meant I had someone to run to if things went south.

But I have no one.

No one in my corner.

No one to run to.

No one to help me.

No one to save me when Jason inevitably takes things too far.

THIRTY-SIX

LEIGHTON

My fingers brush against something at the edge of the bed, and I let out a small sigh of gratitude for the asshole in front of me. His college baseball bat. The one he keeps under the bed in case there's ever a home invasion.

I don't know where I'll go, but if I make it out of this house, there's no way I'm coming back. I don't deserve this life. I don't deserve a man who would hurt me. And I'm done pretending I do.

I wrap my fingers around the bat in as firm a hold as I can manage and slowly rise to my feet. Apparently his pants are giving him the same amount of grief they gave me because he doesn't notice me swing until it's too late.

The bat hits him hard in the side of the head, and I drop it before he has time to react. I run as fast as I can out of the room, down the hallway, but only make it a few steps down the second flight of stairs before fingers wrap around my hair and jolt me backward.

I lose my balance on the steps and slip down the remaining ones, crumpling at the bottom in agony. Tears fall against my cheeks, and for long moments I'm paralyzed. From pain or fear, I'm not sure because both are so overwhelming I can barely breathe.

"Did you think I'd let you run from me, Leighton?" Jason crouches over me, wiping the blood from his lip before wiping it along my cheek.

In a quick movement I barely see coming, he tears the front of my robe open and shoves me down until I'm flat on the rug at the bottom of the stairs. The bitter taste of blood fills my mouth, but I can't move to tell where the source is.

I let out a choked cry, but my fight is gone. What's the point? I tried, and I failed just like I always do.

He palms my breast painfully, giving little regard for the pain he's causing me, but I let him do it. That makes me all kinds of pathetic, but he's already proven he can best me, and all the fighting has brought me is more pain, so what's the point?

He flips me onto my stomach with ease where he would normally complain about the extra weight I carry. Either that's always been a lie, or the liquor has given him some kind of superhuman strength.

Somehow I don't think it's the latter.

Jason's hands push the robe up over my ass, and he lets out a growl. "Who did you wear these panties for, Leighton? Did you know they would be there tonight? Did you fuck them in the toilets like a common slut?"

I shake my head against the rug as a choked sob breaks

through. "No, I promise."

"I don't believe a word that comes out of your mouth." He tears the panties from my body, the fabric biting into my hips before finally giving way.

It's not until the hard wood of the bat brushes up the back of my leg that I realize he brought it down with him, and a cold sweat breaks out over my whole body. I don't need to be in his mind to know what he's thinking.

"Jason, please don't do this," I beg. I claw at the rug, trying to get any kind of control on this situation, but the agony through every inch of my body tears away any strength I had left.

"I'll do whatever the fuck I want, Leighton. Do you know why?" His hot breath whispers across my cheek as his body pins mine to the floor. He's so heavy on top of me I can barely drag in a breath, and for a moment, for the slightest of seconds, I wish for death. Wouldn't it be easy if he just killed me? Finally I wouldn't be in pain. Finally I would be *free*.

But almost as soon as the thoughts enter my mind, so does the fight. I haven't had the chance to live. I've spent my whole life scared. I've spent my whole life living for everyone else. I've never had the chance to live for me.

"I'll do whatever I want because I own you. You will be my wife. You will be my property. And I'll do anything I fucking well please to what belongs to me."

The blunt end of the bat moves between us until it's wedged at my entrance. There's no way he can get that inside me at this angle, not with his entire body on mine. He has to reposition himself if he wants to make this work, and that's going to be my only chance to run.

"I'm going to stretch your whore cunt out, and then I'm going to fuck your ass raw. Then maybe you'll have some fucking respect."

Every word out of his mouth is more vile than the last. Has he always been like this under the surface? Was the boring man who only wanted to have missionary sex in the dark just a farce to lead me into a false sense of security? Is this what I always had to look forward to? A monster hidden behind a fitted suit and a good family?

He shifts slightly and my body screams. I can't pinpoint any one source of pain, because everything hurts. Everything feels broken beyond repair.

He lets out an annoyed breath, obviously struggling to figure out our positions in his inebriated state, and when he lifts his body from mine, I twist against the pain until I'm on my back. It's not much better of a position than the one I was in a second ago, but if I can just get enough leverage, I might be able to get away.

He lunges at me, the bat slamming down in the middle of my stomach and sending shooting pains through my body. A gurgled scream tears from my already sore throat, but that doesn't stop him from landing the next blow, this one on my pelvis.

Stars dance in my vision as pain screams down my legs, and I don't get a chance to move before the bat makes contact with the same spot again. I scream so loud it pierces my own ears.

If he keeps going like this, I'm going to pass out from the

pain. There's no doubt about it. And then what's he going to do to me?

I can't let that happen.

I'm about to force my body to roll away from his next hit when the telltale sound of his ringtone blares through the house and makes him pause mid swing. I've found myself cursing that phone over the years because it normally interrupts the limited time Jason would set aside for me, but right now I'm grateful for it.

He mutters something under his breath and glares down at me. "Stay there." And then he disappears down the hallway.

I stay stuck to the ground for long seconds, listening to each step he takes, and then I run. I manage to grab my clutch from where I dumped it on the entrance table and wrap my coat around my bare body, before slipping from the house.

I don't bother with shoes because I'm sure whatever I catch from the streets of New York would be less painful than the pain Jason could inflict on me if I'd wasted any time finding footwear.

My feet hit the sidewalk in heavy slaps. The streets are quiet for a Saturday night, and it occurs to me how freaking cold the concrete is below my feet. I'm grateful it's a fairly quiet night on the usually bustling city streets.

I'm sure if the paparazzi got photos of the police commissioner's daughter running bloody and bruised through the streets of his city, he'd be less than pleased.

I hail the first cab I see and throw a hundred-dollar bill at him to prove I'm not going to run on him the second he stops the car, but he still looks at me speculatively. I don't blame him, I haven't bothered to look at myself in any kind of reflective surface, but I can feel blood dripping down my face and the bruises from where he hit me starting to form.

I rattle off an address I have no right knowing let alone going to. But I don't have a choice right now. Nowhere else in the city is safe.

"Are you sure you don't need to go to the hospital, miss?" The cab driver, a middle-aged man with a cap over his eyes, asks.

"No, I'm okay," I whisper. My throat burns from all the screaming I've done, and right now I can't handle any more pain than what I'm already feeling.

He nods and pulls to the curb.

I look up and let out a sigh before quickly thanking him and climbing the steps to the front door. I hesitate for a second before rapping my knuckles on the heavy wood, but when the door swings open I barely manage to keep myself standing.

"I'm sorry, I didn't know where else to go."

THIRTY-SEVEN

ELIAS

Wyatt's bloody as hell by the time he pulls the Ferrari into its spot, but the blood lust only kept that look of longing out of his eyes for half the drive before it came back.

He's quiet and tense as we walk up the steps of the brownstone we share, and I unlock the door without a word. There's not much to say.

Leighton made her choice, and whether we believe it's the wrong or the right one, *she* believes she's doing what's in her best interest, and once someone has made their mind up about something, it's very fucking hard to change it.

I throw my bow tie and keys on the table before following Wyatt through the house, but I still see her everywhere. How is that possible? She was here for less than twelve hours. But somehow she's buried her way into every surface, every fiber of the place, to the point it doesn't feel like home without her.

I shake my head at my own stupid thoughts. It's impossible for us to feel this fucking deeply about a woman we've spent such a short amount of time with, and that has left us on multiple occasions for an abusive piece of shit, but that doesn't seem to matter.

Wyatt collapses into the armchair and stares at the blank television. He's taking this harder than even I expected. He's always been the one of us to feel things more deeply, even if we both have pretty low capacities for such things, but this is worse than I've seen him.

"You should take a shower," I say as I unbutton the top few buttons of my shirt, finally allowing myself to breathe. I may wear a suit most days but I fucking hate the things.

"Yeah."

I sigh and close the space between us. We've been through a hell of a lot together over the years, but I'm not sure that anything I have to say can bring him any peace right now. "She just needs more time, Wy. You saw how her mother treated her, constantly making reference to her weight, making jokes at her expense like she wasn't there. And the way that cunt held onto her, his grip a little too tight. This is a cycle of abuse she's been in for a long time, and you know just as well as I do that those are hard to break."

He nods and lets his head fall back against the chair. "Fuck. I know that." He runs his bloody hand over his face. He watched his father beat his mother for years. He saw the cycle firsthand every single fucking day of his childhood. He knows it's not as easy as just leaving a situation like that, no matter how easy it may seem to people on the outside looking in.

"She knows where to find us. We'll keep an eye on her, make sure he doesn't escalate, and if worst comes to worst, we'll take matters into our own hands."

He opens his mouth, I'm assuming to ask what I mean by that. We've already floated the idea of kidnapping her, and it's definitely not off the table. But before he can get the words out there's a tentative knock at the door.

Our eyes clash. Who the fuck would be here at this time of night? No one even knows where we live, and that's by design.

I tug the Glock from the back of my waistband and move carefully through the house before taking a steadying breath and opening the door slowly. I keep the gun out of sight in case it's just someone meant for our neighbors knocking on the wrong door, but what I find is so much worse than even I could have thought.

Leighton stands on the doorstep, her bare feet on the concrete, her face bloody and bruised, blood trickling down her bare legs, with a coat wrapped around her tightly. She trembles uncontrollably, her tear-stained cheeks shivering with each second that passes.

"I'm sorry, I didn't know where else to go," she whispers.

I stare at her for another second before her legs give way. I lunge for her, managing to get my arms around her just before her knees hit the harsh steps.

She hisses out a breath at the contact, but there's not much I can do about it. I lift her into my arms and carry her quickly into the lounge room where Wyatt is standing in front of the couch, his eyes blown wide.

"What the fuck happened to her?" He approaches us carefully, but Leighton flinches at his hard tone instinctively.

"Soften your voice," I say as evenly as I can. "Pretty girl, I need to check your injuries so I can make a call about how to treat you. Okay?"

She nods against my chest, her brows pulled together with pain.

As carefully as I can manage I sit her in the seat Wyatt was in just a few minutes ago, but every move seems to hurt her. Little winces, hisses of pain, flinches with every touch. Without even opening her coat I suspect there isn't an inch of her that isn't bruised.

The emotions crashing over me are conflicting at best. Relief that she knew she could come to us, that she *wanted* to come to us. Anger that that asshole is still fucking breathing after hurting her like this. Fear that she's hurt worse than I can help her with.

Wyatt crouches down beside the chair, his eyes moving over the skin we can see, and his eyes mirror my own. Worry is above all else, but Jason just signed his fucking death warrant. I will not have him breathing the same city air as Leighton after this.

"How did you get here, angel?" he asks quietly, pushing blood-soaked strands of hair from her eyes.

"A cab," she croaks. "I ran for a few blocks before I saw one and luckily they stopped. I didn't expect him to while I was looking like this."

I clench my jaw to stop myself from reprimanding her. She didn't do anything wrong. She ran from her situation and came to us as quickly as she could. I just wish that didn't involve running while she was injured or getting in a cab alone while vulnerable.

"Can I take your coat off?" I nudge at the edges that she's holding closed for dear life.

She nods, and I carefully peel the expensive fabric off her shoulders, but I'm not prepared for the sight that greets me as Wyatt helps me pull it from behind her.

She's black and blue from head to toe, and naked as the day she was born. Angry bruises are forming over her stomach, her thighs, too fucking close to her pussy and dread washes over me as I meet Wyatt's eyes.

Did he violate her?

THIRTY-EIGHT

LEIGHTON

V iolent trembles vibrate through my body, but I don't think I'm cold. I'm not sure what I am right now.

Scared.

Alone.

Relieved.

In agony.

It's all morphed into one, and I can't make heads or tails of any of it.

All I know is I've never felt more sure of a decision in my life as the one I made to come to Wyatt and Elias. Realistically I know I didn't really have any other choice. Where else was I going to go? No one else I know would help me. But I guess I knew these two men would keep me safe, and when you've spent your whole life afraid of the people around you, that means a whole hell of a lot.

I look away as they peruse the bruises Jason left. I don't want to see them, not unless I want to lose the contents of my stomach.

The room falls silent for so long I almost look up to make sure they haven't left, but I know they haven't. Their warmth is just a breath away, and although I can't look them in the eyes, just having them close is enough to put me at ease.

Elias lets out a steadying breath, and I finally manage to look up at him. Emotions whirl around in his eyes as he looks at me, but none of them scare me. "Leighton, I need to know what happened. Can you tell me?"

I nod, and I find a throw wrapped around my shoulders, while another rests over my legs. I didn't notice him move, but Wyatt has silently given me my modesty without me having to ask him. "Thank you." I give him a tight smile, but even that hurts. "We got home from the gala, and I went to the bedroom to get changed. I was coming out of the closet when I ran straight into him, and then he…" I choke.

Wyatt takes my hand and gives it a gentle squeeze of support. "It's okay, angel. Take your time."

"He started calling me every name under the sun, saying he knew what we did, and that he was going to use me the way I deserved to be treated." A violent tremor runs through my body causing me to hiss out in pain. "He got me on the ground, but then I felt the bat he keeps under the bed, and I managed to get him with it so I ran. But I wasn't fast enough. He caught me on the stairs, and I fell down most of them. By the time I hit the bottom, I was pretty banged up. I couldn't move, and he used that to his advantage."

Elias squeezes his eyes shut, the anger burning behind them should probably scare me, especially seeing as I've just fled from a man intent on beating me within an inch of my life. But the only thing that scares me about the two men crouching in front of me is how intense the feelings I have for them burn in my chest.

"He had me pinned to the ground, he kept shoving the bat against my...against me." I'm not sure why I can't bring myself to say the words. The men in front of me are intimately aware of that part of my body, but at this point getting the story out is more important than analyzing that. "And then he was hitting me with it. My stomach. My thighs. My pelvis. It hurt so much." Tears fall against my cheeks, the salt in them burning the cuts. I must look like a real fright, but you wouldn't know it from the way they're looking at me.

Wyatt takes a steadying breath, but he manages to keep his face mostly passive, I think for my benefit more than his.

"His phone rang in the other room, and I guess he thought I was too injured to move." I shake my head. "I probably am, but I guess my fight or flight responses took over, and all I could think about was getting out of there."

I look down at my bloody hands in my lap. I need a shower, but it's going to hurt, and I'm really not sure how much more pain I can handle right now. As it is, the adrenaline is running out, and the agony threatens to take over.

"You're so fucking brave, Leighton." Elias gently pulls my face up until I'm staring into his eyes. "I need to make a call. I want a real doctor to look you over, but I don't want to take you to the hospital and risk him or your parents coming."

"Okay," I whisper.

Wyatt moves into my view with a gentle smile. "Can you trust us to take care of you tonight, angel? I can't imagine how much pain you're in right now, and all we want to do is help."

"I trust you."

"Good girl."

The words move through me, and despite the agony I lean into the praise. I did the right thing coming here. I made the right choice.

Elias disappears out of the room, and I allow my eyes to drift closed, exhaustion threatening to pull me under. Sleep has never sounded better if I'm honest, but a warm hand against my cheek forces my eyes open again.

"I know you're tired, angel. When Elias comes back I want him to check you for a concussion, and then maybe you can rest for a little while until the doctor arrives."

I nod but hold his gaze.

He leans forward and presses his forehead against mine. "Thank you for coming to us, Leighton. Thank you for trusting us to keep you safe."

THIRTY-NINE

WYATT

Seeing Leighton's beautiful skin smattered with angry purple bruises is a new kind of torture. I know that's kind of fucked up because a week ago I was thinking about how fucking good she looked covered in our marks, but this is different.

Those were created in passion, proof of the night we shared and the bliss we tore from her sweet body. But these…

I pinch the bridge of my nose to try to calm the raging beast in my chest. I need Jason wiped off the face of the earth. I need to make sure he can never hurt Leighton ever again. But I'm not sure how I'm going to let her out of my sight ever again to make that happen.

Elias checked her for concussion when he came back from making his call, and as soon as he confirmed she was okay to rest I moved her to the couch.

She protested about getting blood on the suede, but I honestly couldn't give a shit about the fucking furniture right now. Her head lays across my lap, her body curled in on itself as her mind drags her under to unconsciousness. But she's anything but peaceful right now. The crease in her brow, the little flinches, how she winces when she moves, it's all evidence of the night she's had.

Was this our fault?

Did he hurt her because he saw the way we looked at her?

Did he know we cornered her on her way back from the bathroom?

Did *we* do this?

I brush my bloody hand through her hair gently, needing more contact than I deserve right now. I never got the chance to clean up from the fight, and while I loathe the thought of that fuckers blood on my woman, I can't drag myself away from her right now. I'm not sure when I'll be able to.

Elias paces restlessly in front of us, his eyes flicking to her every so often to remind himself that she's here and that she's safe. Hurt, but safe. We haven't spoken since she slipped into her restless slumber, wanting to give her the chance to rest before the doctor gets here.

The doctor and Crew.

I have no idea why the leader of the Legion is making a house call because he never has before. Anytime he's loaned us one of his doctors, he just sends them our way, and we never speak about it again, but this time he's coming, too.

"You need to sit down," I whisper, watching Leighton's face to make sure my words don't startle her. It's strange caring for someone to this degree, because I never have before. Not my ex-wife. Not any woman I've ever dated. No one. Except for my mother all those years ago. The woman I watched my father beat to death when I was twelve. Maybe that's why.

"I can't."

"Don't you think it might freak her out if she wakes up, and you're pacing around here like a fucking wild animal at feeding time?"

He huffs out a sigh and collapses into the armchair Leighton was in not too long ago.

"Are you sure we can't wash the blood off her?" I ask.

He shakes his head and moves his eyes over her body. It's mostly covered right now by blankets and one of my shirts, but what lies beneath will be imprinted on my soul for the rest of my fucking life. The cuts. The bruises. The brutality she faced. I'm fucking scarred from it, and that fucker never even touched me. "Crew said we should wait." He sighs and presses his eyes closed. "He also said we should think about getting some photos of her injuries, in case we need them down the road."

"No," I growl, my hand pausing in her hair.

"I know. I said that, too. But then he asked what the fuck we're going to do when the police commissioner comes knocking on our doorstep demanding we give his daughter back. Or when the fucking governor of New York starts poking around. If we can prove what Jason did to her, then we have leverage."

I look down at Leighton. The bruises on her jaw are deepening, the cut on her hairline still weeping with blood. She didn't

243

deserve this. She didn't deserve to be beaten by that asshole. How can I agree to have documented proof that this ever happened? And how can we ask that of her?

"I know, Wy. Believe me, it makes me fucking sick to think about it, but I think he's right. The police rarely poke around in our business because of our direct association with the Legion, but do you think Jason is just going to let this go? Do you think her mother is going to allow her daughter to embarrass the family by slumming it with the likes of us?"

I open my mouth to argue, but he's right. We need leverage. We need a reason to keep her with us, and we need to be able to keep her away from Jason at all costs. It seems a small price to pay to ensure her safety. "Okay," I concede.

"We need to ask Leighton. I won't do it without her permission, but I think it's the right thing to do."

I brush my fingers over the bruise on her cheek, noticing how hard the area feels compared to earlier tonight when we had her trapped between us. "Is this our fault?"

Elias is quiet for long moments, so long that I start to question whether I spoke or just thought about the worry that's been playing in my mind.

"Do I think his act of violence tonight is a direct result of our presence? Yes. I think he saw how we looked at her, and how she avoided looking at us, and put two and two together. But do I think this is the first time he's hurt her? Do I think that if we hadn't been there tonight that he would never lay hands on her again? No. Men like that hit women to feel strong, to feel superior, and that pissant would constantly feel like he's in his father's shadow. Hitting Leighton is his chance to taste that power."

I'm well aware of the reasons men hit women, but it doesn't make it an easier pill to swallow to think that we did this. She was hurt as a direct result of our actions.

Before I can voice the thought to Elias, there's a light knock at the door.

Leighton startles awake, her eyes wide and afraid as she looks around the space with panic. I think she's going to be jumpy for a while, but I'll do anything to make her feel at peace again.

FORTY

LEIGHTON

My eyes flick open at the sound of knocking.

Where am I?

Why does my body feel like it's been run over by a truck?

Wyatt's worried eyes meet mine and allow me a moment of calm before the night comes crashing down on me.

The gala. Coming home. The awful things Jason said. How little regard he had for me.

"You're okay, angel. You're safe," Wyatt says as he gently runs his fingers through my hair in a comforting gesture. "The doctor is here to check you out, and then we can go to bed."

Bed.

A new panic washes over me. I ran from my home tonight with nothing more than my purse and phone, both of which are useless to me. Jason and my parents would have frozen my accounts by now, and if what Jason said last weekend when he thought I was asleep is true, my phone will allow him to track me anywhere I go. The moment I step foot out of this house he'll be able to get to me.

I have nowhere to go.

I can't stay here. Not when this is the first place they'll look for me.

Jason knows I was here last weekend. Even if I never confirmed it, I'm sure he could tell by my reaction to his insults.

How long do I have before they come?

Will they come tonight?

Tomorrow?

Will Elias and Wyatt hand me over?

Fingers brush along my jaw, dragging my attention back to the man whose lap I'm lying in. "I need you to breathe for me, angel. Nothing can hurt you here. I won't let it."

I suck in an unsteady breath, but he seems pleased nonetheless. "Sorry," I croak. As if every other part of my body doesn't hurt enough, my throat feels like I've swallowed razor blades.

"You don't need to apologize to me, angel, or anyone for that matter."

Before I can respond, Elias walks back into the room with two men. The first carries a leather bag, his salt and pepper hair shining in the light, and his brown eyes look around the space with recognition.

The other wears an all black suit and walks with an air of

confidence not many can replicate. His mismatched eyes meet mine, and although his demeanor is terrifying, he gives me a kind smile.

Elias rounds the couch and kneels down beside us, his fingers brushing across my cheek. "Leighton, this is Dr. Garrison, and this is Crew."

My eyes widen, because while I've never seen a photo of him, I've heard whispers of the leader of the Legion. A man so captivating, with one blue and one green eye, and sin oozing from every pore.

"He won't hurt you, Leighton," Wyatt whispers. "He can help us keep you safe."

I look to Elias for some kind of confirmation, but he's too busy chatting quietly to the doctor.

Before I can ask Wyatt any questions, Crew approaches me cautiously, almost as if he's approaching an injured animal. "It's nice to meet you, Leighton." He crouches in front of me, bringing his large frame to my level. "Elias has told me a great deal about you."

Heat rushes to my cheeks at the thought, but I can barely hold this man's eyes let alone ask any questions about that statement. "It's nice to meet you."

Wyatt pulls my face around until I meet his eyes. "We need to ask something of you, and I want you to know you can say no if you want, however we do think there are benefits to it."

I nod slowly, nerves bursting to life in my belly. It's different to the anxiety I get when I'm around Jason because while I may not know them very well, I'm almost positive they would rather cut their own hands from their body than hurt me.

"It's likely that Jason knows where you are, which means your father will before long, too," Elias says, carefully watching my reactions. "We think the only way to keep them from showing up here and trying to take you back is if we have proof of what Jason has done."

My brow furrows with confusion. They're right. Jason will know exactly where I ran, and that's why it probably wasn't the smartest place to come, but I don't regret the decision. This is the only place I knew I'd feel safe despite what just happened to me.

"Would you be okay if we took some photos of your injuries? That way if they show up here we have a reason to refuse to hand you over that not even the police commissioner can disagree with."

The blood drains from my face as dread washes over me. They want to take photos of me like this? They want to have proof that this happened to me? To use as leverage?

Wyatt brushes his fingers through my hair, bringing me back to the moment and away from the panic that was beginning to build. "I was skeptical, too, angel. But I don't know that we have another choice because there's no way in hell I'm handing you back to that asshole just so he can do this again or worse."

Nausea rolls through my stomach at the thought, and I find myself nodding before I can fully think it through. I trust them to do what's best for me. I probably shouldn't. Not when they're associated with people like the Legion, but something in my gut tells me I can trust them, and that's all I need right now.

"Okay," I whisper. "I think…I think that's probably wise."

Wyatt gives me a soft smile before carefully helping me sit up. "We'll have the doctor do your examination in my room, and then we can take some photos of your injuries."

FORTY-ONE

WYATT

Leighton sleeps restlessly between Elias and me. Apart from the night the three of us spent together, Elias and I don't make a habit of sleeping in the same bed, but neither of us could drag ourselves away from her tonight.

Dr. Garrison and Crew left an hour ago, and I was finally able to wash the dried blood away from her soft skin. But that just uncovered more bruising.

I've seen conflict in many different forms. I've been to war for God's sake. But I've never seen someone covered with as many bruises as Leighton is.

She has a broken rib or two, a sprained ankle that she somehow managed to run with, a dislocated shoulder which she screamed as he popped it back in breaking the heart I thought was long gone, and several gashes that needed stitches.

In short, that asshole did a real number on her, and the pain Elias and I are going to inflict on him in return will make him wish he was never fucking born.

I glance over her and see Elias's eyes open as well. Neither of us have been able to leave her side, and I can't see that changing anytime soon. I already texted Brock, our club manager, to let him know we likely won't be in this week, and that he'll need to hold down the fort until we return. But I'm not even sure that's going to be enough time.

"You need to sleep," Elias says, brushing his fingers along Leighton's cheek.

"I can't."

He sighs. "Nothing is going to happen to her. Crew has a team set up around the house and around Jason's, his father's, and the commissioner's houses. If they come for her, we'll know about it."

"It's not just that. This is our fault, El. We talked her into coming home with us last weekend. We wouldn't let her go when she left. We followed her to an event we knew they would be at together, and we knew she wouldn't be able to guard her reaction to us. We did this. This is our fault."

"No, it's not. We didn't hit her. We didn't force ourselves on her. We didn't push her down the stairs. But do you know what we will do? We will keep her safe."

"What if we can't?"

"Do you really think the governor and the commissioner are dumb enough to go up against the Legion? Crew is making it clear that Leighton is under their care, and any harm that comes to her from here on out will lead to heads rolling. We can keep her safe, Wyatt. I promise."

"Maybe we should take her away. Even just for a little while.

She can recover, and then she'll be in a better position to face all of this."

He shakes his head as his eyes flick to the sleeping angel between us. "If we take her out of the city, we all but admit we're doing something wrong."

My next words are cut off by a whimper as Leighton twitches, her body tense and afraid even in sleep. "No. Please, no," she cries.

I squeeze my eyes shut to shove down the anger that threatens. I can't show her that. I can't let her see the monster that I've hidden from her. She deserves a knight in shining armor, not two demons who will burn the world down to protect her.

Elias pulls her gently against him, wrapping his large body around her much smaller one. "It's okay, pretty girl. You're safe."

Her eyes flutter open and meet mine before letting out a relieved sigh as she realizes it was just a dream. If only she understood that we'll never let anything happen to her. I guess we'll just have to prove how true that is.

The sun streams through the window and illuminates Leighton between us. After her nightmare, neither of us were able to go to sleep, so we both spent the night staring at her, watching for fear, and promptly taking it away from her wherever we could.

She only woke a few more times, each nightmare pulling her back to consciousness before she realized she was safe and went back to sleep. The pain medication the doctor gave her will likely have her drowsy for the next few days before we can start weaning her off it. But he said it's important that she takes it, that her body needs to rest without being tense with agony.

Elias rolls out of bed first, checking the cameras around the house from his phone. He does this most mornings, a habit he got into when we came back from Afghanistan, and he's never been able to break it, but this morning he stares at it a little harder, assessing each frame with careful precision.

"All clear?"

He nods, and his eyes flick over Leighton's sleeping form, as if he hasn't been staring at her all night. We're in uncharted territory. We've never cared like this. We've never put anything or anyone above ourselves and our own interests, but that all changed when our angel walked into our lives and changed them forever. "I'm going to go make some coffee and breakfast so we can feed her when she wakes up. She's overdue for painkillers as it is."

"I'll wake her up soon."

He disappears from the room without another word, and I run my fingers over the smattering of bruising across her cheek wishing I could take the pain away for her. She didn't deserve this.

Her eyes flutter open, and there's a split second where fear crosses her gaze, but when they settle on me it's quickly replaced with a small smile.

"Good morning, angel."

"Hi."

"Elias is making you some breakfast so you can take your painkillers. How's your pain?"

She rolls onto her back and winces slightly as she tests her movements. "I think it's a little better than last night." But the deep set of her jaw and how her brows furrow with each small move tells me a different story.

"Leighton," I whisper, cupping her face gently as I move to hover over her. I'm careful to make sure none of my body rests on hers, but that she can feel my heat as much as I can feel hers. "You don't have to lie to us. You don't have to downplay your injuries because that's what you've had to do in the past. We want to take care of you. We want to make sure you're okay. And we're never going to be upset with you for being in pain."

Her eyes shut and tears brim around the edges. "You say that now."

A growl rises in my throat, but when her eyes pop open, there's no fear. Surprise maybe, but she's not afraid of me. "No, Leighton, that's where you're wrong. You've had one foot out the door since the moment we met, but Elias and I have had both feet in the whole time. We will do anything to keep you safe, burn this entire fucking city to the ground if we have to. Does that sound like we're going to be mad at you for taking your time to recover?"

She shakes her head, but there's an edge of doubt etched into her brow. We'll have to work on breaking all the bullshit her family and Jason have ingrained in her mind so she'll see the incredible woman that's caught some of the most ruthless men in the city.

FORTY-TWO

LEIGHTON

E very morning I wake up expecting to be sent back to the life I escaped, but instead I'm faced with two men falling over themselves to help me, even when they can see it's driving me insane.

I haven't heard from Jason or my parents, but I'm not sure if Wyatt and Elias have and just haven't told me. They've done everything they can to allow me to heal without any added stress, but with each day that passes, the more my stomach sinks.

They have to know they're not just going to let me go, that whatever time they're giving us is nothing more than a farce to lead us into a false sense of security.

It's been a week since I ran from Jason, and the bruises are finally starting to heal. Something else I expected was for them to look at me with pity, to see the bruises I allowed a man to inflict on me and see nothing but a weak woman. But it's the opposite case.

They look at me with admiration in their eyes.

I bring the throw around my shoulders and watch Elias move around the kitchen preparing dinner. I've offered to help over and over again, but they haven't allowed me to lift a finger since I got here. Instead he bundled me up on the couch with the Kindle they bought me and a hot cup of peppermint tea to soothe my anxiety.

I never told him I was anxious, but somehow he knew.

Wyatt went out an hour ago to get me a few things, even after I told him they'd bought me enough, and I could make do with what I had. The morning after I showed up here bloody and broken, a new phone, laptop, the Kindle I'm holding, and a week's worth of comfortable outfits showed up at the base of Wyatt's bed, along with enough skincare and makeup to last months.

Logically I know he can take care of himself and that nothing is going to happen to him while he's outside the house, but it's the first time they haven't both been hovering over me, and it's making me nervous. What if Jason approaches him? What if my father hires someone to hurt him? What if they have him followed and come back here for me?

"I can hear you thinking from here, pretty girl, and you're meant to be resting," Elias says without looking up.

I sigh and push the blanket from my lap. "I can't help it."

He finally flicks his gaze to meet mine, but there's no anger there. Just understanding. One of the craziest parts of the last week has been how different things have been from my usual life. No one has yelled at me. No one has called me fat or tried to restrict what I've eaten. No one has looked down on me. It's been the complete opposite of my whole life leading up to this point.

He places the knife down on the cutting board and crosses to where I'm sitting. He crouches in front of me until his eyes are at the same level as mine. "We don't expect you to break out of a lifetime of habits in a week, Leighton

We know it's going to take some time, especially after all you've been through."

I drop my gaze and let out a stuttered breath. I'm not used to telling others what's on my mind. I've spent years holding on to every thought, every feeling, and to put my trust into these men has been both terrifying and the most liberating experience of my life, but I know I have to keep going. "What happens next?"

"What do you mean?"

"I mean, I can't keep expecting you to do everything for me. At some point I'm going to have to face the music because there's no way they're going to let this drop."

He sighs and gently tips my face up until I meet his eyes again. "You let us worry about that, pretty girl. We have it well in hand, and if at any point we don't, you'll be the first to know. Okay?"

"I can't just let you take care of me. It's not fair to you," I argue.

A flash of something I haven't seen since the gala crosses his face, and my breath hitches in my throat. Dominance. He may have been gentle with me for the last week while I've been healing, but the same ruthless man is still lurking in the shadows, waiting for his moment to take over again. "Do you know what I think you need, pretty girl?" he croons. "I think you need to be punished for running from us."

The words send a cold wash of dread through my body, the automatic reaction of someone who has been hurt the way I have been, but it's quickly replaced with heat. For the last week, they've done everything for me. They've helped me bathe, they've fed me, they've held me through nightmares, and they've taken care of my every need. But they haven't touched me the way I want them to. A gentle kiss to the forehead here, and a light touch of my thigh while we watch television. But nothing like the first night we spent together, and I hadn't realized how badly I've needed it.

"I'll wait until Wyatt gets home. He'll want a say in your punishment."

I nod, and the most natural words I've ever spoken fall from my lips. "Yes, Sir."

FORTY-THREE

WYATT

My outing today was only partially about getting more supplies for Leighton. If that was all it was, I would have had our personal assistant do the shopping like we did the first day, but I needed an excuse to leave the house that wouldn't worry her.

As it is, Elias messaged me an hour after I left to let me know she'd been watching the door like a hawk since I walked out it. I don't like that my absence is making her uneasy, but there's something I have to do.

I stroll through the modern office building, past cubicles of interns who look like they haven't slept in a week, and men in suits whose self-importance is higher than any man's should be. I walk right past the pretty redhead behind the reception desk whose tits are sitting a little too high for the outfit she's wearing to be considered work appropriate.

"You can't go in there," she rushes out but before she can even get around her desk, I'm pushing my way into Jason Collins's office.

He looks up from behind his desk, startled by the intrusion, but when he notices who it is, anger crosses his face. "What the fuck are you doing here?" He snaps, shoving himself to his feet as if it does anything to improve the obvious difference in power between us.

"I came to deliver a message. Stay away from Leighton. Forget about her. Tell your parents you love someone else. I don't really give a fuck as long as you never breathe the same air as her again."

"And if I don't do that?" he challenges as he crosses his arms across his chest.

"Have you heard from the PI you hired to watch us lately?" I raise a brow as a smirk settles across my lips.

His face pales, but to his credit, he doesn't flinch.

I toss my phone into the middle of the desk, the image of his PI's dismembered body up for him to view. I didn't get to do the dirty work myself, but Kaos and Kovu were more than happy to take that job off my hands.

Jason's hand covers his mouth as he tries to hold in his reaction to the gruesome image, but his body jolts as he gags. "You're fucking psychotic."

I smile. "You're right, I am. And imagine how psychotic I'll be if you ever come near Leighton again."

I pluck my phone off the desk and walk myself right back out the way I came. It's not that I think Jason will drop this with one little threat, but he won't be able to say I didn't warn him when I finally tear him limb from fucking limb.

E lias's famous spaghetti goes down too well, and Leighton seems to think so, too. She finishes her plate faster than she has anything else since we brought her into the house. I'm not sure if she was just extra hungry tonight, or if some of her hang-ups about her weight are starting to fade now she's been away from the poison in her life for a little while.

I push my own plate away from me. "We should have moved a pretty girl into the house sooner if it meant you were going to cook so much."

Elias glares at me, but when a small giggle fills the space we both turn our attention to our angel. She shakes her head as she wipes her face delicately with a napkin.

Her smile is as bright and unguarded as I've ever seen it. For the first time since we met Leighton, she's not censoring herself. When she finds something funny, she laughs. When she's upset or in pain, she cries. And the fact we've given her that makes my chest tighten.

"Oh you think that's funny, brat?" Elias smirks. He rises to his feet slowly, never taking his eyes off her as he does.

"No." She presses her lips together, but she can't hide the amusement in her features.

He lunges for her before she can react, quickly throwing her over his shoulder. I'm about to snap at him to tell him to be careful when I notice how gently he actually did it, including how slowly she made contact with his shoulder, without resting any weight on her broken ribs.

"I think it's time for that punishment we discussed, pretty girl." He starts toward his bedroom, and I follow after them, readying myself for an argument. He's always been the one to correct behavior in our subs and normally I wouldn't challenge him, but Leighton is hurt. The mottled bruises are only just fading, and I hardly think a spanking is what's best for her right now.

But then the sweetest words fall from her pretty lips. "I think so, too, Sir."

Elias carefully deposits her in the middle of his bed and stares down at her. She's swimming in one of his old t-shirts despite all the clothes we bought her, and I can only assume it was him who chose her outfit today. Her hair hangs loose around her shoulders, and her eyes stare up at us with lust.

"Are you sure she's ready for this?" I ask quietly.

"She needs to get out of her head. She needs to hand over control for a while, and we're in a position to help her with that."

I turn my attention to Leighton, looking for any signs of doubt, but when I meet her eyes, there's nothing but trust in the deep-brown pools. The idea that this woman, this angel, could trust us is mind-blowing. She knows we're not good men, we can't be with the company we keep, and yet she puts all her trust in us anyway. She knows we'll keep her safe above all else. "What's your safe word, angel?"

"Red, Sir."

"Good girl. Just like last time, I want you to say it if you're in any pain, or you're uncomfortable with anything we're doing."

"Yes, Sir."

I groan and turn my attention to Elias who stares down at her with rapt attention. He crawls across the bed slowly, and Leighton can't help but watch his approach. He reaches for her and draws the shirt from her body, revealing nothing but a silky G-string and plains of soft skin. "You're so fucking beautiful, Leighton," I murmur.

A deep blush spreads across her cheeks as she pulls her bottom lip between her teeth.

Elias brushes a single finger across her collarbone, the light touch eliciting a trail of goose bumps in its wake. I've never been with someone so completely receptive to our touch like she is, and it's fucking addictive.

"How's your shoulder feeling, pretty girl?" He presses a gentle kiss to her cheek.

"It's fine today, Sir."

He scrutinizes her for a moment, making sure there's no sign of deception in her words before he gives her a single nod. "Your punishment will not be a spanking today."

She opens her mouth to respond, to argue even, but she quickly snaps it shut again.

"We're going to give you a lesson in control."

Her eyes widen in understanding, and I find a smirk tugging at the corners of my lips before I can stop it.

My specialty.

FORTY-FOUR

LEIGHTON

I'd almost forgotten how domineering these men can be.

Almost.

They stare down at me with lust in their eyes, both taking every inch of my body in like it's the most delicious treat laid out for them, and it's hard to remember all the reasons I'm self-conscious about my body.

If only the voices in the back of my mind would give me one night. One night to feel powerful, to feel sexy, to feel anything other than all the disgusting things my mother has called me over the years. But I think there's every chance I'll hear her voice every time I look in the mirror for the rest of my life.

Elias climbs up to the head of the bed and carefully drags me against his chest the same way Wyatt had the last time we were together.

The other man's eyes roam my body hungrily as he shucks his shirt and pants in just a few quick movements, not wasting any time as he crawls up the bed toward me.

"Do you remember your rules, angel?"

"Some of them, Sir."

"Well there's only one I need you to remember tonight." He grips my chin between his fingers and forces me to look into the intensity of his eyes. "Do not come unless we tell you."

Elias presses his lips against my ear and chuckles. "And if we tell you to come, you come without hesitation."

My brows furrow in confusion. That second part shouldn't be too hard to follow, not if the last time we were together is anything to go by, but I can't see how that would be part of a punishment.

Wyatt smirks as he drags the flimsy fabric down my thighs. "Orgasm denial isn't the only form of torture, Leighton."

Before I can respond, his fingers brush along my slick folds, and I let out a soft moan. Sex shouldn't have been on my mind over the last week, not when Jason tried to force himself on me, not when my pelvis and thighs have been black and blue from the brutality of his attack. And yet every moment I spend with Elias and Wyatt I can't think of much else.

His calloused palm moves up my thigh as his fingers tease me with gentle touches designed to drive me insane.

Elias kisses my neck, my shoulder, the shell of my ear, and between them I'm overwhelmed with sensations. Each kiss, touch, nip, brush of skin sends me closer and closer to an edge I crave so badly but know will be ripped away from me at the very last second.

Wyatt repositions himself between my legs until he's lying on his stomach with his head resting against my thigh. His ministrations of my clit are unhurried and gentle, not quite enough to get me close to the abyss, but enough to make me pant with longing.

"Mm, our pretty girl is getting out of her head," Elias praises as his fingers begin brushing circles over my hardening nipples. "Perhaps it's time we discuss what you're being punished for."

I nod against his chest, too blissed out to form a response.

Wyatt teases my entrance with the tip of his finger, and I can't help the groan of frustration that escapes my throat. I need more. I need everything they can give me. I need it all.

"You ran from us, angel," Wyatt says as he pushes the finger deeper before withdrawing it and moving the tip over my overstimulated clit.

"I'm sorry," I moan, trying my hardest to hold still.

"Tell us why," Elias demands, the deep timbre of his voice against my ear dragging a lustful gasp from my chest.

"I had to, Sir. I didn't have a choice."

"You absolutely had a choice. You could have waited for us to wake up. You could have discussed things with us. But instead you left a note and ran."

I flinch at the disappointment in his tone, but Wyatt quickly brings my focus back before my mind can drift off by plunging his finger inside me, tearing a scream from my throat.

"Why did you sneak out, little one?"

I squeeze my eyes shut, trying desperately to get my bearings, to focus my mind enough to answer his questions cohesively. "Because I was worried you'd talk me out of leaving," I admit to not only them, but myself as well. At the time it was just automatic, I didn't allow myself to think about it too closely. But now? Now it makes sense.

Wyatt and Elias bend me to their will with such ease, but never in a way that hurts me. They don't tear me down at every opportunity, they build me up. If I'd given them the chance to talk me out of leaving, I may have listened.

"Would that have been such a bad thing, angel? Even before all this you were miserable, were you not?" Wyatt asks as he presses a second finger in alongside the first one, stretching me deliciously.

I catch my bottom lip between my teeth as I try desperately to find an answer to their questions that won't ruin lives. That won't ruin *my* life when this inevitably comes crashing down.

I'm too caught up in my own thoughts to notice the withdrawal of his fingers, but I don't miss the harsh slap on my pussy and the pinch of both nipples that tears a cry from my lips.

"You're thinking too much, pretty girl," Elias croons as Wyatt pushes his fingers back inside me and gently massages the spot that threatens to detonate me.

"I have nothing without them," I cry out the admission I was hoping to hold to myself. "The conditions on my trust fund require me to marry someone my parents see fit. They stopped me from getting any work experience after college, they wouldn't let me get a job, and no one will hire me without their say so." The painful thoughts are only the tip of the iceberg, but they're all I can give them right now. The rest is too much, and considering their alliances, I'm not sure what they would do with the information if I gave it to them.

Wyatt looks up at me with wide eyes while Elias tenses behind me, but I don't know which part of my admission has dragged this reaction out in them.

"Did your trust fund always have those parameters?" Elias asks behind me as Wyatt continues his assault on my G-spot. I'm careening toward the edge, but I'm not silly enough to think they'll give me the release I crave.

I let out a moan and try to close my legs around his hand. I need just a little more and maybe, just maybe...

I can taste the first wave of my orgasm, but it's quickly stolen from me with a slap to my folds for good measure. The startled yelp only seems to make them both chuckle before they each return to work overstimulating me.

"We asked you a question, angel," Wyatt reminds me.

"No." I shake my head. "It was part of the agreement my parents made with Jason's father." Just saying his name while they touch me like this feels wrong, but not in the way you would think. I don't want to taint this moment with thoughts of him. I don't want him to have anything to do with the time I spend with these men.

Wyatt looks over my shoulder, and they seem to communicate silently for a few seconds before all their attention returns to me.

"You've been such a good girl for us," Wyatt praises. His fingers pump harder inside of me and he adds pressure to my clit until I can barely breathe.

"Wasn't that easy, little one?" Elias presses a kiss to the crook of my neck as he pinches my nipples with just the right amount of pressure until I'm dancing across the tightrope of pleasure and pain.

I nod against his chest, the soft fabric of his t-shirt the only thing between us. Why isn't he naked?

A few more flicks of my nipples and a little more pressure on my clit, and I'm right there, so close my body instinctively clenches in preparation. But again it's torn away, and this time tears prick at my eyes. Irrational tears that have no place in this room or with these men, but I can't help but let them fall against my cheeks.

I expect them to be mad at me, or to stop what they're doing, but the sight of my tears makes them double their efforts and when I'm at the edge again they don't withdraw, they don't pull me back, they allow my body the release it craves.

"That's it, angel, come for us," Wyatt's eyes are red hot with desire as he coaxes my body through wave after wave of pleasure.

When I sag against Elias, and he wraps me in the blanket Wyatt hands to him, I feel lighter than I have in years, like somehow the release of my own emotions and my body's release were all I needed to be able to breathe.

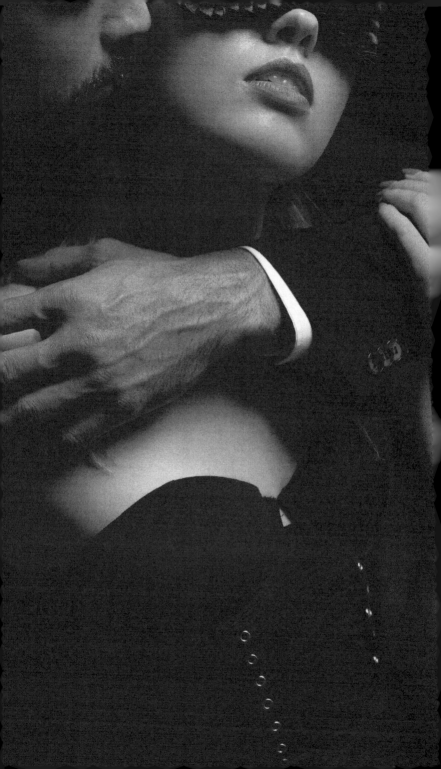

FORTY-FIVE

ELIAS

I stare down at Leighton's sleeping form in my arms in awe.

I never liked cuddling. Not when I was a teenager, not with my ex-wife, and not with any of my subs. If I were in a position where I had to provide aftercare, of course I would, but it wasn't something I enjoyed.

But this? This is everything.

She feels tiny in my arms, so fragile and vulnerable that all I want to do is put my body in front of hers against anything that could ever hurt her, but she's proven how fucking strong she is, too.

I'm sure she doesn't see it that way, the dejection in her voice as she admitted why she didn't feel like she could leave was proof enough of that, but when I look at our girl, I see a fighter, a woman I want to give the whole fucking world to.

Wyatt pads back in with a bottle of water and a bag of crackers for when she wakes up. She's probably still full from dinner, but I'd feel better if she ate something after what we just did. She needed that release. She needed to cry and let out all the emotions she's been holding on to, and the evidence of that is how peacefully she sleeps in my arms.

He climbs onto the bed beside me and peeks at her over my shoulder. "You were right," he says.

"When am I not?" I smirk, pushing some of the hair from her eyes. "But what in particular this evening?"

"About the punishment. I thought you were fucking crazy when you suggested it, that she wouldn't be able to handle it after all she's been through."

I nod. "She needed the outlet."

"I went to see Jason today. Told him if he comes near her I'll kill him."

"We're going to kill him anyway."

He laughs. "Yeah, but he doesn't need to know that."

I can't say I'm surprised he went to see the asshole. I've been considering it myself, but I can't bring myself to leave Leighton yet. Everyone sees Wyatt as the nice one, the soft one even, but he's the loose cannon. He doesn't have the same control I do, and that's what makes him fucking lethal in a fight. But it has also got him in trouble over the years, which is why I wish he'd spoken to me about it before he went.

"There's a part of the story she's not telling us," I muse, looking down at the sleeping angel in my arms. It's an apt nickname for her, one that so accurately describes her. But it's not lost on me how much she doesn't belong in this world.

We're going to ruin her. She's too soft for our hardness, too innocent for our deviance.

But we wouldn't be the villains of the story if we let her go.

Wyatt nods. "I picked that up, too."

The question is, why? She has nothing to lose and everything to gain by telling us the truth. By now she should realize she's safe, and we're not going to let anything happen to her. But she's still holding something back.

Leighton isn't a liar. She wouldn't lie to us unless she believed it was for the best. One glance at Wyatt confirms he's thinking the same thing, his brows pulled together as he stares down at her. No sub has ever captivated us like this. Hell, I don't think I've ever held someone like this as they slept. I would have put any other woman down as soon as they drifted off. But not Leighton.

"What are we going to do?" I ask quietly, not wanting to wake her from the sleep she so clearly needs. "We can't keep her locked up in the house forever, then we're no better than Jason."

"But then she's just a sitting duck waiting for them to confront her." He sighs and brushes his fingers through his messy hair. "If they get in her ear, she'll run again."

That certainly is the risk. There has to be a reason she kept some of the details to herself, but I'm sure the people in her life wouldn't hesitate to use it against her to force her back to a life she clearly doesn't want to live.

"He'll kill her if he gets her back," Wyatt says quietly. "Look how he escalated by seeing us near her for one night, imagine what he'd do knowing she's been here with us for a week."

I release a stuttered breath and press my eyes closed. I have no idea how to keep her safe while giving her the freedom she needs.

But we'll have to find a way, because her happiness is all that matters to us now.

TRUST IN THE FALLEN

FORTY-SIX

LEIGHTON

I thought after my punishment things would start to heat up, because honestly despite the earth shattering orgasm they gave me, I still crave them with every breath.

But they haven't touched me.

They're more affectionate than they were before, always finding a way to be touching me, always kissing me before they leave a room, but at night when they strip and nestle me between them, they never take it further.

It's been ten days since I ran from Jason, and I still haven't heard from him or my parents. Each day that goes by without a word from them is putting me more on edge. They've never given me this much freedom. Even in college, Jason was there, too, watching my every move, making sure I didn't do anything to disrespect the family.

I eye Wyatt over the glass of whiskey he handed me a few minutes ago. He's typing away on his laptop, too focused on whatever is on the screen to notice me staring. Every now and then his palm runs up my calf in a soothing pattern that I'm not sure which of us is getting more from.

Elias had to go to the club for the first time since the night I showed up on their doorstep covered in blood and bruises, although he complained about it to no end.

I find myself missing him as soon as he walked out the door, and I'm worried about him. I know what my parents are capable of. Despite their public displays, they're just as evil as the scum of the city.

"Something on your mind, angel?" Wyatt asks without looking up from the laptop.

I open my mouth to respond but quickly snap it shut. How the heck did he know I was watching him?

"You've been staring at me for the last ten minutes." He looks up with a smirk, catching me red-handed. "Why don't you tell me what's happening in that pretty head of yours?"

"It's nothing."

He shakes his head and closes the laptop slowly, keeping his eyes on me with each movement. He places it down beside him and reaches for me. Before I've consciously made the decision to go to him, he plucks me from my spot on the couch and deposits me with my legs straddling his and my glass of whiskey trapped between us.

I let out a surprised squeal and planted my free hand on his shoulder to steady myself. His woodsy scent washes over me, and I barely manage to swallow the moan being close to him drags from my chest.

His rough hands glide up my bare thighs, shifting my hips closer until his hardness rests against where I'm aching for him. "Try again, little angel."

I sigh and take a sip of whiskey, hoping it will give me the courage I need. All my life I've been warned against speaking my mind. I've been told that everyone else knows best and that I need to stay quiet and trust them. How am I meant to break a lifetime of habits in just a few weeks?

"I'm worried about Elias," I admit.

Wyatt's answering smirk is filled with amusement, but he's not laughing at me. If anything, he finds my concern endearing rather than silly. His fingers trail higher up my thighs until they tease the edge of the shirt I'm wearing. Despite the fact they've bought me a bunch of outfits, each time I step out of the bathroom after a shower, one of their shirts is laid out on the bed for me, and being enveloped by their scent is almost as comforting as being in their arms, so I'm more than happy to oblige. "I'm sure Elias would be smug as shit about your concern, but you know he can take care of himself, right?"

I nod, because I *do* know that. He was a SEAL for goodness' sake. He's built like a linebacker and as unflappable as any man I've ever met, but they can't truly know what they've stepped into.

Because you haven't told them. The voice in the back of my head speaks up and guilt floods through me.

Wyatt's hand lifts to hold my face, his thumb brushing along my cheek in an intimate move I would have found foreign a couple of weeks ago. But not anymore. Not when these men find any excuse to touch me. Not when I've felt wanted for every single second that I've been here. "I can't help if you don't tell me why you're worried."

"It's just that my father, he's not a good man." I flinch at my own stupid words, but Wyatt waits patiently for me to elaborate, never showing even an ounce of impatience. "People think because he's the police commissioner that he believes in law and order, but he doesn't. There are things he and Governor Collins are working on, initiatives that are really scary, and that could ruin a lot of lives. And I don't want you getting caught in the crossfire."

I expect him to look at me like I'm being stupid, because that's exactly how Jason would be staring at me right now, but there's nothing but softness in his eyes. He plucks the glass from between my fingers and deposits it beside his own.

"We can take care of ourselves, angel." He flips us so fast I barely catch the squeal before it tears from my throat. His huge frame presses mine into the couch, the evidence of his erection pressing into my belly. "But the fact you're worried about us makes me want to fuck you so fucking hard you can't breathe."

I gasp at his words. You'd think I would be used to their filthy mouths by now, but growing up in such a conservative home has obviously left its mark. I take a steadying breath, pulling all the false bravado I can manage and look him right in the eye. "Then why don't you?"

His eyes flare with heat. "Is that a challenge, Leighton?"

I shrug under his weight, but the heat in my cheeks will be more than enough for him to know I'm anything but nonchalant.

Before I can take another breath, his lips crash down on mine, his need bleeding into every press of his lips. His tongue demands entry, and I open willingly, needing to feel all of him against all of me.

He shoves the shirt I'm wearing up my thighs and quickly tears my panties from my body, the bite of the fabric only making me kiss him harder.

I run my hands down his back, clawing at his shirt until he pulls back for long enough for me to push it over his head.

His hands travel over my ribs, careful as he brushes the ones that haven't quite healed yet. He catches my lips again in a ferocious kiss, like he won't be able to breathe if he isn't kissing me. And honestly, that's exactly how I feel right now.

I reach for his sweatpants and shove them down as far as I can before he takes over, discarding them across the room.

He pushes a hand between my legs and when his fingers move over my wet folds, he groans deeply. "Is all this for me, angel?"

"Yes," I breathe.

His fingers pinch my clit, and I cry out in a mixture of pleasure and pain. "Yes, what?"

"Yes, Sir."

He smiles down at me, his eyes glinting with satisfaction that makes my stomach flutter. I've spent my whole life trying to please everyone around me, but with them, it's as easy as breathing. "Good girl."

He lifts one of my legs, pressing it against my chest while he keeps close attention to my reaction. He lines up his length with my entrance and sinks forward slowly.

We let out a collective moan, and he drops his forehead to mine. His hips drive back and forth, unhurried, never allowing his gaze to stray from mine for even a second.

There's something so intimate about the moment, about how he holds my body as if it's the most precious thing to him, how he peppers kisses along my cheeks before returning to staring into my eyes, how he drives into me with deliberate movements that bring me closer to the edge with each thrust.

"Fuck you feel so good, angel," Wyatt grunts right before he crashes his lips down on mine again. It's the first time I've been with one of them without the other, and while I've wondered how, and if, a real relationship between three people could work, I haven't been brave enough to ask the questions that sit on the tip of my tongue.

But right now none of that matters. All that matters is the man thrusting into me like he'll die without me, and it's that thought that brings me right to the edge.

"Come, Leighton. Come right the fuck now," he demands through gritted teeth, and I follow his command without hesitation.

The orgasm that crashes over me steals the breath right from my lungs. I claw at Wyatt's back, trying desperately to hold on through the violent tremors that rack through my body.

His muscles tense under my hands, and he lets out a roar as his release fills me.

Wyatt collapses on top of me, but he's careful to keep most of his weight from me. His face buries into my neck while mine does the same to his.

For a moment I allow myself to consider what a life with these men could be like. How would it feel to be cherished every day? What would it be like if I never had to go back to Jason, if I never had to see my parents again?

Bliss.

Someone clears their throat in the doorway and we both look up to see Elias leaning against the frame in a fitted suit, a smirk etched into his full lips. "Did I miss all the fun?"

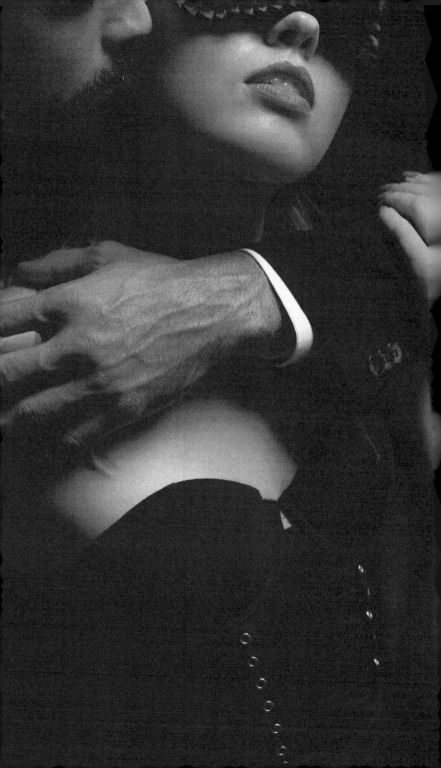

ELIAS

I heard their moans from the porch steps, and for a moment I hesitated, not wanting to interrupt their time together.

We haven't discussed how this is going to work with Leighton yet, but Wyatt and I had a brief conversation a few days ago, agreeing if we were going to make this work, we were going to each need time with her alone, as well as together.

But I couldn't stay away even if I wanted to.

I let myself into the house and take careful steps toward the moans. As soon as I step through the doorway to the living room I find the source.

Wyatt's body thrusts into Leighton's, holding her close. Her eyes flutter open and closed, so wrapped up in her pleasure that she doesn't realize she's being watched.

Not for the first time I wonder how deep her deviant streak runs. She's shown time and time again that she can handle our darkness, and I have no doubt that when we finally give her everything, she'll take it in her stride without hesitation. But there's one thing I'm not so sure about.

The club.

The memory of her reaction to the sin and debauchery as we carried her through to our office is burned into my mind. She looked horrified.

Will she ever truly be able to accept that side of us?

And if she can't, will we be able to give it up?

Before I can think much further on it, Leighton tumbles over the edge, her body clinging to Wyatt as she falls, and he's right behind her.

I consider stepping out of the room, letting them enjoy their afterglow, but I've always been a selfish motherfucker, and my cock is aching to sink inside Leighton's perfect pussy. We agreed to let her come to us, to not push her after Jason tried to violate her, but it's been a fucking challenge. Watching her walk around our home in nothing but one of our shirts, her ass peeping out to tease us, and let's not even fucking mention how she presses the delicious globes back into my cock as she sleeps.

Jesus, I've never had more cold showers than I have in the last week and a half.

I clear my throat, and they both peer up at me. Wyatt's shit-eating smirk tells me the smug son of a bitch is glad he was the one that got her alone first, and Leighton's blush is equally tempting as it is amusing.

"Did I miss all the fun?" I rasp, my own arousal clear in my voice.

"Right on time, brother." Wyatt waves me over as he rolls Leighton on top of him, not allowing his cock to slip from her cunt. He's never had any interest in coming inside a woman much less holding said cum inside her, but Leighton is the exception to the rule. His disappointment when she told us she was on birth control mirrored my own, and I can't help but wonder how long it will take for us to convince her to come off it.

I round the couch and take a seat beside them, taking a moment to press a kiss to the top of Leighton's head. I'm not ashamed to admit I missed her tonight. That's why I'm home so early after all. I couldn't handle being away from her any longer. I never thought I'd be one of those assholes who can't be away from their woman, but here we are.

"Take his cock out, angel," Wyatt instructs, and she doesn't hesitate to do as she's told. At least she's learning.

Her fingers brush over my hard length, and her eyes flash with lust despite having just been fucked.

She fumbles with my belt, trying to work out how to unbuckle it without moving from her position on Wyatt's softening cock. The furrow of her brow and the way she tucks her bottom lip between her teeth as she concentrates almost makes me take over just so I can be inside her sooner, but I allow her to continue until she finally flicks the clasp open with a satisfied smile.

A deep chuckle escapes my throat, but it doesn't distract her from her task as she unbuttons my pants and promptly unzips them.

Her eyes widen when my hard cock pops through the zipper. I often don't bother with underwear, preferring how it feels without them, but if this is going to be her reaction every time, I might set fire to my whole fucking underwear drawer.

Wyatt's mouth opens to give her an order, but she's already climbing from his lap to mine before he can get the first word out.

"Is my girl desperate for my cock?" I tease, capturing her hips in my hands and relishing in the softness of her skin. Her hair falls around her shoulders and down her chest. Her rosy nipples peek out through the strands, and I itch to pinch them, to have her writhing beneath me as I torture them.

"Yes, Sir." She nods and I swear if my cock gets any harder it could cut through diamonds.

"Go on then, take what you need from me." It takes every ounce of control I have to lean back against the cushions and remove my hands from her hips. Wyatt and I are not in the business of handing over control, but she needs this. She needs to know that we're willing to make concessions for her if she can just be honest with us.

Leighton only hesitates for a second before gripping my aching length in her tiny hand and positioning it at her entrance. She's fucking soaked, the mixture of hers and Wyatt's releases evident as I slip inside her with ease. But fuck me is she glorious.

Her cunt is my very own brand of heroine.

Her head falls back as she takes every inch of my cock, a soft moan filling the room.

She rolls her hips slowly at first, figuring out what feels good for her, and it occurs to me this might be the first time she's ever been on top. I haven't asked a lot of questions about her experience, but I know it's limited, and from what I know about her jackass ex-fiancé, I doubt he was up for more than some missionary and maybe doggy style if he was feeling adventurous.

"You're taking him so well, angel," Wyatt praises and she looks up at him, a small smile touching her lips.

Our girl has a praise kink I'm more than happy to satisfy.

She lifts her hips a little higher before carefully lowering herself again. Over and over in a maddening rhythm that is simultaneously too much and not enough.

Each move she makes is uncertain, but she doesn't let it stop her, and pride bubbles to life in my chest. When I look up at Wyatt he's got a similar spark in his eyes.

"Do you like riding my cock, pretty girl?" I rumble, finally giving in to the temptation and moving my hands to rest on her hips. It doesn't seem to matter how much I touch her, it never seems like enough.

"Yes, Sir," Leighton moans.

Wyatt's fingers move down her body, stopping at each nipple to pinch it lightly, causing her pussy to pulse around me. Jesus. She's like a goddamn paradise.

They continue their path as I guide her up and down, relishing in each rise and fall that brings her closer to her release.

The moment Wyatt's fingers brush over her clit she lets out a gasp that almost throws me over the edge. Holy fucking shit. I pride myself on control, but I have none when it comes to her.

Her movements become more jerky as she struggles to keep them consistent.

"Do you want me to take over, little one?" I ask, digging my fingers into her hips a little harder. I need her to say yes because I'm barely fucking holding on as it is. I need to fuck her. I need to own her. I need to pump her full of my cum. I need it fucking all.

She nods through a moan, and I don't need her words right now.

I thrust my hips up in a sharp movement that tears a scream from her throat as I set a punishing pace.

Leighton's hands move to my shoulders, using them for balance but doesn't she realize I'll never let her fall?

"Fuck," I grit out.

"I'm close," she cries out, and I swear if I wasn't so focused on getting her to oblivion, that declaration likely would have been enough to throw me into my own.

"Good girl," I croon. "You're taking me so good. Are you going to come for me? Are you going to be a good little whore and soak my cock?"

She doesn't get the chance to respond before her orgasm tears through her. Her entire body trembles with the force of it, but I hold her steady, dragging every single ounce of pleasure from her before I let myself follow her.

I pump my cum as deep into her as I can, praying to a god I don't believe in that it's the zero point one percent that beats the birth control and takes root.

I know how fucked up that is, but if we could plant our seed in her, there's no chance of her running. She'd be trapped with us, and that's all I fucking want.

FORTY-EIGHT

LEIGHTON

I pace up and down the living room restlessly.

When Wyatt laid out a dress I've never seen before, one my mother would have a heart attack if she saw me in, on the bed this afternoon and told me to get ready, it set off a chain reaction of stress and anxiety.

Where are we going?

Do I look like someone who likes surprises?

Is it safe for me to go out?

The questions peppered my mind all afternoon as I did as I was told. I applied the expensive makeup they bought me last week, somehow knowing the exact shades and colors I prefer. I curled my hair and pinned some of it up in a messy style that matches the dress they picked out.

And I slipped into the black satin number that leaves very little to the imagination. The one-shoulder design is about the most conservative thing about the piece of fabric charading as a dress. It drops to just above my knee with the highest slit I've ever seen in my damn life. To the point when I put it on, I had to take my panties off, which I'm sure was probably the intention now I think about it.

The dress clings to me, and when I expect to hate it when I look in the mirror, my mouth pops open in surprise.

I look good.

Like really good.

And I think it might be the first time in my entire life I've thought that.

I'm not sure if it's the result of three weeks of not being told I need to lose weight, or how often Wyatt and Elias remind me how beautiful they think I am, but whatever it is, I could get used to feeling like this.

"Jesus." Wyatt whistles from the doorway causing me to stop in my six-inch strappy heels. "I don't know if you're going to get out the door looking like that, angel."

"You picked it for me," I challenge.

A wolfish grin crosses his face. "Oh I know. It looks even better on you than I had hoped."

I look down at myself, a small smile playing on my lips. I never would have worn a dress like this before I met them, never would have given it a second glance if I saw it in a store, but the way it fits, it's almost like it was made for me.

A set of footsteps in the hallway drags my attention back to the doorway, and I catch the moment Elias sees me.

His jaw tenses, and lust creeps into his steely gaze. "Absolutely not."

I open my mouth to argue, but I'm quickly cut off by Wyatt's booming laugh. Did he plan this? Did he know his best friend was going to react like that to seeing me in this dress?

"You don't like the dress?" I pout and for a moment and second guess my decision to tease him, something I never would have done to anyone in my life before.

But when he turns his glare from Wyatt to me, it's not anger behind his eyes, it's pure need. He prowls toward me, barely pausing to step over the ottoman that separates us.

Out of instinct I step backward as he approaches, but with each step I take back, his stride eats up the distance between us until I'm caged between his hard body and the wall.

"Oh I love the dress, pretty girl, but so will every other motherfucker we see tonight, and do you know what will happen to them if they leer at you?"

I suck in a breath and shake my head.

"I'll have to tear their fucking eyes from their sockets."

I open my mouth to respond, but what the heck do you even say to something like that? Instead, I take a deep breath, steeling myself to be confident, something that certainly doesn't come naturally to me, and I carefully run my hands up his suit-covered chest.

His eyes darken, but he makes no attempt to stop me.

"I like this dress," I whisper into the space between us. "And the only people I care about looking at me in it are in this room."

He groans and presses closer to me, trapping my arms between us as he pins me to the wall. "Fuck, Leighton. Keep saying shit like that, and we'll never make it out the front door."

Wyatt clears his throat behind us, and I can't help but laugh when I meet his smug smile. He's proud of himself. "We should get going."

Elias lets out a low growl in his throat, and if I were wearing panties, they would be soaked from that sound alone. I mean, they would have been pretty wet when Wyatt couldn't take his eyes off me, and when Elias informed me I couldn't wear the dress, and then when he came at me like a predator hunting its prey…you know what, let's just assume my panties will likely be permanently soaked anytime these two men are around.

The club doesn't look any different than it did the first night I saw it, but *I'm* looking at it in a whole new light.

Instead of being horrified by the man chained to the Saint Andrew's Cross, being whipped by a woman almost half his size, I'm intrigued. Instead of shying away from the curious gazes that watch Wyatt guide me through the main lounge, I find that I like being on his arm, and instead of thinking about how filthy the place is, I can't help but notice how beautiful it actually is. The red leather accents, the dark woods, the soft plush carpet beneath my heels. Whoever designed this place did so with intention, and it's beautiful.

304

Elias walks a few steps ahead of us, but every time he glances back our way I swear I notice a hint of nervousness. Which is ridiculous. Given his relationship with the Legion, I'm pretty sure he kills people from time to time, why would he be nervous about bringing me here?

"He's nervous you'll run when you see the other side of us," Wyatt murmurs against the top of my head, pressing a gentle kiss there before pulling back.

I glance up at him to tell him that's ridiculous, but then I remember how I must have looked when I was here before and quickly shut my mouth.

"Don't worry, angel. I know you're not going anywhere, but he needs a little reassurance, okay?"

I nod.

They didn't tell me where we were going until we pulled up out front in the same spot the cab dropped me off the night we met, but this time there was no apprehension. Something about being with these men makes me stronger, makes me the woman I always dreamed of being but never got the chance to be growing up in a toxic household.

They explained some basic rules before we came in. Don't speak unless spoken to. Address all Doms with respect. Don't make eye contact. And I've been trying to keep my eyes low as I look around.

Elias leads us through to the back area, which I didn't see the night we met, and I can't help the small gasp that escapes my lips. I'm not sure what I was expecting, but this isn't it.

Couches line the walls, facing into small rooms only separated by windows.

A couple sit watching a scene, their hands gently moving over one another as they observe a woman on what I think may be a spanking bench. I've done a little research over the last couple of weeks when Elias and Wyatt have left me to my own devices, but it's all a bit of a blur.

The backs of the woman's thighs are red, and there's a little jewel peeping out from between her ass cheeks.

There's a tall man, thick with muscles, standing near her head. His shirtless chest is covered in tattoos, and his dark gaze is fixed on her as she swallows his cock.

I thought the idea of watching other people have sex would repulse me. I've never even watched porn for goodness' sake, but the wetness gathering between my thighs tells me I was wrong.

Just like I was about so much else.

Wyatt chuckles beside me, and I realize I've stopped walking to take in the scene. Elias hovers a few feet ahead of us, and I don't miss the concern lighting his eyes.

"Do you like the look of that, angel?" Wyatt croons, his arm tugging me in beside him tighter.

I nod, unable to tear my eyes from the scene.

The man moves a hand to her blonde hair and grips it in a tight hold before yanking her off his cock.

He drops into a crouch until their eyes are level, and he says something to her that makes her body tremble.

Wyatt's hand moves up and down my back with featherlight touches, and I long for Elias to do the same, but he still looks so uncertain, and I'm not sure what to do to make him feel better.

The man rounds the spanking bench and presses down on the plug in her ass, causing the woman to shift, desperately trying to get more friction.

"Would you like it if we plugged your ass, angel? You know how badly we want to train you to take both of us. I bet you can't wait to be filled with two cocks, unable to breathe because you're so full of us."

A strangled moan falls from my lips followed by a deep blush. We're in public. I can't do this...can I?

Wyatt swats my ass, tearing a gasp from my throat. "When I ask you a question, Leighton, you know I expect an answer."

"Yes, Sir. I want that." I force my voice to remain steady despite the way my whole body trembles with need and desire.

FORTY-NINE

ELIAS

I've never been nervous in my whole fucking miserable existence.

Except for tonight.

Wyatt assured me over and over again that I had nothing to worry about, that Leighton could handle the darkest of our desires, but I had a hard time believing that our angel could ever want to be defiled the way we crave.

Hell, both our ex-wives left us because of those desires, and Leighton is a hell of a lot more innocent than they were.

I can't bring myself to look back at her and Wyatt. What if she can't accept this part of us? Can we give up the club? Can we give up the life we made for ourselves?

I didn't want to bring her through the dungeon tonight, not when her reaction to the main floor had been so bad the first night she was here, but Wyatt insisted.

He said we can't just give her some of the story because that's just setting ourselves up for failure, and although it went against my very core, I agreed with him.

But that sense of dread only gets stronger the closer we get to the door. Things are usually much more intense on the other side, and although I don't think she's run out screaming yet at the sight of women kneeling before their Dominants and a man being whipped, that doesn't mean we're out of the woods yet.

As soon as I catch sight of the scene in front of me, my stomach plummets. Not because it's particularly brutal, but because it's exactly the kind of thing Wyatt and I would like to do to Leighton.

Sienna, one of the regular submissives, is strapped to a spanking bench with the backs of her thighs red from a flogger. The angry welts look sore, but her pussy is soaking, the evidence of how much she enjoyed that particular punishment. Her ass is plugged, and Micah is fucking her face without mercy. The tattooed man is one of our most experienced Doms, so I have no concern for her safety, but I'm worried about what Leighton might think.

I finally force myself to turn back to them, to see the horror on her face, but that's not what I find.

Her eyes are glued to the scene, a deep blush across her cheeks, and her lips slightly parted. But there's nothing but interest in her pretty eyes. She's not horrified, she's intrigued.

I look up at Wyatt whose smug smirk is firmly in place. Asshole.

He whispers something against the shell of her ear, and her body trembles at whatever he says, before nodding.

What is she nodding about? Did he ask if she wanted to leave? Or if she wanted to watch a while longer? Or…

Before I can ask any more questions of myself, Wyatt is leading her toward me. She keeps her eyes low as we instructed her, not making eye contact with anyone around us, but Wyatt doesn't stop beside me, he guides her further into the dungeon.

It's not until he's pushing one of the private rooms open that I realize what's going on. Has he somehow convinced her to play? Or are we using the room to talk her down from whatever metaphorical cliff she's standing on the edge of?

I trail after them, closing the door behind me and watching as Leighton takes in the space around us. This room is one of the more basic ones without a theme, and I'm fucking relieved Wyatt didn't try to take her into the playpen or the medical room. She's not ready for that yet, especially if she's freaking out.

But when her eyes settle on me, not quite meeting my eyes, it's not fear or disgust playing in the deep pools. It's lust.

"Our little angel wants to play," Wyatt informs me, carefully guiding a single finger down her bare shoulder.

I'm still fucking cursing him for picking that dress out for her, because she looks entirely too tempting in it, and I've already had to stop myself from killing no less than ten motherfuckers who looked at her with interest.

"Do you now, pretty girl?" I approach her carefully, watching for any signs of hesitance, but there are none, just trust.

I don't know what the fuck the two of us did to deserve for her to trust us, but fuck, I'd do it over and over again every day for the rest of my life if she'll keep looking at me like this.

"Yes, Sir." A small smile tips up the corners of her lips, and I let my eyes fall closed for a second as I let go of all the fear I walked in here with.

"Angel, why don't you tell Elias exactly which parts of that scene we just watched you would like to recreate."

A soft shiver moves through her body, but she doesn't pause, and he certainly doesn't have to ask her twice. It's like the woman standing before us is a completely different person to the one we met a month ago. "All of it, Sir. The bench, the spanking, the plug. Everything."

A growl climbs up my throat, and I don't get the chance to swallow it before I advance on her. She backs away from me slowly, but she's not really trying to get away. She's just pretending.

I pin her against the spanking bench, the soft leather pressing into the backs of her thighs as I trap her there. "Do you want to be a good little whore for us, pretty girl?"

She moans as her lips part. Her sinfully pink tongue darts out to wet her cherry-red lips, and there's nothing I want more in the world than to nip it. "Yes, please, Sir."

"Such manners." Wyatt chuckles from his spot across the room. I hadn't noticed him move, but realize what he's doing immediately.

In one hand, he has a plug, and the other a vibrator as he dumps their packaging into the trash. Leighton doesn't move her eyes from me, and that may be the biggest sign of trust she's given us. She's in a foreign place filled with things she doesn't know all that much about, and instead of trying to see what he's doing, she keeps her eyes trained on me.

"What's your safe word, pretty girl?"

"Red."

"And what do you say if you're approaching your limit?"

"Yellow."

"Good girl," I rumble. "Do you want to strip for us? Or do you want to be fucked in your pretty dress like the desperate little slut you are?" I'm testing the boundaries, seeing how far I can push her before hesitance creeps into her eyes, but she doesn't falter.

"I want to wear my dress, Sir."

I groan and flick my gaze up to where my best friend is attaching soft leather cuffs to the bench. The smirk on his face tells me he's happy with her response, and honestly, so am I.

I press a gentle kiss to her lips, relishing in her softness, before I carefully turn her to face the bench.

Leighton bends without instruction and allows Wyatt to wrap the cuffs around her wrists. "Not too tight, angel?"

"No, Sir."

He drops a kiss to her forehead and stands, joining me behind her to appreciate the view. "Look at our girl." He runs a hand up the back of her thigh, carefully pushing the satin dress up as he goes.

We let out a collective groan when he pushes it over her ass, and we find her bare pussy waiting for us. There's no way I would have let her out the door if I'd known she wasn't wearing any panties. Any of these motherfuckers could have seen what's ours.

"No panties, angel?"

She shakes her head, but she can't look over her shoulder with the way her hands are bound in front of her.

"That's very naughty, Leighton," I admonish. "I think you need to be punished."

A soft moan fills the room, and my cock hardens immediately. Fuck. I have no idea how I'm going to last. I need her almost as badly as I need my next breath.

I cross to the cupboard where the paddles are kept and pick out a leather one. We're already making a big jump from hand to paddle. There's no way in hell she'll be able to handle a wooden one straight out the gates.

She watches me with interest and a little bit of trepidation, but she's not afraid.

Our angel knows we would rather die than hurt her.

FIFTY

LEIGHTON

Desire burns in my blood like wildfire, and I can't help but shift slightly in an attempt to get any kind of friction where I need it.

Wyatt chuckles behind me and moves his rough palm over the globe of my ass. "Are you already impatient, angel? Because you've got a long way to go before we're going to give you any relief."

I groan, but the idea of my orgasm being held just beyond reach only makes the wetness gathering between my thighs grow.

His hand leaves me for a moment, but he's back a second later. Something wet touches my puckered hole and I instinctively try to wriggle away, but the binds and his hands on me hold me in place. "It's just lube. We need to prepare you to take the plug you wanted so badly."

I let out a steadying breath. I was so sure of the decision as I watched the scene unfold in front of me, but right now I'm second-guessing myself. I've never had any interest in anal sex. I mean sure, it's hot in books, but in real life?

Elias crouches down in front of me, his thumb moving over my cheek in soothing circles. "You know we'd never do anything that would hurt you, right, pretty girl?"

I nod. "Yes, Sir. I'm just nervous."

He smiles at me. "I know, but we've got you, and you've got your safe word."

I let out a breath. I know that. I know they won't let anything hurt me, and they've shown me that over and over again. They've taken such good care of me every step of the way. They nursed me back to health, helped me walk to the toilet, bathed me, and fed me when I didn't have the energy to do it myself.

A single finger presses against my back hole, and I take a deep breath, trying desperately to calm my nerves.

"Good girl," Elias praises. "Let him in. I promise it will feel so good after the first little bit."

I lean into his hand and keep my eyes on him as Wyatt breaches the ring. I suck in a breath, but after the initial burn, I find myself relaxing into the sensations.

He withdraws for a moment but quickly returns with a second finger, and I breathe through the added pressure. It's not unpleasant by any means. It just feels kind of strange.

Elias leans forward and catches my lips with his in a kiss full of need and desire. Before I met them, I had no idea kissing could set me alight like this, but every single time their lips press to mine, it takes my breath away.

Wyatt's fingers disappear, and I let out a keening moan at the loss, but they're quickly replaced by something cool and foreign.

Elias pries his lips from mine when I flinch, and he gathers my face in his hands again. "I want you to take a deep breath for me, pretty girl, and when Wyatt tells you, let it out slowly."

I nod, words lost in the lust coursing through my body.

The plug presses further against the puckered hole at the same time I drag in a deep, ragged breath.

"Okay, angel, let it out," Wyatt instructs, and I do as he says as slowly as I can manage.

The plug slips inside me with ease, and once it's seated, it doesn't hurt at all. If anything, it feels kind of good.

"Such a good girl for us," Elias rumbles, pressing one last kiss to my lips before standing and joining his best friend behind me.

It's hard not to feel vulnerable when I'm spread open for them like this, but I'm nowhere near as anxious as I imagined I would be.

A soft buzzing fills the room, and I tense for a beat before I force myself to relax again. They won't hurt me.

Vibrations trail up the back of my thigh, over the globes of my ass before continuing down my other thigh. I may never have been allowed to own one, but I know it's a vibrator of some kind and tingles of anticipation spread through my body.

"Here's what's going to happen, pretty girl," Elias rumbles. "Wyatt is going to shove this vibrator in your pretty little cunt, but you are not to come. I don't care how desperate you are, you will not fall over the edge. If you do, you will not be allowed to come for a week. Do we understand each other?"

"Yes, Sir," I gasp out as the head of the vibrator presses against my clit.

"I'm going to give you ten spanks with my hand, and ten with the paddle. If you're a good girl and take your punishment, you *may* be allowed to come once you're taking both our cocks like the little slut you are."

A whimper escapes as Wyatt pushes the vibrator inside me, pressing it in and out a few times for good measure before holding it as deep as he can push it. The vibrations tear a strangled cry from my throat, and for a few long seconds I panic. I'm not going to be able to hold off my orgasms. There's no way. Not with my ass full of a plug and the vibrator pressing on both my clit and G-spot.

"Color check, Leighton," Wyatt says as he brushes a comforting hand down my back.

I hesitate for a second, contemplating whether I really want this to slow down, and the truth is, I don't. I love the freedom their control gives me. I love not having to make decisions but always having a way out if I need it. I may be bound to this bench right now, but I've never been more free. The invisible shackles of my old life were heavy and impenetrable, but these aren't, and for that reason I murmur, "Green."

Elias lets out a pleased noise, and I settle myself against the bench. The soft leather against my stomach and chest heats with the temperature of my skin, and I allow my body to relax into it despite the nerves bubbling in my gut. "Count with me, pretty girl."

The first slap of his hand takes my breath away, but it doesn't burn like I expect it to. "One."

The second comes down on my other cheek, and I hiss out a breath. "Two."

The next five are in quick succession, each one coming a moment after I say the last number until there are only a few left with his hand.

By the time the final one comes down, I'm panting, tears brimming in my eyes. The mix of pleasure and pain they're inflicting on me is overwhelming, but I'm not tempted to say my safe word, not when it feels so freaking good.

"You ready for the paddle, Leighton?"

"Yes, Sir."

Wyatt uses the few seconds while Elias picks up the leather instrument I watched him choose from the drawers across the room to push the vibrator in and out of me while twisting the plug in my ass.

I cry out, the sensations almost too much for me to handle as my release dances just a breath away. It would be so easy to fall over the edge, to succumb to my body's baser needs, but I drag my bottom lip between my teeth and bite down, praying a different kind of pain will bring me back from the edge.

The first smack of leather on my heated ass takes a few seconds to hurt, but when it does, it *burns*. "One."

Another three hits in rapid succession tear the air straight from my lungs until I'm gasping the counts out. My entire body is on fire, the battle between pleasure and pain overwhelming me until I'm not sure how I'm going to drag in another breath.

"What are we up to, pretty girl?" Elias demands, and I allow the tears to fall against my cheeks. It's too much and not enough all at once.

"Four," I gasp through ragged sobs. Tears track down my cheeks through the next four smacks of the leather. My ass burns so hot I swear it's seconds from setting alight, and I can't drag in a breath through my cries. It's too much. I can't do it.

The word is on the tip of my tongue, but for some reason I can't spit it out. Instead I continue to count. I'm not sure if the words falling from between my lips are legible, but they seem happy with it, and all that matters to me is this moment and the wholeness that settles in my chest.

If these men could be the rest of my life, I'd be the happiest woman on earth.

FIFTY-ONE

WYATT

There are moments I think she's going to say her safe word, and I wouldn't blame her.

Elias isn't going easy on her seeing as it's her first time on the bench, and the tears dripping from her cheeks to the soft carpet are the evidence of how much pain she's in.

But she never says it.

She takes every spank with grace and counts even when her voice is hoarse from sobbing, and I've never been prouder of anyone in my life.

Elias looks down at her as he delivers the final smack with nothing but admiration in his eyes. I see what he may not have realized yet, because it mirrors what I feel in my heart. We've both fallen madly in love with this woman, and there's no way we could let her go now even if we wanted to.

She's ingrained in our very being, our hearts beat in time with hers, and at this point, losing her would be like cutting off a limb.

Elias moves his hands over her ass cheeks gently, rubbing the heat in while also soothing her ragged sobs. I want to tear the bindings off her and hold her against my chest. I want to wipe the tears from her cheeks and soothe her pain. But we're not done yet, not unless she tells us we are.

"Color, pretty girl?"

"Green," she chokes on a sob.

I meet Elias's eyes and shrug. If she says she's okay, we can't force her not to be, and we know better than most how freeing it can be for a submissive to release the emotions building in their chest, so who are we to argue?

"You took your punishment so well for us, angel," I praise.

I move the vibrator in and out of her, careful not to put too much pressure on the places that will set her off. She's already on edge, even through the pain she was pulling away every now and then, trying to get away from the assault of the vibrator, but even as sadistic as we are, I don't want to set her up for failure when she's being so good for us.

"Are you ready for more?" Elias asks.

"Yes, Sir."

He grins as he circles the bench and crouches in front of her. He gathers her face in his hands and presses a gentle kiss to each cheek, lapping up the tears as they fall. "Because you've been such a good little whore for us, I'm going to give you a choice. Do you want us to fuck you with you on the bench like this? Wyatt could fuck your pretty pussy while I fuck your mouth? Or do you want us both filling you at once? Do you want me to take that delectable ass for the first time while Wyatt fills your sweet cunt?"

She groans in response, her body shifting in a bid to get relief. Her entire body trembles with the need to come, and if it were me, I'd be torturing her to forced orgasm after forced orgasm, but this is Elias's punishment, and I'm not going to get in the way of that. "The second one," she whispers. "Please, Sir."

I groan and palm my aching cock. I've been rock hard since we walked in, my dick pressing painfully into the zipper of my pants.

"Seeing as you asked so nicely." He carefully undoes the cuffs around her wrists and massages each one to make sure the blood is flowing as it should be, but Leighton doesn't move, waiting for instruction.

I pull the vibrator from her pussy and throw it in the sink across the room before scooping her up and carrying her to the four-poster bed on the other side of the room. Elias and I have fucked enough women to know what he's about to instruct us to do.

I hold her close to my chest, relishing in the feel of her against me. "You sure you're okay, angel?" I whisper against the top of her head.

"Yes, Sir. I want to keep going."

I carefully perch her on the edge of the bed, mindful of how fucking sore her ass must be right now. Once this is all over, I'll rub some cream into her ass and the back of her thighs to hopefully help with the bruising, but she won't be sitting comfortably for at least a day or two.

Leighton watches me with keen interest as I push my jacket off my shoulders and dispose of it across the room, followed by the rest of my clothes until I'm standing before her naked.

I position myself at the top of the bed against the headboard and lift her carefully onto my lap. I grasp the base of my cock and move it to her entrance before taking a deep breath and lowering her onto me. We let out a mutual groan of satisfaction as I seat myself inside her, holding her still while Elias strips.

"How does he feel with that plug in your ass, pretty girl?" he asks as he shucks his pants in a pile near my own.

"So good. Oh god, so good."

I chuckle and press my lips to her jaw. "Now come on, angel, you know God is not here right now."

Elias picks up the lube from the table beside the bench and brings it over to the bed. He crawls up behind Leighton and sinks his teeth into the place where her neck and shoulder meet.

She lets out a startled cry, but by the way her cunt tightens around me, she fucking loves it. Our girl sure does love some pain on the side of her pleasure.

He presses the plug in and out a few times, causing her breathing to stutter before withdrawing it and throwing it off the side of the bed to deal with later. Right now all that matters is fucking our girl until she can't breathe.

I pull her against my chest, giving him some extra room and after a few seconds his cock is lined up against her ass.

She clenches down on me instinctively, and I turn her face to capture her lips. The kiss burns my very soul, each swipe of her tongue against mine is another mark she leaves on me, and I don't give a fuck if I'm bloody and broken in the end so long as I have her in my arms.

Elias slowly presses forward, and she lets out a choked moan. Her pussy tightens around me, so much so I'm sure she's about to choke it right off. "Good girl," Elias praises as he runs a gentle hand down her arm. "That's it, you're taking us so well, little one."

Each murmur of praise makes her pant harder, and I'm beginning to believe she could come from nothing but that. Perhaps something for us to try in the future.

Elias seats himself inside her, and we give Leighton some time to adjust to the feeling of being stretched. Neither of us are small by any stretch of the imagination, and we could hurt her if we start fucking her like we want to without giving her time.

Leighton's face is buried in my neck, her breaths coming in hard and fast as they brush over my bare skin.

"Angel?"

"I'm okay. Green." She pants. "Please start moving. I need to come, Sir. I need to come so badly."

"Holy fuck," Elias grunts, pinching his eyes closed to get hold of himself. If we ever fuck her like this again, which seems very fucking likely, we may have to gag her so she can't say shit like that.

FIFTY-TWO

LEIGHTON

If I thought it was possible to combust with need, I'd be pretty freaking close right now.

The heat of being trapped between them, of their bodies pressed against mine, holding me with such reverence, it's almost too much.

But it's also not enough, which is why I started begging for them to move.

The burn is almost overwhelming. Elias is a lot bigger than the plug they used on me, and I'd be lying if I said it didn't hurt. But it's also intoxicating. I've never felt so full, and so complete, like the three of us joining like this is all I've ever wanted, and now that we're together, I can't imagine anything tearing us apart.

An emotion I've never felt before bubbles to life in my chest and tears spring to my eyes as the rush of emotions and sensations clash, tearing a moan from my throat.

"Jesus fucking Christ, angel," Wyatt groans as he lifts his hips at the same time Elias pulls back. They set such a seamless pace, and I'm grateful for them taking the lead the way they have. My body can barely remember to breathe right now, let alone move.

"You feel like heaven, pretty girl. A perfect little whore for us," Elias grunts from behind me.

"Are you going to come for us?" Wyatt whispers against the shell of my ear. "Are you going to milk our cocks with your orgasm?"

I nod my head against his chest even though I'm not sure I can. I need the release so badly, but there are too many sensations, I can't focus on any of them for long enough to get to the place I need to be.

Elias wraps an arm around my body and wedges his hand between Wyatt and I, but I don't realize what he's doing until his fingers find my sensitive clit.

I scream out at the added pressure, trying desperately to escape it, but they're holding me too tightly, and I'm at their mercy.

"That's it, Leighton," Elias coaxes. "You wanted that orgasm so fucking badly and here we are serving it to you on a silver fucking platter. Take it," he snarls.

And that's what throws me over the edge. My vision spots until all I can see is a sea of darkness and the stars of the sky. The intensity of my release steals the air right from my lungs, and I'm just along for the ride.

Wyatt and Elias's movements speed up, all the softness they showed me is gone, and the monsters I've come to know are in their place.

One orgasm rolls into another, until I'm not sure if it's multiple, or one never-ending one. Either way, my body is no longer my own, and I'm more than okay with that as long as they don't stop.

As long as they never stop.

They drive into my body with such force I know I'm going to be feeling it for days, but I don't care. I hope this moment is burned into my skin, that their touch permanently marks me so I never have to go a day without feeling them.

"You're squeezing me so tight, angel," Wyatt grunts. "I'm going to fill your sweet pussy." His cock pulses inside me and hot spurts of cum slam into me as he lets out a roar of his release.

Elias's grip on my hips tightens, and a moment later he fills my ass with his seed. The deep growl that erupts against my back might be the hottest sound I've ever heard and will likely feature in my dreams for the rest of my life.

We collapse in a heap, Elias careful not to put too much pressure on my back. "Goddamn, Leighton." He kisses a trail along my shoulder.

"You can say that again, brother," Wyatt groans. "I think you sucked the fucking life from my cock."

I giggle and rest my head in the crook of his neck, allowing myself a moment to just enjoy being wrapped up in their embrace. Being sandwiched between them is everything I ever could have hoped for, and if I spent every day for the rest of my life exactly like this, you'd never be able to wipe the smile from my lips.

I suck in a breath to give myself courage to say the words I feel so deeply I'm not sure I can keep breathing without getting them off my chest. "I love you," I whisper.

They both still, and I squeeze my eyes shut.

Stupid.

It's too soon.

Of course it is, we've only known each other a little over a month, we've never even discussed what our relationship is. How could I be so freaking stupid?

Wyatt carefully gathers my cheeks in his palms and forces me to look into his deep eyes that mirror my own heart. "I think I loved you the moment I first laid eyes on you, angel. So fierce and yet so vulnerable. I knew then that you were our missing piece, and that you would complete us just like you have."

He carefully turns my face, and Elias's hand replaces his. "You're everything, Leighton. You're the air I breathe and the reason my heart beats. You brought light into our lives when all we've seen is darkness for so long, and for that, I'll love you with every single beat my heart has left because you're everything to me."

Tears gather in my eyes, and I allow them to fall, not shying away from the happiness in my chest for once in my life. For once, I'm being selfish, and I'm taking what I want, to hell with the consequences.

Once Wyatt helps clean me up, and he rights my dress with the added addition of his coat to keep my trembling body warm, we exit the private room.

I look around at the scenes playing out around us in a new light. I look at the woman being forced to come over and over again and wonder if that's something I could come to enjoy. I look at the woman with a ring gag spreading her lips for the woman standing over her with a strap-on dripping with saliva and instead of being afraid, I'm kind of turned on.

The woman I was the first time I was here and the one I am now aren't the same, and I'm never going to be her again.

"We just need to check in with Brock, and then we can take you home." Elias tugs me into his body and presses a kiss to my temple.

"I need to go to the bathroom anyway." I gesture to the door we're approaching.

They both hesitate but nod. "Okay, when you're done, come out here and sit. We won't be long." Wyatt gives me a forced smile. I'm not sure they'll ever be okay with letting me out of their sight again, and despite living my entire life with overbearing people looking over my shoulder, I find it kind of endearing.

I step into the modern bathrooms and let out a breath. Tonight has been a lot, but in the best kind of way. I'm addicted to the way they make me feel.

I pass the marble-clad basins to the stalls.

Once I'm done, I walk to the basins and wash my hands, admiring how healthy I look. For years, I starved myself to be the size my mother demanded of me, but what she failed to understand is that you can be healthy and curvy. Not everyone can be a size four or below, and that's okay.

I bring my fingers to my lips and touch the smile. Life has changed so much in such a short amount of time, but I can honestly say I've never been happier.

I'm so distracted by my own thoughts that I don't realize I'm not alone until my mother steps up behind me, and before I have a chance to react, a painful prick digs into my neck.

Just as the world starts to fade away and my bare knees hit the cool tiles, I hear her whisper, "You've had enough fun, you little bitch. It's time to come home and fulfill your duty to your family."

FIFTY-THREE

ELIAS

I don't think I've ever walked through this place with a genuine smile on my face, because I don't think I've ever been genuinely happy since we bought the place.

Not that the club doesn't bring me happiness, it was just the rest of my life that was a permanent dumpster fire, but right now I'm on top of the goddamn world.

We need to talk to Brock about what's going to happen moving forward.

Since we bought the place, we've both worked seven-day weeks, along with dedicating time to our other ventures and helping the Legion with some of their dirty work from time to time. But we don't have the same kind of capacity that we used to. We have someone waiting at home for us that we want to spend our time with.

I push my way into our office that Brock has been using during our absence and stop dead at the sight of four officers standing over our manager, his face pressed into the carpet by the oldest looking one. The hatred in his dark eyes burns my skin as he glares at me.

Two of the other officers approach us slowly, their hands on their guns in their holsters. "Elias Ford and Wyatt Keller, you're under arrest for embezzlement. You have the right to remain silent. Anything you say or do can be held against you in a court of law."

I only get to glance over my shoulder for a second before I'm thrown to the ground, my shoulder hitting the carpet painfully as one of them wrenches my arms behind my back.

This can't be happening.

We've always kept our business shit above board. We had to, considering who we were getting in bed with.

Wyatt grunts as he's thrown to the ground beside me, but he doesn't share my confusion. He's fucking mad. The rage in his eyes rivals that of a bull staring down a red flag, but he doesn't fight against the young police officer who puts his hands in cuffs much more gently than mine had.

"Leighton," I whisper. What if she doesn't know what happened? What if she thinks we abandoned her.

"This is her dad," Wyatt tells me quietly. "The police commissioner is dirty as they come."

My eyes widen. "It's a trap."

For the first time the anger in his gaze falters, fear bleeding into the blue.

This isn't a coincidence. They planned this to take her from us.

But they have to know these charges won't stick, and when we get out, we're coming for our angel.

FIFTY-FOUR

LEIGHTON

Nausea crashes into me as soon as consciousness comes, but the memories are slower to return.

We were at the club. Elias and Wyatt showed me the night of my life, gave me everything I ever could have wanted, and then…

Nothing.

It's like there's a whole chunk of time I can't account for and no matter how hard I push my mind, the memory just isn't there.

I haven't been able to force my eyes open yet. It hurts too much to think about, let alone execute, so I haven't bothered trying.

At least not until someone clears their throat from beside the bed.

As soon as I open my eyes I realize why I didn't want to open them in the first place. The smells were too familiar, the cold ambiance too obvious for me to allow myself to accept.

I'm at my parents' house in my childhood bedroom.

My eyes settle on my mother staring down at me disapprovingly. The memory crashes into me all at once, almost stealing the air right from my lungs.

"You drugged me," I croak.

"I did what I had to do to get you back where you belong."

"I don't belong here," I snap.

"No, you're right. You belong with Jason."

"He beat me!" I shout, unable to keep a lid on my emotions. "He threw me down the stairs and tried to rape me." The memory of it brings panic so stifling my chest feels like it's about to collapse. What if she sends me back to him? What if I can't escape again?

"You can't rape a partner, dear. You give blanket consent just by being with them." She looks down at me like I'm the one talking crazy. What in the eighteenth century is she on about?

"You've been married to a cop your whole life, mother. I'm sure you're aware that's not what the law says."

She rolls her eyes. "It's irrelevant what the law says, Leighton. Women like us do what we're told when we're told to ensure our husbands have everything they need."

I stare at her because surely she's lost her ever-loving mind. She cannot seriously believe the crap that's coming out of her mouth right now. Can she?

344

I mean, I knew my parents' marriage was a performance, a show to make sure the right people saw their lives as together and happy while they barely spoke in the privacy of their own home. Heck, I can't remember the last time I saw them have a conversation between just the two of them. I'm not even sure they would remember.

But this is going above and beyond what even I thought they were capable of.

"You drugged and kidnapped me. That's against the law." The words fall from between my lips before I can think them through.

"I'm your mother, I know what's best for you, and I'm just making sure you fulfill your duties. You made a promise to Jason, and you will follow through with it."

"No, *you* made a promise to Jason's parents. I never got a say in it." I'm done being the quiet wallflower she raised me to be. It never got me anywhere before, and I'm sure it won't get me anywhere now she's resorted to such insane tactics.

Finally feeling strong enough, I push myself up to a sitting position. At least she didn't tie me up, but maybe that never occurred to her when I've always fallen in line before. I never challenged her, always did as I was told like a good little girl because she told me I had to. She told me I didn't have a choice. But I did. And I do now.

"Again, irrelevant," she snaps tersely. It's rare for my mother to lose her cool, but I can see her teetering on the edge now. "You know why we made that deal with Jason's father, and why you have to follow through with it now." She raises her eyebrows waiting for me to challenge her. "Or do you want to go to prison for murder?"

I open my mouth to argue but quickly snap it shut as that night comes roaring back to me. The night everything changed. The night I became a pawn in a game of chess I never agreed to play.

Seven Years Ago

*T**he cool November air settles on my bare skin as I walk through the deserted forest. The party shouldn't be too much further. Or at least that's what Jack said when he invited me.*

I have to admit it was kind of weird when he asked me to come to one of his infamous bonfires out of the blue, but he's the captain of the football team, and I'm just some loser he's never seemed to notice before so I wasn't going to ask any more questions than where and what time.

But perhaps that was my first mistake.

Pine needles crunch beneath my boots as I walk, each sound around me making me jump higher than the last. I'm about to turn back and cut my losses when I finally hear music on the other side of a clearing.

At last.

I walk past a few of the cheerleaders I have some classes with, but they don't look my way, and I decide it's better I don't engage with them. They've never been that mean to me, probably because of who my family is, but I've seen them bully some of the other kids in our class, and I'd like to remain off their radar.

I walk farther into the trees and try not to look at any one person for longer than I need to. There are alcohol bottles lying around, cigarette butts carelessly discarded, and the strong scent of weed lingers around me.

I shouldn't be here.

And I certainly shouldn't have snuck out tonight to come.

I'm just about to turn around and head back the way I came when a firm hand grasps my bicep causing me to jolt.

I look up and find Jack looking down at me with a wide smile. His bright green eyes shine with excitement like he's genuinely happy to see me, and I can't help but notice his floppy brown hair is slightly styled tonight. "You made it!"

"I did," I say quietly, immediately reprimanding myself for not saying something wittier. I don't belong here with these people. I'm the police commissioner's daughter. He would kill me if he were to find out I was around drugs and alcohol, but it's a little late now.

"Would you like a drink?" he asks, wrapping an arm around my shoulder and dragging me toward a group of people I recognize from school.

I shake my head. "No, thank you."

"Oh come on, Leigh, you gotta loosen up a little," he teases, but it doesn't seem mean. He thrusts a beer bottle into my hand, and I take it from him despite the fact I've never drank before in my life. I guess there's a first time for everything, and I'm young. What's the worst that could happen?

347

*A*n hour and three drinks later, the warmth rushing through my body is almost enough to make me take my jacket off, but the sensible daughter my mother raised me to be can't quite force her arms to go through with it.

Jack hasn't left my side once, keeping a hand on my jeans-clad thigh at all times, and it feels nice. It feels nice to have someone care enough to touch me after being invisible all these years. It makes me think that maybe my mother was wrong when she said I was too plain and plump for anyone to show any interest in.

"Do you want to take a walk?" he asks, nodding to the fire. "The smoke always gets to me after a little while."

I hesitate for a second, but I find myself nodding before I've really thought it through. "Yeah, a walk sounds nice."

He takes my hand in his much larger one and leads me through the trees until the party is nothing more than a faint sound in the background. He's silent for a long time, and I'm happy with that. I've never had a lot of friends, so I'm not so great with small talk, especially with the opposite sex.

"I'm glad you decided to come tonight."

I look up at him and meet his intense eyes. They seem darker than they did earlier, but I put it down to there being no light this far away from the party. "Me, too."

He stops us and brushes his fingers down my cheek. "I've been wanting to do this all night." And then his lips are coming down on mine. My first kiss, and it's with the captain of the football team.

I fumble for a moment, trying to catch my balance as his kiss deepens, but he just drags me against him, holding me steady.

The warmth from the alcohol seems stifling now as his body presses into mine, but there's no way I'm pulling away now.

He presses me against the tree beside us, trapping me between his hard body and the rough bark, but I'm too lost in our kiss to care. At least until his hand moves up under my shirt, brushing over my bare skin.

I startle and try to break the kiss, but he shoves me backward more forcefully, his lips and teeth becoming rougher with each swipe.

Suddenly the heat is replaced with a cold sweat as the reality of my situation washes over me.

I just allowed a guy I didn't know to get me drunk and walk me far away from the party, where he could do anything to me, and I would have no witnesses, other than those that saw me laughing and smiling at everything he said all night.

He can do anything he wants to me, and I won't have a leg to stand on.

"Jack, slow down," I plead between his kisses, trying desperately to shove against his chest but to no avail.

"Hold still," he growls, capturing my hands in one of his and shoving them up above my head. The bark of the tree digs into my wrists, but he doesn't seem to care.

Jack's free hand pushes back up under my shirt and grasps my breast in a rough hold, making me cry out.

"You like it rough, huh?" he snarls. "I bet you do. I bet the

police commissioner's daughter has a dark side she's begging to unleash."

I shake my head. "No. I don't. I don't want that."

"Too bad." He throws me to the ground, and before I can even think of crawling away from him, his body comes down on top of mine.

Why aren't I fighting back? Why is my body frozen even though I know self-defense? Even though my father has been drumming it into me for years?

Jack's hands settle at the button of my jeans as he easily undoes them and shoves them down my legs despite how hard I kick.

I feel around the dirt for something, anything, to defend myself with, and when my fingers grasp around a large rock, I let out a stuttering breath.

Jack comes back down on top of me, one hand holding him up while the other unbuckles his belt, and I know this is my only chance.

I take a deep breath, lift the rock, and slam it into his temple as hard as I can manage.

His weight collapses on top of mine, crushing me no matter how hard I try to push, he's too heavy for me to shift.

Footsteps crunch through the pine needles, but I can't see who's coming. What if all this was for nothing? What if someone is coming to finish off the job?

"Leighton?" a familiar voice says a moment before Jack's

weight is lifted from me.

Jason Collins stands over me with worry in his eyes. He crouches down and touches my wrists where Josh was holding me a little too tight, and rubs gentle circles into them before checking Jack's pulse.

His eyes widen as he turns back to me. "He's dead."

FIFTY-FIVE

WYATT

"This is fucking bullshit." I slam my palm against the brick wall, unsurprised when I don't feel the pain. I stopped feeling twelve hours ago when we realized we were being set up by the father of the woman we love.

I should have believed her when she said he was a bad man, but I was too fucking cocky. I thought he couldn't touch us, not when the Legion is in our back pocket, but that seems very fucking irrelevant right now.

Elias sits with his back against the wall. At least they put us in the same holding cell. I thought they would have separated us, but apparently the police commissioner wasn't quite smart enough for that, even if he has stopped us from having our one phone call.

I don't know how he's blocking that request seeing as it's our right to have it, but he's found a way to make every officer in this godforsaken place ignore our very existence.

"Sit down, Wy."

"No." I pace up and down the cell, the same three steps I can take back and forth got boring eleven and a half hours ago, and yet I can't bring myself to stop. "What if they've taken Leighton back to Jason?" I voice the fear I've had since the second we stepped into the office. "What if he hurts her?"

Elias presses his eyes closed and lets out a ragged breath. "She's strong. She knows we'll come for her." But I'm not sure which one of us he's trying to convince. There are a lot of thoughts racing through my mind right now, worries I'm not sure if I can voice. What if she thinks we left her?

"Wyatt, you need to sit down. You're not doing yourself any favors pacing around here."

"I don't know how you can seem so fucking calm," I snarl. "They set us up. They set us up so they could get Leighton away from us so they can take her to her fucking abusive ex-fiancé. Or are you forgetting that she showed up on our doorstep bloody and covered in bruises a month ago? Did you forget how her dislocated shoulder had to be set in the middle of our living room, and we had to ask her if we could take fucking photos of her injuries to prove what a cunt Jason is?" Every word that comes out of my mouth is louder than the last, but I can't fucking help it. I'm losing it. I've always been the easy going one. But right now I'm ready to kill every motherfucker in this building if it means I can get my woman back.

Elias stands so fast I barely catch his movements before he slams my back into the wall. His fist holds my collar tightly as he growls. "No I haven't fucking forgotten. I was there. I fucking held her through just as many nightmares as you did. But you know what else I know? I know that the more we freak out, the more shit they have to use on us. I know the calmer we are, the more likely they are to give us the fucking phone call we keep asking for. And that means we're more likely to find Leighton quicker." He shoves me, and I collapse against the wall, all the fight burning away from my limbs. "Settle the hell down. We need to be able to move quickly when we get out of here. And we won't be able to do that if we spend the whole time we're in here panicking."

All the fight drains from me, and I don't bother pushing myself up.

I've never felt as helpless as I do now as I think of all the ways he could be hurting my angel right now.

FIFTY-SIX

LEIGHTON

I always knew my mother was a cold, vindictive woman, but as I stand in the middle of my childhood bedroom holding a piece of premium cardstock, reading over the words printed in delicate script over and over again, I realize she never loved me either.

Mr. and Mrs. Lionel Chalmers
together with
Mr. and Mrs. James Collins
request the honor of your presence
at the marriage of their children
Leighton Grace Chalmers
and
Jason James Collins

The rest of the invitation is irrelevant once I reach the date. Saturday. This Saturday. Five days from now, I'll become Mrs. Jason Collins and begin my life as nothing more than an accessory to him the same way my mother has always been for my father.

I have no idea how they've pulled this together so quickly, or if they were always planning to get me back when they did. I've been here three days, but it's been two since anyone has said a word to me. I've just been locked in this room with nothing but my own thoughts.

Unsurprisingly, I'm not allowed near a computer or phone because they know I'll call Elias or Wyatt. Just the thought of them makes my chest ache for them.

What do they think happened to me?

Do they think I left them?

I wince at the thought and throw the invitation on the desk with the thank you notes I'm meant to be writing. These people haven't even given us a gift yet. I'm not sure how my mother expects me to thank them for one.

The key in the door drags my attention away, and I immediately move to the other side of the bed, making sure to have something between me and whoever is coming through the door.

The last person I expect to step through it is my father with Jason's just a few steps behind. There are few people I want to be locked in a room with less than these two evil men, but there's no escape. Believe me, I've tried, but they went as far as nailing the windows shut to keep me here.

"Leighton," my father greets me as he shuts the door behind them.

"Father. Governor Collins." I nod at each of them with disgust as if they're not two of the most respected men in the city.

"You've caused a lot of issues for us as of late." The senator starts rifling through the few thank you cards I've actually bothered to write.

"The broken ribs and dislocated shoulder your son gave me when he pushed me down a flight of stairs and tried to rape me were pretty inconvenient for me, too." I never would have been brave enough to speak to them like this before, but I'm past caring. What's the worst they can do?

Oh wait, they're already doing it.

They've already torn me away from the men I love, they're already forcing me to marry a man I despise, I'm already going to live a life of misery by his side because of a stupid mistake I made in self-defense when I was fifteen. There's nothing else they could do that would hurt me more.

They each stare at me for a moment, like they can't believe I spoke out against them. No one is ever brave enough, but those who have nothing left to lose can say whatever the heck they want.

"There's no need for your lies and exaggerations, Leighton," my father says, dismissing me completely. I shouldn't be surprised. When Jason called our fathers after he found me with my jeans and panties around my ankles and Jack's lifeless body crushing mine, they blamed me for it. They told me if I wasn't such a slut it never would have happened and now they had to clean up my mess.

"We didn't come here to argue with you about what my son has and hasn't done wrong." The governor steps toward the bed, and for the first time I notice the file he has tucked under his arm. "I'm sure you recall the reason the deal was made for you to marry Jason."

I nod, not bothering to say anything in return.

"I took care of a mess for you, made sure you wouldn't spend the rest of your life in prison for a silly mistake, and you would marry my son, linking our families and allowing us to go into business together."

He's not telling me anything I don't already know, but anyone who knows James Collins knows there's nothing he loves more than the sound of his own voice.

"But it's become clear that you need a little more…incentive." He tosses the file into the middle of the bed and I reach for it hesitantly.

As soon as I flick it open, my stomach plummets. No. It can't be. The photos staring back at me are mug shots of Wyatt and Elias. There's a bruise on the latter's cheek that wasn't there when he left me at the club. Have they hurt them?

"Your little boyfriends are rotting in a cell waiting for sentencing. I'm not sure if you're aware how closely they work with the Legion, the same group who is blocking all our attempts to…clean up the city."

I flick through the file, seeing a few shots of them with Crew and other men I only recognize from the newspapers as the other members of the Legion. None of this is a surprise to me, but I act shocked nonetheless. I want them to get to the point with as few stops as possible so they can get the hell out of my space. "You mean your attempt to introduce human trafficking into the city?" I raise a brow.

That shocks them. Both men's mouths drop open in surprise.

"That's not what—" my father starts, but I quickly cut him off.

"Yes it is. You don't need to lie to me when Jason's the idiot who doesn't close his office door during the phone calls he insists on having on a loudspeaker."

It feels good to render these men speechless, but it's not going to make any difference to whatever outcome they've decided on when it comes to my fate.

"Regardless," the governor snaps. "This is the deal. You do as you're told. You marry Jason, spend your life being a dutiful wife, and never have any contact with those men again, and we'll set them free this afternoon. If not—" he shrugs. "I guess they'll spend their lives in a prison cell regretting every second they spent with you."

I open my mouth to argue but quickly snap it shut again. There's nothing I can say that will change their mind. No argument I can make. I have no contact with the outside world, no way to call anyone to help them. They have me backed into a corner I can't get out of.

"Do we have an agreement?" my father asks.

I nod and immediately turn away from them so they can't see how much pain the idea of never seeing Elias and Wyatt again brings me.

The door clicks shut, and I collapse to the carpet as I allow tears to fall down my cheeks.

Nothing like signing your life over to the devil to break your heart.

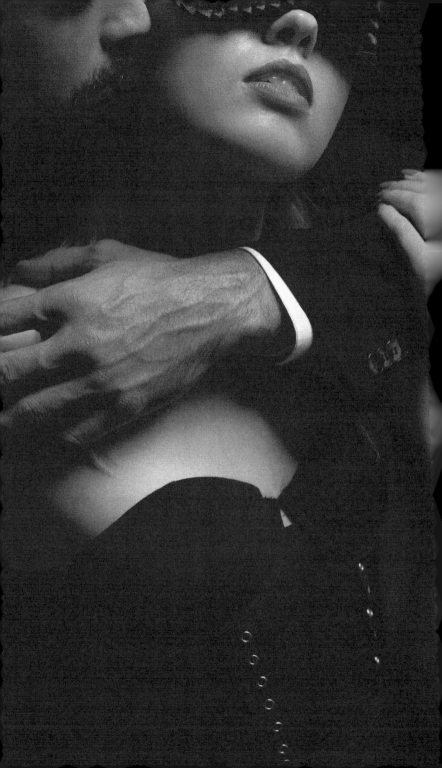

FIFTY-SEVEN

ELIAS

At this point nothing that's happening is legal, and that's coming from someone who does shady shit for a living.

We've been here for days, and we haven't been allowed a single call. We haven't been allocated a lawyer. And we're definitely past the seventy-two-hour holding period. But not one police officer gives a fuck about any of that.

If I ever needed proof the cops in this city are corrupt as fuck, here it is.

Wyatt goes between pacing up and down the cell restlessly and lying on the lumpy cot in defeat. I hate seeing him like this, especially after the glimpse of happiness we were given. A flicker of hope our cold, dark souls never dared to hope for.

I press my eyes closed at the thought of Leighton.

They could be doing anything to her right now, and we wouldn't know, we wouldn't be able to protect her, because we're stuck in here.

It's been hours since we've spoken because I'm more than aware of the fact that anything we say in here is likely being recorded, and we're not dumb enough to let them get us on a real charge. They have no proof we've embezzled shit, because we haven't. We keep our business affairs above board so the cops never have a reason to come sniffing around the other shit we do. But they know that. They just had to get us here so they could hold us, regardless of whether we actually did anything wrong.

A single set of footsteps in the hallway drag my attention from the spot on the wall I've been staring at for the last hour or so, and I don't think I've ever been so happy to see Crew as I am right now.

A police officer trails after him, taking three steps for every one of Crew's. "You have no right to have kept them for this long without pressing charges," Crew barks. "Do you idiots actually know the law, or are you making shit up as you go along?"

If you set aside the fact that Crew and the other members of the Legion run this city, he's still one scary motherfucker, and the cop is shaking in his boots every time his mismatched eyes flick to his scrawny frame.

It's the middle of the night, so I assume this guy is the only one around, and I bet he's panicking.

"And you know you're meant to provide a phone call and a lawyer, right? Neither of which have been provided."

He steps in front of the cell we're being kept in and looks us both over. "You two look like shit."

Wyatt rolls his eyes. "That's what happens when you're kept in a cell with no access to a shower for however many days we've been here."

"We're leaving." Crew turns to the police officer and raises his brow expectantly as he fumbles with a ring of keys. I have no idea if this guy has the authority to let us go, but hell, I'm not going to argue with the fucker.

Once Wyatt and I step out of the cell and pass the officer, Crew turns to the cop and says, "You can let your bosses know they'll be hearing from our lawyers. I hope they're ready to pay handsomely for this little stunt."

Before he can stammer a response, Crew is leading us out of the building with his head held high like he didn't just basically walk into a police station and break two of their prisoners out with nothing more than a few barked orders. It's little wonder he's able to keep the five families under control.

We pile into the blacked-out SUV, nodding quickly to Bishop before he pulls away from the curb, giving no mind to the traffic he cuts off.

"Nothing like a jailbreak on a Wednesday night to get the heart pumping." He smirks, looking at us in the rearview mirror. "Wow, you two look like ass."

I roll my eyes but don't miss Crew's snicker. Like father, like son, I suppose.

"Sorry it took so long. It took us some time to figure out what the fuck was going on, and every time I demanded to see you we were blocked with some bullshit reason," Crew tells us.

"So you resorted to picking on the weakest link in the

department to break us out?" I ask.

"It's not breaking you out when they had no grounds to hold you in the first place. There were no charges placed, and therefore you should have been released well before now."

"Do you know where Leighton is?" Wyatt asks, his voice breaking as her name passes through his lips.

Crew nods and sighs. "We do. That's part of what took us so long. We were trying to find her as well so our workforce was a little split." He turns to us with something clutched in his fingers. "The security tapes at the club were doctored, but the idiots didn't think to wipe the neighboring buildings. From what we can tell, they knocked her out and carried her out around the same time the cops took you down."

My stomach sinks, and my eyes clash with Wyatt's who looks about ready to throw up. We never should have left her on her own. What if they've hurt her?

"They're keeping her at her family's estate upstate, and we're working on extracting her, but they have the place locked up like Fort fucking Knox," Bishop says. "Kaos and Kovu have been there the last two days scoping out the joint, but we can't get a lock on where Leighton is without setting every alarm in the fucking place off."

"That's not the worst of it." Crew passes the piece of card he was holding back to us, and a snarl climbs up the back of my throat as I read over the words.

No.

No fucking way.

There is no way in hell our sweet angel is marrying that abusive piece of shit.

FIFTY-EIGHT

LEIGHTON

T his is like the nightmare I can't wake up from.

Every morning my mother has some other wedding-related task for me, and every morning I contemplate whether this is a life I can actually live.

The small blessing is that I still haven't seen Jason since I've been back.

I know that can't last. I have to walk down the aisle tomorrow and see him at the other end. There was a blissful moment when I thought that wouldn't be my life. I thought there was a chance I could have a future with the men I loved. Marriage may not have been an option, but we could have had a happy life. We could have loved each other, and maybe we could have even had a family. Our kids could have had two dads who loved them and would do anything for them, and I would have died knowing I'd lived a full life.

But that's not how this story ends, and that's just something I have to accept. Not all fairytales have happily ever afters.

"Are you listening, Leighton?" My mother scowls as she holds out the third hideous wedding dress of the morning.

I'm surprised I'm getting a say in this at all. I thought she would have chosen one for me, and I would have seen it for the first time not long before I walked down the aisle, but my mother has always been full of surprises.

"Yes, Mother."

"So? What do you think of this one?"

"I hate it."

She huffs out a sigh and puts it back on one of the four racks filled with white dresses that were shoved into my bedroom this morning. "You're not being very helpful."

"I agreed to go through with this. I never agreed to help the process along."

She rolls her eyes and picks up another dress, this one marginally less hideous, but the high neckline and long satin sleeves make it an immediate no. "This one?"

"Are there any that don't look like a marshmallow exploded during production?"

She turns on me, her eyes wide with surprise and anger. I never would have dared speak out against her before my time with Elias and Wyatt, but now it all seems irrelevant. "I don't like who you've become since you've been back."

I shrug and lean back against the chair I'm perched in. "That'll happen when you drug, kidnap, and blackmail someone. Their attitude tends to change a tad."

370

"You are not being blackmailed," she huffs. "You are facing the consequences of your own mistakes. This is something you committed to a long time ago, I don't understand why you're making such a big deal out of it."

"Because Jason is already using me as a punching bag, Mother. He's already cheating on me. He already doesn't value the goddamn vows he's going to make me tomorrow. That's why I'm making a big deal out of it." I eye the racks and pick out the only one I don't completely loathe, a ballgown with a sweetheart neckline and a lace bodice. It's really quite beautiful, too bad I'll hate the thing for the rest of my life because of what it represents. "This one is fine."

Before my mother can respond I get up and walk into the ensuite, quickly closing the door behind me. I may not be able to run very far, but I will not sit here and be told to be happy about marrying Jason when I never had a choice in the matter.

N ight falls, but I don't bother turning on any of the lights in the bedroom.

I stare out at the expansive yard, green from all the rain we've had in the last couple of months, dreaming of the life I could have had. The one I *almost* had.

I wish we had more time. I wish I got to say a proper goodbye so I could tell them how much I love them. I wish we had a chance to see where things could have gone for us. Maybe things wouldn't have worked. Maybe a relationship between three people is too much, and there's a reason traditional relationships have just two. But I wish I could have found that out for myself.

371

But more than anything, I wish I could see them one last time. Even if it was from afar I would have the chance to commit every single inch of them to memory, where they'll always live.

A tear falls against my cheek, followed by another, and then they fall freely, but I don't bother wiping them away. What would be the point when they'll just be replaced a second later?

The door opens without the courtesy of a knock, and I'm quickly reminded that even the illusion of privacy will be out of reach from here on out. At least until they trust I'm not going to run back to Elias and Wyatt, I imagine I'll be locked up.

"Leighton?" Jason's voice cuts through my chest like a knife, but I don't turn around. I don't want him to know how much this is affecting me. "I know you're mad. I know I hurt you, and I'm sorry."

"Until next time," I whisper.

"There won't be a next time," he says adamantly, the door clicking closed behind him.

My stomach bottoms out at the thought of being locked in here with him, but then I remember as of tomorrow I'm his property, so what does it matter? If anything, he's less likely to hurt me right now because of all the important people that will be in attendance at the wedding of the year tomorrow.

I wonder what all those socialites and politicians, businessmen and lawmakers think of how quickly this thing has been pulled together. They probably think I'm knocked up, and we don't want a pregnancy out of wedlock to look bad for either of our families. I'm sure the gossip will be out in force through the church.

"That's what all abusive men say, Jason. No man is ever going to admit they plan to hit their partner again." I wipe my cheeks and finally turn to face him.

He's come straight from work, still in his fitted suit, but his tie hangs loose around his neck. "I didn't come here to fight, Leighton."

"I don't know why you bothered to come at all. We'll see each other tomorrow and every day after that."

"Because I thought we should clear the air. I wanted to apologize for all the things I've put you through, and let you know things are going to change after the wedding."

I quirk a brow up in question, waiting for him to continue.

"There will be no more other women, and I'll never lay a hand on you again."

A laugh falls from my lips as I sit back on the window sill.

"I'm not kidding," he growls.

"I know you're not, but you are lying."

"I don't see the distinction."

"Kidding is a joke. Lying is a deliberate deception. There's a very clear difference. We both know you're going to cheat again. There's a reason you never wanted to have sex with the lights on, and I'm willing to guess it has nothing to do with your own insecurities. You'll just get smarter about it."

I think back to the conversation I overheard between him and my father. "You'll probably start traveling more for work, start messing around with women in other states where it's less likely I'll catch on. And I'll sit at home waiting for you. Alone."

He opens his mouth to argue, but I shake my head slowly. I'm not done yet. This might be my last chance to say my peace, and I'm not going to waste a second of it. After tomorrow, I'll be his obedient little wife and expected to behave myself.

"And you'll hit me again." I shrug like the thought doesn't have ice-cold dread sinking into my bones. "Maybe you'll keep your word for a while, but one day I'll forget to pick up your dry cleaning, or I'll speak to one of your colleagues at a function for too long, or I'll do something else you don't like, and we'll find ourselves in the exact same position we did before I left."

Jason looks shell-shocked. Probably because I don't ever call him, or anyone else, out on their bullshit. But it feels good. It feels really freaking good.

In the back of my mind, I see Wyatt, a proud smile playing on his lips as I stand up for myself, and the tears threaten to fall again, but they can wait until Jason leaves.

"I'll see you tomorrow," Jason sighs and turns his back on me, obviously accepting the fact he's not going to win this argument.

"I'll be the one in white."

FIFTY-NINE

LEIGHTON

I peek through the doors and down the aisle.

There are hundreds of people finding their seats, most of which I don't know from a bar of soap. But they were invited to my sham of a wedding.

I look down at the dress I'm wearing and sigh. This isn't what I would have picked for myself if I'd had a real choice, but at least I don't look like the Ghostbusters are coming to get me.

I wish I could say I was ready for this. That I was ready to hand my life over to Jason. But I'm not, and I probably never will be.

"You're doing the right thing, Leighton," my father says from behind me, but I can't bring myself to look at him. He's in a navy blue suit I'm sure my mother picked out for him, with his police medals pinned to the lapel like he's an upstanding citizen. If only they all knew he was as rotten as the criminals he claims to protect the city from.

I nod, choosing not to respond when I know I have nothing to say that won't land me in more trouble than I'm already in, but nothing about this situation feels right.

We go through our lives imagining our wedding day. We see our big white dresses, and the church filled with our loved ones. We see the love of our life standing at the other end of the aisle and our loving father by our side as we try not to stumble toward our happily ever after. But that's not what my wedding day looks like, and my heart aches for the little girl who dreamed of today. I let us both down.

The music starts playing, and I take a deep breath.

I can do this.

I can do this if it means Wyatt and Elias are safe.

Even if it means I'll never know the meaning of freedom.

My father grips my elbow, and it takes every ounce of my willpower not to flinch away from his touch, but he doesn't notice my discomfort, all he cares about is looking like the dutiful father of the blushing bride.

Every step down the aisle burns me from the inside out as panic takes hold. I've never liked being the center of attention, but least of all right now when I'm a few breaths from a panic attack.

Jason stands at the other end, his eyes locked on me like I'm the most beautiful woman he's ever seen in his life, but he can't see me past the lace covering my face. That much I'm glad for because I can't pretend to be happy to be walking to the end of my own freedom.

I didn't get a choice in my hair and makeup, surprise surprise really, but the tasteful updo is exactly what I expected my mother to choose for me, my chocolate-brown locks pulled away from my face the way she likes. My makeup is simple and light. There's nothing Margaret Chalmers detests more than too much makeup on a young face.

The music seems a little too loud. The guests stares a little too intense. And the future ahead of me a little too real. But before I know it, I'm standing in front of my almost-husband with nowhere else to go.

I kiss my father's cheek as I've watched every bride I've ever seen married do, before turning to Jason.

He lifts my veil away from my face and gives me a tight smile. He knows how little I want to be here, if only he would do the right thing and call this off.

"Welcome," the priest says. "We're gathered here today to join Leighton Grace Chalmers and Jason James Collins in holy matrimony."

Each word he speaks is another nail in my heart, and I barely make it through the vows he makes me repeat after him. It's a lie. It's all a goddamn lie, and I want to scream that from the rooftops. I want to tell every person in here why we're here.

I want to admit to killing Jack in self-defense because whatever future awaits me if that were public knowledge still has to be better than what I'm about to go through with.

"At this time, should anyone present know of a reason this couple should not be joined in matrimony, speak now or forever hold your peace."

Jason looks at me with confusion, and when I look at where our parents are sitting in the front row, they look just as confused as we are. Was that meant to be in there? I haven't ever heard those words in a wedding before. I thought they were outdated and excluded decades ago, but maybe the priest is confused.

"I object," a voice at the back of the church booms, and when I meet the mismatched eyes of Crew, I almost burst into tears.

Another man stands a few pews away, his wild blue eyes and messy chocolate-brown hair, paired with an open-collared shirt make him stick out from the people around him. "I object."

Two more men I don't recognize, one that looks a little like Crew and another who looks like he could kill someone with nothing more than a well-placed look in their direction, stand and object.

But then I see them and every other person in this godforsaken church ceases to matter.

Wyatt and Elias are standing by the back door, their eyes firmly locked on me as they utter those same two words the other men had, and my heart bursts to life.

I step away from Jason and toward the aisle, ready to run down the way I came, but I'm not expecting someone to grab me before I can make it past the first pew.

A man I recognize as one of my father's security guards glares down at me, and then I feel the cool metal press into my side, and my stomach plummets. He has a knife.

"That was a mistake, Miss Chalmers," he murmurs against my ear. "Did you really think your father and the governor didn't plan for an interruption like this? And now that you've shown yourself as a two-bit whore, I guess we'll have to get rid of you."

He turns me around and pushes me toward the back exit, keeping the knife pressed against my lower back.

Every step I take away from the men I love hurts.

But at least I got what I wanted.

All I wanted was to see them one last time, I just hoped it would be for more than a moment.

SIXTY

WYATT

The plan is solid.

And more than that, the plan is completely nonviolent, which is kind of surprising since Kovu is the one who came up with it.

The other options included, ambushing Leighton's car to the church, going into the church and shooting every motherfucker standing between us and our woman, and killing Jason before *he* could make it to the wedding.

And yet it was the crazy fucker who said, "Why don't we just object?"

It wasn't hard to get the priest to add the line, one look at Kaos, and he was more than willing to do anything we asked, and just adding one extra sentence wasn't so bad, right?

Maybe not for him, but for the family who hired him, it was a whole other story.

I have no idea how they pulled this fucking wedding together so quick, but I'm sure it was in an attempt to stop us from coming up with our own plan.

Elias and I stand at the very back of the church, but no one has paid us any attention. We're both dressed for the occasion, and we slipped in as the bride was on her way up the aisle, so there was no reason for anyone to look back this way.

The Legion filtered in with all the other guests, because although they are connected to us, I'm sure everyone thought they had better things to do than to crash a wedding. I'd say that was their first mistake, but god, they've made a whole host of them that could earn them a bullet to the brain.

"I really hoped the first time we saw our girl in a wedding dress she would be meeting us at the other end of an aisle," I grumble.

Elias shoots me an annoyed glare that softens almost immediately. "Me, too."

Neither of us thought we would ever get married again, but as soon as I saw Leighton that first night I could see her walking toward us in all white, the vision of an angel. And we will get that chance. We just have to get her out of here first.

Every step Leighton takes up the aisle is hesitant. She doesn't want to do this, and she won't have to go through with it.

The priest says his line, and some of the weight that's been pressing against my chest lifts. We had a contingency plan if he turned on us, but I'm grateful we don't need to start shooting people yet.

Each member of the Legion stands and objects, and as the

room realizes who they are, my smile grows. These fuckers have never been in the presence of pure evil. Sure they've been around plenty of people who pretend to be good but have pitch-black hearts, but people like us and the Legion, we're dark all over, and we're not afraid to show the world.

As soon as Elias and I object, Leighton's eyes burn into mine, the relief in the deep pools is evident even from so far away.

She pulls away from Jason and starts toward us, but when guests start standing to get a better look of what's going on, I lose sight of her.

One look at Elias confirms he has, too, and I press the earpiece on. "Anyone got eyes on her?"

"I'm blocked in," Kaos grunts. "No visual."

"Same," Kovu says.

"Some guy has her. Tall, security I think," Bishop tells us.

I step around the crowd of people trying to get a better look. I shouldn't be surprised that we weren't the only ones with contingency plans, but I'm annoyed nonetheless.

"I need you all to stay calm and remember the backup plan." Crew's voice is tense, and I search for him in the hoards of people. Who needs this many guests at their goddamn wedding? I'm willing to bet Leighton can't name two-thirds of these assholes.

"What's going on?" Elias asks.

"He's got a knife on her."

Panic slams into me like a goddamn freight train. This wasn't

385

part of the plan. It wasn't even something we really planned for because we thought they needed her.

But what if we were wrong?

What if their contingency plan is to take a player off the board all together?

SIXTY-ONE

LEIGHTON

Fear coils around my throat tighter than any hand ever could, making it impossible to drag in a breath as I'm shoved out the back door with my father, the governor and Jason on our tails.

I knew today would be a nightmare, but I never imagined just how badly it could go. I thought the worst thing that could happen was having to consummate my marriage at the end of the night.

But I was wrong.

Very freaking wrong.

I'm shoved into the back of an SUV before I can think to look back, and it takes off so quickly I slide off the seat. My head slams into the window so hard my ears ring painfully, and my vision spots.

"Where the fuck are we taking her?" Jason yells from the driver's seat. Wasn't he part of whatever plan they're executing?

"Just drive. This is our chance to take out those Legion assholes," my father barks at him from the passenger seat.

I look at the guard next to me, his cold, dark eyes intensely staring at me. He presses the knife tighter into my side, and I suck in a breath. This was a trap? They used our wedding as a goddamn trap?

Jason takes a sharp corner and sends me flying into the hard body beside me, jamming the knife right into the boning of the bodice beneath my ribs.

A startled yelp escapes my throat, and three sets of angry eyes turn on me. "Shut the fuck up, slut," the governor snarls, a world away from the man who had come to me a few days ago to insist on me playing along with this little game of theirs.

They knew Wyatt and Elias would come for me.

And they knew they would call on the help of the Legion.

Something warm drips down my face, and when I reach up to touch it I find blood, but no one in this car is going to care that I'm bleeding.

At this point I doubt they'd care if I died.

"Take a left here," my father instructs and another sharp turn sends me flying into the window. "Head over the bridge to the business district. We have a warehouse there we can lure them to."

I stare at the back of his head, wondering what the hell is going through his mind right now. What kind of father uses their only child as bait? What kind of man forces his daughter to marry a cold, vicious man in the hopes their wedding will be their opportunity to take out their enemy?

The Legion may be ruthless killers, the glue that holds the underworld together, but at least they're honest about it, unlike the men in this car parading around as saints.

The next turn throws the three of us in the back seat to one side, and I realize too late the agony that burns in my side as the knife slices through the lace and straight through my skin.

"Shit," the guard mutters but doesn't bother pulling the blade from my side.

My father turns his dark gaze on us, his eyes locking on my wound as blood starts pooling around the knife. "We only need them to think she's alive. Don't worry too much about it."

Tears fall against my cheeks, but I'm not sure what they're for.

The agony?

The heartbreak?

The hopelessness?

The men I love who are about to walk into a trap to save me?

It all hurts too much so that when I allow my eyes to flutter closed, nothing but an abyss of darkness waits for me.

SIXTY-TWO

ELIAS

"**W**hat the fuck was that?" Crew barks as we pile into a blacked-out van.

"I have no fucking clue." Bishop shucks his jacket and throws it onto the pile of bags at the back. "We knew this was a possibility, I just didn't think Leighton would be used as bait."

I rub my hands down my face.

Fuck.

"Should have gone with my plan to blow the place up." Kaos shrugs from the driver's seat, and despite the possibility we could have hurt our girl, I don't disagree with him. There would have been fewer variables to prepare for, but we assumed the police commissioner would care more about his reputation than anything else. As soon as he had a knife pulled on his daughter, it became abundantly clear that wasn't the case.

Wyatt drops his head into his hands and lets out a pained roar, the sound so deep it's almost inhuman. We were so close to getting her back.

"What do we do now?" Bishop turns to his father for guidance.

"You don't have to keep helping us," I say. "We appreciate it, but it's becoming more and more clear this is a trap, and if I had to hazard a guess, it seems like it's more of a trap for the four of you than it is for Wyatt and I."

We *need* their help. But I can't ask them to throw it all away for us. They've worked too fucking hard to get to where they are, and I won't let them sacrifice that.

"How many times have you pulled us out of the shit, Elias?" Crew raises a brow.

"This is different."

"No, it's not. It's exactly the same. You walked into a burning building to save Kaos when he got himself stuck under that beam last year," Kovu pipes up.

His best friend turns a glare on him, but he nods his agreement before looking back at the road ahead. "Where am I going, Crew?"

"Is the tracker in Leighton's dress operational?" he asks Bishop.

Tracker? What tracker?

"Yep. They're on the bridge out of the city."

"They think they're luring us to our own deaths." Crew nods as he thinks. "Head back to the compound, Kaos. They'll be expecting us to be on their tail, and we don't know that they don't have a trap set up. We'll wait until the tracker stops moving and then work out our next steps."

Wyatt looks like he's about to argue, but I shake my head. I want to run head-on into their trap as badly as he does if it means we get to our woman sooner, but we have to be smart about this if we want to get her out safely.

Leighton is our number one priority.

I just hope they don't hurt her while we're waiting to strike.

The hours drag by, each one feeling longer than the last.

Wyatt feels it, too. I don't need him to say the words for me to know that.

His eyes are drawn, his usual happy-go-lucky self is long gone, and he looks more and more defeated with each minute that ticks by.

It didn't take long for us to put together a plan. Wait until nightfall. Follow the tracker to their location. Burn the whole fucking thing to the ground the second we get our woman out. We can't allow them to live after all they've done, especially because they're only going to keep coming. They won't give up. Every time Leighton walks out the front door she'll be afraid this will be the time they come for her.

Absolutely fucking not.

They can't take her from us if they're dead.

"Will you stop fucking pacing? You're making me dizzy," Kaos snaps at Wyatt.

"All this sitting around is driving me crazy," he sighs and collapses on the couch next to me.

It's rare for the Legion to let anyone outside the four of them into their compound, but we are two of a few select people that even know this place exists. We've been here a couple of times, and every time we come here, I'm shocked at how huge the place is.

It is a row of nondescript homes they joined together to make each of their apartments, the home base for operations, and the basement doubles as a pretty good torture chamber. What more could you want?

"The guys we have around the warehouse they have her in have confirmed the security presence is massive. They can't get near the place." Bishop walks into the room and drops down on the other side of me.

"Do we have any confirmation that Leighton is actually in the building?" Crew asks from where he's perched on the edge of his desk. We converged on his office, something I'm sure he's none too happy about, but it's bigger than Bishop's and the other two affectionately call the basement their office.

Bishop's eyes flick to mine as he nods. "We have footage from a nearby factory that caught them carrying her in. It looked like she had passed out."

I rub my hand over my face. This is taking too long.

"They're not going to make it easy for us," Kaos says with a smirk.

"When have we ever liked the easy missions?" Kovu chuckles.

Usually I'd agree. But usually my stake in the mission isn't quite so high.

SIXTY-THREE

LEIGHTON

A cold shiver pulls my mind back to consciousness, but I can't drag my eyes open immediately.

The pain in my side is excruciating, and each breath is harder to take than the last. I think back to my high school anatomy class, trying to figure out what organs are around that area, but my mind is too muddled.

I guess I can thank my father and his asshole security detail for that.

There's something around my wrists, rope I think, and they're tied behind my back. The tulle of my dress cushions an uncomfortable metal chair, but it doesn't totally protect me from how cold the surface I'm tied to is.

"They're not coming," the governor growls. I'm used to seeing him in front of others, not having spent all that much time with him without a roomful of people, but he's never sounded so...evil. Is it all a farce? Is the nice family man who wants to clean up the streets of New York with my father all a lie?

"Yes, they are," my father placates him. "They won't leave her here."

"Maybe you overestimate how much those idiots care about your whore daughter."

I hold my breath, hoping that maybe, just maybe, my father will jump to my defense. But instead he laughs. "For men like them, it's the principle of the matter. They may not give a fuck about her, but they won't want to be so publicly bested by us."

Another set of footsteps cross in front of me, and I hold my breath. They'll stop talking if they know I'm awake.

"How are we going to explain her death to the public?" Jason asks.

"She'll be a casualty of war between us and the criminals of this city. My whore daughter will be the face of our plans to take the current administration in this city down, and bring in a new future." My father speaks like he's been thinking about this for a long time, like somehow this could have all been planned. But surely that's not the case.

"Do you think the public isa going to buy that?"

My father chuckles a dark sound that's nothing like the laugh I remember from my childhood. "People are idiots, Jason. They're easily manipulated. That's how the Legion got to their position, and that's how we'll steal it right out from under them. Soon enough we will take over their role within the city. We'll get the whores off the street, sell them off to the highest bidder, all while we sit in our government offices reaping the rewards of both sides of the law."

I can't help the gasp that falls from my lips. Not only does he plan to overthrow the Legion, but he plans to keep their role while also continuing to serve and protect?

The back of a hand meets my cheek and drags my heavy eyes open. "Looks like our little whore is awake." Jason leers down at me with a sickening smile.

My gaze flicks around the cold warehouse, small puddles of water litter the concrete floor from leaks in the roof. The wide expansive space is almost completely empty, which only makes my stomach drop further into the floor.

I glare up at the man I was supposed to marry today. How I ever thought I'd be able to spend my life with someone as heinous as him, I have no idea. But then again, I was never really given much of a choice.

"You watch her. We'll be back shortly," the governor instructs his son before he and my father turn toward the small door ahead of us that's dwarfed by a huge roller door. I don't know a lot about my family's property portfolio, but this isn't something I would have expected to find in it. But then again, I suppose I didn't expect my law-abiding father to use me as a pawn to get what he wants.

Jason drags a metal chair in front of me and straddles it with the back resting against his chest. I think he thinks he looks cool right now, doing something a criminal mastermind would do in a movie, but he actually looks like an idiot, and it's on the tip of my tongue to tell him that. But if I want any chance of getting out of here, I need to play this smart.

"Were they worth it, Leighton?"

A small smile tugs at the corners of my lips before I can train my expression. Too late to lie now I guess. "Yes. They were worth every second."

His lips form a snarl, but he remains seated. "Did you know they were coming today?"

I shake my head. "Nope. I walked down that aisle thinking I'd never see them again."

"Says a lot about what kind of slut you are, wouldn't you say?"

I shrug. It stung the first few times those insults came from their mouths, but now they roll off me like they're not designed to hurt me.

"Do you think they'll come rescue you?"

"Your guess is as good as mine. But I hope not."

His eyes widen in surprise. "You don't want them to?"

"I don't want them to get hurt," I correct him.

He watches me for long moments, almost like he's seeing me for the first time. Every breath burns more than the last, and stars dance in my vision. The blood loss must be getting to me, but I can't afford to pass out again, not when I'm here alone with Jason, and I might be able to see or hear something useful.

"Do you think they'll come?" I ask. The silence is excruciating, and it makes it impossible for me to stay conscious. I need to keep him talking if I want to stay awake.

He nods. "I don't know why they would bother, but I think

they're dumb enough to come for you." He stands from his seat and approaches me.

As soon as his fingers wrap around my chin, nausea rolls over me. The thought of his touch would be enough to make me want to throw up the tiny breakfast my mother allowed me to have this morning, but the actual act is that much more revolting.

"I'm curious, Leighton. Did your whore pussy like having two men dote over it? You've always been hard to please so I'm curious to know if two cocks was enough to do it for you."

I glare up at him, unable to do anything to escape him. "You never tried pleasing me. You only cared about getting your dick wet, you never cared if I came or not."

His eyes flare with anger, and before I can think to flinch away, his fist hits my cheek so hard the chair rocks on two legs.

I try to keep it upright, knowing the landing will hurt like hell, but it's to no avail. I crash to the freezing cold concrete. My shoulder jars painfully, and I can't swallow the scream that claws its way up my throat. The impact takes my breath away, but it's the kick that lands right in the stab wound that makes darkness fall across my vision.

I fight for consciousness. Fight through the agony. But after the third kick, I can't handle it anymore, and I succumb to the stars in my vision.

The last thing I see as I drift into the darkness is Wyatt's blue eyes and one of Elias's rare smiles. The ones I could have grown old looking at and still dream of every night.

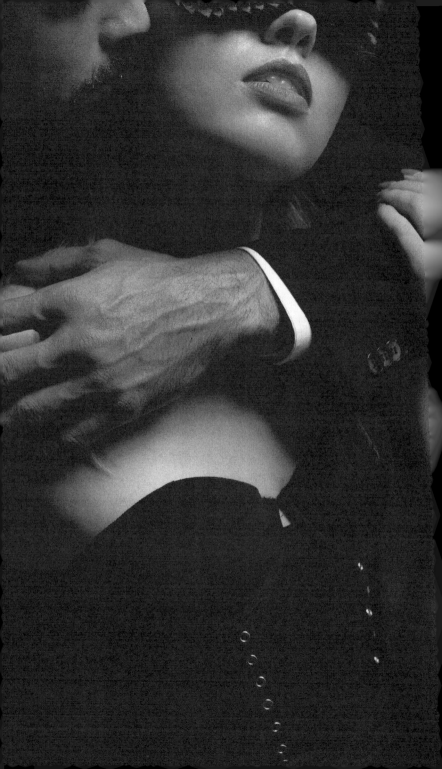

SIXTY-FOUR

ELIAS

The car ride feels longer than any fucking trip across the bridge I've ever experienced, and I've lived in the city my entire life.

Bishop sits in the driver's seat while Wyatt and Kovu are in the car behind us. Crew is running point from the compound because we're all too aware of the fact this is probably a trap, and we can't take every member of the Legion with us.

Kaos went on ahead on his bike and will travel the last mile on foot to cause a distraction.

We went over the plan so many times there should be no possible way anything could go wrong. But you don't work in this industry for as long as I have and not know shit almost never goes to plan, but the stakes have never felt quite so high before.

Bishop parks the car a few blocks from the warehouse and waits for Kovu to bring the car behind us to a stop.

We climb from the cars and meet between them, but none of us rush to say anything. We have a fair idea of the radius the police commissioner has set up, with cops no less, to keep his daughter captive, but the Legion's guys got into position a little over an hour ago, so there's a chance things have changed.

"You ready for this?" Kovu smiles. He looks like a kid in a candy store, and that's exactly what this will be for him. He loves the kill. The blood. The devastation. He fucking lives for this shit. And usually we do, too. But not when Leighton is on the line. Not when we have no idea if she's okay or not because even after nine hours, we still haven't been able to get a visual on her past the grainy footage of them carrying her lifeless body into the warehouse.

The street we're on is quiet, almost too quiet, but then this area always is on the weekends. The only work happening is normally criminal, and we know how to keep quiet so we don't get caught.

"As ready as I'll ever be." The words fall from my mouth before I can actually consider what they mean. Am I ready for what we might see when we get into that warehouse? They've had her for hours, more than enough time to hurt her, and it's become abundantly clear they don't care about keeping her alive.

Wyatt meets my eye and gives me a small nod. He's been quiet since we left the church, and I don't blame him. Generally, he feels things more deeply than I do, but the only exception to that rule is our angel.

When it comes to Leighton I feel just as deeply, I'm just as close to the edge, and if shit goes south, I'll be just as broken.

I tug my gun from my waistband and check it's loaded before shoving it back into place. My trigger finger is itching with the need to kill those who dared to take our angel from us.

In the distance a loud explosion sounds, and seconds later the ground beneath our feet rumbles. Looks like it's go time.

Bishop shakes his head and lets out a sigh. "I didn't give him enough explosives to make that much noise."

Kovu smirks. "But I did."

The crazy fucker bolts before he can hear anything Bishop has to say, and Wyatt and I follow after him, leaving Bishop behind as the getaway driver. He'll get the heads up from Crew once we take out the men surrounding the warehouse so we can make a quick exit once we have Leighton.

The warmth from the explosion licks at my skin as I turn the corner, and the warehouse comes into sight.

Kaos blew up a neighboring building, one he made sure was empty and owned by someone with more money than God, so he wouldn't miss the piece of shit that was rotting by the docks. The fire burns bright, distracting the cops surrounding the building as we knew it would.

I have no idea what the commissioner told them they're doing out here and if they actually know they're holding his daughter against her will, but when something catches alight, their first instinct is to investigate.

I catch sight of Kaos as we approach the warehouse with our guns drawn. The heavy metal in my hands calms me, allowing me to focus on the task at hand instead of all the things that could go wrong, and the list is pretty fucking extensive.

One of the police officers turns toward us and opens his mouth to shout for help, but I pull the trigger before he can get a single word out, the silencer muting the sound.

Wyatt takes down another as we approach the building, and we wait for Kaos to join us.

"You good?" Kovu asks him.

"You know me. Any day I get to blow shit up is a good day."

I let out a chuckle and carefully test the door to make sure it's unlocked. It doesn't really matter if it's not because I'll just blow the fucking handle off, but that will alert whoever is inside to our presence and give them a chance to prepare for us.

The handle turns all the way down, and a sigh of relief whispers past my lips. At least something is going right.

Kovu nods toward the side and I nod. We think there's another entrance around the back, but the plans for this place are about fifty years old so there's a chance things have changed.

We wait for thirty seconds, each one feeling longer than the last before I twist the handle again and throw the door open.

The first thing I see is Leighton and so much blood my stomach lurches at the sight.

The second is the gun held against her temple, her scumbag father holding it steady.

And the third is the swarm of men coming toward us. They're not uniformed, but I wouldn't put it past them to be police. I have no idea how the commissioner would have explained why he was holding a gun to the head of his own daughter, but hey, I don't pretend to understand the going-ons of other peoples' minds, that's not my wheelhouse, and I'm happy to stay the fuck out of it.

"Gentlemen," the governor steps forward from behind Leighton's father with Jason at his side. His gray hair is messier than it was at the church, like he's spent the day running his hands through it, and his eyes are more crazed than normal. "I'm surprised it took you so long to find us."

I ignore the jab and nudge Wyatt before he can say anything as we take a few steps forward and allow the heavy steel door to close behind us.

"Where's your boss?" the police commissioner asks.

"Crew had other shit to do." Kaos shrugs. "So I guess your plans to take us all out are probably not going to happen tonight."

The earpiece we each have fitted crackles, and Crew's voice comes through the line. "Don't antagonize them. We want to get Leighton out of there safely, not with a bullet wound because you were talking shit."

I drag my eyes over our angel, over her blood-stained dress, her bruised arms, the open wounds across her face. They didn't just kidnap her. They beat her, and from the looks of things, the asshole with the knife in the church stabbed her.

My finger itches to pull the trigger, to end the miserable existences of these men, but I won't risk Leighton.

How long has she been bleeding? Have they patched the wound? Or has it just been bleeding for hours?

"What's he paying all you assholes to bear witness to him holding his bleeding, barely conscious daughter against her will?" Wyatt asks, looking at the men moving toward us, each with their own weapon drawn. "Because this ain't no law and order I've ever been a part of."

The men don't pause, continuing to move until there are just a few feet between us. "You're the criminals here," one of them says.

Kaos chuckles and rubs his jaw. "You don't know much about what your bosses are doing behind the scenes it seems."

"Don't listen to them, they're lying," the commissioner growls.

"We just want Leighton. Hand her over, and we'll leave peacefully," I bargain.

"You think I'm going to hand my only child over to the likes of you?"

A laugh falls from between my lips. "You were willing to marry her off to someone who beat her, so I figured your standards can't be that high."

SIXTY-FIVE

WYATT

What the fuck is he doing?

I glare at my best friend. We had a plan, and pissing them off isn't a part of it. We just have to stall until Kovu can find another way in and get the element of surprise on our side, then we take all these motherfuckers out before getting our girl and getting the fuck out of here.

Simple.

Elias loves a fucking plan. He thrives on the goddamn things and gets mad when I don't follow them to the letter, and yet here he is, with more at stake than ever before, fucking up the plan we meticulously thought out and discussed for hours.

The commissioner's face glows red with anger as he shoves the gun tighter against Leighton's temple. She's barely conscious, held up only by his grip across her chest as he uses her as a shield. "How dare you?" he snarls. "Jason is an upstanding citizen—"

"Who beat your daughter mercilessly," Elias finishes for him. "I have the photos of that by the way. If anything happens to Wyatt and me tonight, or to Leighton for that matter, those photos will be released to the press. They have a date stamp and a written testimony from Leighton on the night it happened."

I look at him out of the corner of my eye. That was our last resort. The thing we were going to throw out to them if all else fails. Why the fuck is he compromising the whole fucking plan?

"We also have footage of your security staff holding a knife against your daughter's side as you escorted her from the church. I can't imagine that will look very good for your career."

Kaos turns to me, his brows pulled together in confusion. I'm glad I'm not the only one out of the goddamn loop.

The earpiece crackles to life again, and I expect to hear Crew losing his ever-loving mind at Elias going off script, but instead he says, "Elias is doing as instructed. It's taking Kovu longer than expected to get around the back so we need a diversion."

I release a breath and try my best to settle my erratic heart. I thought I'd feel relieved once Leighton was in front of me, but this is worse than not knowing. Seeing a gun held against her temple, her body limp and bloody, it takes everything I am not to cross the cold concrete floor and tear her from her father's arms.

"There's no way to prove my son had anything to do with that. For all the press knows you hurt her and made her write that letter," the governor says.

Elias nods like he agrees, but he and I both know we covered our bases over and over. "Normally I'd agree with you, but we also have the footage of Leighton fleeing, barefoot in nothing but a coat from the scene, her in the taxi, her on our doorstep, and of her writing the letter, all with time stamps of course." I smile. "So I think that's what most would call checkmate."

Silence falls over the dimly lit warehouse, but silence is the last thing you want in a situation like this, because silence usually means desperation, and desperation leads to mistakes. The last thing we need when our woman is in the hands of the enemy, and she already looks worse for wear.

The safety of a gun clicks off nearby, and I hold my breath as I stare at my angel. She can't die. I can't let her die.

"Sorry, gentlemen. I'm a little late to the party," Kovu's voice booms through the warehouse, but it takes me a moment to figure out he's on a small platform on the other side of the space, his gun trained on the men in front of us.

"Start shooting," Crew instructs. "Let's get this done and get your girl the fuck out of there."

I take out the two men directly in front of me, not hesitating to put a bullet right between their eyes as Elias and Kaos do the same.

Kovu takes out a couple of the men who were circling around us, while gunshots ricochet off the tin walls.

I look up just in time to see a guy aiming at Elias with his finger tight on the trigger, and manage to knock my best friend out of the way. The bullet misses us by inches, and I let out an unsteady breath. This mission is about saving Leighton, but there's every chance in the world one of us may not come home from this.

He gives me a quick nod before turning back to the task at hand.

Kovu lets out a maniacal laugh as he sends bullet after bullet into the enemy, never missing a target. The crazy motherfucker has no formal training, he wasn't in the SEALs like Elias and I, but he's the best fucking shot I've ever seen.

I take careful steps closer to where Leighton is pressed against her father, and the governor and Jason are a foot ahead of them. I can't believe any of these assholes are still standing in this room with bullets flying around bothering to pretend their plan is still operational.

Elias is at my side, his gun trained on Jason. I fucking wish we had the time to drag his death out, to make him feel every fucking pain there is to feel in this world as amends for the pain he caused our angel, but I'll settle for a bullet in the head if it means we get her back.

"That's quite close enough," the commissioner snaps, tugging Leighton against himself tighter.

Her eyes flick open, but her lids are heavy. From how far the blood has spread across the delicate lace of her dress, I'd say she's been bleeding for hours. She's fading fast, and we need to get her the hell out of here.

"Just hand her over, and we can all walk out of here without any more casualties," Elias says.

"And how do you expect I explain this level of devastation?"

He gestures around us with the gun flicking around wildly.

"I think you're going to have a hard time explaining this regardless," I mutter without thought.

The governor moves the gun he had pointed at Kovu toward me and trains it steadily. "I don't think you're in much of a position to be making snide remarks."

"And you are?" Elias asks.

"Here's what's going to happen," Jason pipes up for the first time since we came in. "You're going to drop the guns and let the four of us walk out of here, and maybe we'll let you live."

A booming laugh fills the empty space, echoing off the tin walls, but it takes me a few moments to realize it came from me. "If you think you're walking out of here with our woman, you have another thing coming."

"She's mine," he growls.

"You'd think you were trying to take away one of his toys the way he's carrying on." Kaos chuckles as he steps up beside me.

I glance behind us and see there's no one left standing. Just the four of us against the three of them. They're outnumbered and definitely out-muscled, surely they know this is over.

"That's all she is to him," Elias says.

"That's enough," the commissioner thunders. "Step back, or I will put a bullet in her brain."

Leighton's eyes widen with fear, but immediately droop closed again. She's barely maintaining consciousness. She

417

needs a doctor and quick.

"She's going to die if she doesn't get medical treatment soon," Elias placates.

"Which is why you need to let us walk out of here."

Elias looks at me, and I give him a slight head shake. No fucking way is he walking out of here with our woman. Not in this lifetime or the next is he taking our angel away again.

Her eyes flicker open again, and she meets my gaze. She holds it for long seconds and then mouths three words I feared I would never see fall from her lips again.

I love you.

SIXTY-SIX

LEIGHTON

I'm dying.

I know enough about the human body to know there's no way to lose this much blood and keep living without any kind of intervention, and they haven't even bothered to dress the wound so there's any number of infections to take into consideration, too.

I always thought I would die in a retirement home with the love of my life by my side. I thought I'd be in my eighties, and I'd be surrounded by our children and grandchildren, and it would be a celebration of the long life I got to live.

I never thought it would be surrounded by guns in a dingy warehouse with the men I love watching me fade away. I don't want them to see this. They deserve more than to watch me die in front of them, but I can't hold on any longer.

I've been in and out of consciousness since Jason lost his temper, but each time I come back to, it's for less and less time.

The darkness calls to me, begs for me to succumb, but I'm not ready yet, even if death seems more peaceful than the life I've lived. The happiness I had was so fleeting most would think it wasn't worth the pain, but that's not the case at all.

The time I spent with Elias and Wyatt made every crappy thing that ever happened to me worth it. It makes the pain raging through my beaten body seem like nothing, because I got to know pure joy and to feel true love, and how many people are lucky enough to have that?

Each breath is harder to drag in than the last, and although I know I'm in agony, it's been a while since I've been able to feel the pain.

My time is coming, and despite the chaos surrounding me, I've made peace with my own death.

I force my eyes open one last time and meet Wyatt's intense eyes. They're so deep I swear I could have spent my life getting lost in them, but that's just not the hand we've been dealt.

I tear my eyes away from him and look to Elias. He looks so serious, like always, and the little line between his brows is deep with worry. All I want is to smooth it with my thumb, take away some of the tension so he can relax, something he rarely allows himself to do.

I muster every bit of strength I have and mouth the three words I wish I could say aloud. I wish I could have said them over and over again. I wish I'd been able to say them more than just that one time. But at least that moment was perfect.

I love you.

I allow my eyes to drift closed, and a smile tips up the corners of my lips as my entire body crumples. The body holding mine upright falters, his balance thrown off by the dead weight in his arms.

Maybe that will buy my men enough time to end this.

SIXTY-SEVEN

WYATT

There are moments in my life that I had no idea were going to shape me into the man I am today.

When my father beat my mother to death.

When he died a few years later from a drug overdose.

When my unit was attacked when I was in the SEALs, and I was the only survivor.

When my ex-wife left me.

The morning I woke up and went to the club like any other day, just to meet the woman I knew would be the love of my life.

At the time, I had no idea how those moments would change who I was. But this one right here, as I watch the light flicker out of Leighton's eyes and see the moment she gives up, I know this moment is going to fuck me up for the rest of my life.

I know there will never be a time I can close my eyes and not see this exact moment in time.

I know my heart is never going to recover from losing her.

And I know Elias will never be the same either.

Leighton slumps forward, her weight shifting in the commissioner's arms, causing him to lose his balance. This is it. This is our chance.

Jason and his father take their eyes off us for long enough to look behind them, but that's a mistake, because that gives us each a chance to unload a bullet into one of them.

I hit Jason right between the eyes. It's not nearly as satisfying as I wish it was, but just having the cunt die at my hands is enough.

Elias takes down the commissioner as he fights to get Leighton back in front of him. Too bad for him that Elias is a damn good shot, and so he never gets the chance.

And Kaos takes down the governor with two shots to the chest.

I drop my gun and sprint across the distance. I fall to my knees in front of Leighton and drag her limp body into my lap.

I brush her matted hair from her cheeks. "Angel," I whisper. "Open those pretty eyes for me, baby."

"We need to get her out of here." Elias crouches in front of us, his eyes filled with worry.

Sirens blare in the distance, and I know our time is up. I close my eyes and relish the feel of her body in my arms, allow myself this moment to tell myself she's finally where she belongs, and then I hand her over to Elias so I can stand.

We jog out of the building as the sirens draw nearer.

Bishop's BMW idles a few feet away. Kovu slides into the front while Elias and I take the back seat with Leighton. Kaos jogs off in the direction of his bike, and when I open my mouth to question whether that's safe considering the cops are seconds away, Bishop chuckles. "He loves the chase. He'll draw them after him, so we can get Leighton to the compound to see the doctor."

"Should we take her to a hospital?" Elias asks, his eyes glued to our girl's beautiful face.

"Do you want to explain how the police commissioner's daughter got beaten black and blue, has a stab wound, and is being brought in by a bunch of known criminals?" He raises a brow in the rearview mirror.

He has a point.

I run my fingers over her cheek while Elias holds her head against his chest. "She's too cold," I whisper.

"Her heartbeat is faint, but there's not much we can do about it." He looks down at her, doing the same thing I did just a few minutes ago. "Hold on for us, pretty girl. Hold on, and we'll give you everything. Just please don't leave us." The crack in his voice is enough to force my eyes up to meet my best friend's broken ones.

We can't lose her.

We won't survive it.

SIXTY-EIGHT

ELIAS

It's funny, I never thought much about love.

When I married my ex-wife it had a lot more to do with duty than anything else. We reached the point in our relationship where it was expected for us to tie the knot, and so I got down on one knee and proposed.

I had nothing to do with the planning of our wedding, and the whole day was just as much a surprise for me as it was our guests. And then I repeated after the priest's words I didn't really believe in.

Because to me, love was some fucked up notion about giving your life to another person, and surely that shit wasn't real.

When we divorced, it was more of a relief than anything else. It hurt more that the woman I tied myself to thought my proclivities were a sickness than the fact she didn't love me anymore and was sleeping with my cousin.

But as I stare down at Leighton, her eyes closed and skin gray, her beautiful hair matted with her own blood, I understand what people mean when they say they couldn't live without their love. If I could tear my cold, dead heart from my chest and hand it to her, if that would mean she could keep breathing, I would do it without thought or hesitation.

Because a world without Leighton isn't a world I want to take a single breath in. She's the light that makes all the darkness seem insignificant, the soul that makes Wyatt and I seem a little more redeemable, and I don't want to imagine a second of my life where she's not by our side.

I check her pulse again and try to calm the panic that rises in my chest. Every time I check it, it's a little more faint. She's lost too much blood. Way too much fucking blood.

I want to turn around and drag those cunts back from hell just so I can kill them over and over for daring to touch our angel.

"How's she doing?" Bishop asks, his concerned eyes meeting mine in the rearview mirror.

I shake my head, not wanting to put the words into the universe. I don't normally believe in that woo-woo crap, but right now I'm not taking any chances.

"We're almost there," he promises.

I look over to Wyatt who can't tear his eyes off her face. The angry purple bruises are too similar to the ones she had the night she showed up on our doorstep barefoot and terrified. I thought that night was the first night of the rest of our lives. She came to us because she knew she could trust us, she knew we would keep her safe, but we failed her like we have too many fucking times.

Bishop takes the turn into their underground parking lot a little too sharp, but Wyatt and I absorb the impact, keeping Leighton as still as we can manage.

Crew's waiting in the garage when we come to an abrupt halt and tears the back door open. "Hand her to me. We have all three of our doctors on standby."

I can tell Wyatt is hesitant to hand her over but at this point, our pride doesn't have any right being at the forefront when all that matters is saving her life.

As soon as he has her cradled against his broad chest, he takes off toward the doors that lead to the medical rooms while we're left to climb out of the car.

We're covered in blood, but none of it is our own. It belongs to nameless men and our angel.

I look down at my hands, and the crimson staring back at me has bile climbing up the back of my throat. Even when my hands are clean, I'll still see her blood on my skin, taunting me, reminding me over and over how I allowed her to be taken from us.

Wyatt and I follow Bishop through the maze of corridors and into the medical suite that we've been in one too many times. You can say what you want about the Legion, but they're loyal to those who are loyal to them, and I'd never want to be on the other side.

Three men surround our girl. One slices the white tulle and lace, uncovering the wedding lingerie she intended to show Jason tonight.

My fists clench at my sides at the thought, but the doctor

quickly cuts it off her too, covering her with a sheet for some modesty.

Kovu disappeared as soon as we got back, and Crew and Bishop talk in hushed whispers on the other side of the room, neither of their eyes wandering to our woman.

Every inch of flesh they uncover is more bruised and bloody than the last, to the point it's hard to work out where the source of the bleeding is.

One of the doctors looks up at me, his eyes cold as they stare back into mine. "We'll do everything we can to save her, but it's probably best you're not here for this."

The other doctor drags the paddles toward her, and for a long second, I can't breathe. We're so close to losing her.

"Fight for us, angel," Wyatt's quiet words aren't meant for me, or for any of the men in this room. They're for our girl. They're a plea for her to fight for the life we could have if she can just pull through. If she can just fight a little while longer, she'll never have to fight another day in her life because we'll give her everything.

TRUST IN THE FALLEN

433

SIXTY-NINE

WYATT

It feels like they've been operating on her for hours, but when I look at the clock across the hallway, I see it's only been forty-three minutes since Crew led us from the room.

Every muscle in my body screamed for me to stay, to not let her out of my sight, but Leighton wouldn't want us to see her like that, and I know we'd just be in the way. Every beep of the machines they were hooking her up to would have made us rush to her side and get in the way of the doctors trying to save her life, and that's the last thing they need.

"What are we going to do about the warehouse?" Elias asks. I'm not totally surprised he's gone into work mode. It's his coping mechanism when things get hard. He needs the distraction, and obviously the silence has gotten the better of him.

"We have men there now. We have enough evidence to prove they were planning on trafficking in the city, and that the commissioner was willing to sell his daughter in order to make that happen. We're releasing it all to the press in the morning. All the photos, the timestamps, everything. The scandal will overshadow their deaths, but our men are staging it to look like it was a police standoff against the three of them because of the evidence that was uncovered." Crew runs a hand down his face, the first sign of the exhaustion we're all feeling. "We've planted some evidence at the precinct of one of the sergeants that was there tonight."

"So it'll look like a sting gone wrong." Elias nods along. He and Crew have strategized a million times, but even he's impressed by how quickly this plan has been thrown into motion. "How do we explain Leighton's disappearance?"

"She'll need to make a statement to say her father kidnapped her and that she managed to escape before the sting went down. We also believe we've uncovered the reason they were able to force Leighton into the marriage to Jason. It seems there was a death at a party Leighton attended in high school. The boy had his pants around his ankles and a rock had been used to hit him in the head. It must have landed in just the right spot so it killed him. But they were never able to figure out who the girl was that did it."

"Leighton," I whisper.

Crew nods. "We believe so. We think that when she makes the statement, if it was in fact her, that she should come clean. Say she was young and didn't know what else to do and that she allowed her father and the governor to cover it up. Which further invalidates the two of them for forcing a fifteen-year-old girl into a marriage because she defended herself against some overzealous kid who tried to assault her."

"That'll work." His eyes flick to the door again like he thinks the doctors will be out anytime soon, but from the last update we got after they first evaluated her, it'll be hours yet.

But she's going to be okay. She has to be.

She *has* to be okay.

SEVENTY

LEIGHTON

Whoever said death is peaceful was a liar.

Nothing about the pain raging through my entire body can be considered peaceful, quite the opposite in fact.

I thought the pain would have stopped by now.

The white light was kind of underwhelming, too. Instead of my life flashing before my eyes as I approached it, it just seemed to lurk in the distance, taunting me until it eventually disappeared. No matter how hard I tried to get to it, it floated away before I could reach it. But maybe everyone's experience with the light is different, and mine is just a maddening game of cat and mouse with the damn thing.

A faint beeping sound catches my attention as I search for what feels like the hundredth time, making me pause my pursuit for peace. Am I in Hell? Because surely that's the only place a sound like that belongs.

But I don't belong in Hell...do I? I was a good person. What happened with Jack was an accident. It was self-defense, surely God wouldn't hold that against me.

Or maybe it was my relationship with Wyatt and Elias. I don't think the Bible says anything about loving two men in one committed relationship, but perhaps I missed that Sunday of church.

If that's what landed me here, it was worth it. Every second I spent with them was worth a lifetime of eternal damnation.

"I think she's waking up," a voice in the distance says. Probably some demon come to welcome me to whatever version of hell they have concocted for me.

"Come on, angel, open those pretty eyes for us." Another voice drags my attention from the first.

There's something warm in my hands, but perhaps it's the hellfire that waits for me. Nonetheless I allow myself to imagine it's my men. The ones who showed me how to love and to be loved. Who made the first twenty-two miserable years of my life worth it. The ones who gave me everything I always wanted, even if it was for such a short time.

"Pretty girl," the first voice coaxes.

If this is the Devil's idea of torture, to make me think my men are here, just to have them torn away from me over and over again, he's done a pretty good job of finding my perfect hell loop, I'll give him that.

A hand touches my cheek, and it feels so familiar. Too familiar almost. I'm afraid to open my eyes. I don't want this to be some big cosmic joke. I don't want to allow my heavy eyes to open and be faced with some gross demon and the Devil chuckling in the corner.

Do you think the Devil chuckles?

Doesn't seem like a very devilish thing to do, but then again laughing at the expense of others definitely is.

"Something funny, angel?"

I drag in a painful breath and prepare myself for disappointment. I've had a lifetime of being let down, so surely this one time won't be any worse, even if I am waking up dead.

The harsh lights almost make me drop my eyes closed as soon as they crack open, but I push through. God, this really is Hell. The antiseptic smell. The rhythmic beeping. The lighting situation. The Devil really knows what he's doing down here.

"There she is." Wyatt's voice penetrates my praise for the Devil, and I roll my head toward the sound, but nothing prepares me for seeing his messy dirty-blonde hair and deep blue eyes.

I look the other way, my heart beating hard in my chest with a mixture of fear and hope, something I've so rarely allowed myself over the years and find Elias on my other side, his hands wrapped around mine. "Hey there, little one."

Tears fall against my cheeks, and I don't try to stop them. It would be pointless. Because either I'm dead, and I'm in heaven, or I'm alive, and the men I love saved me.

"Don't cry, baby," Wyatt rumbles, his fingers moving carefully over my cheek, wiping the tears away as they fall. "It's all going to be okay now."

I want to know so badly what happened after I passed out. There are so many holes in my memory from when I lost consciousness, but right now all I want is to stare at them, to tell myself over and over again that they're mine, and nothing is ever going to change that.

The bed shifts, and it takes me too long to realize Elias is climbing onto the small mattress beside me. He carefully pulls my body into his and as soon as my back meets his front, there's nothing I can do to stop the tears from falling.

"We've got you, little one. No one is ever going to take you away from us again," he promises, and I believe every single word.

They came for me.

They saved me.

And they're here, comforting me.

I knew from the age of fifteen that I would marry a man I didn't love, and I'd accepted the fact I would never know what true love was.

But somehow I got lucky enough to feel a love like no other for two men who have given me everything since that very first night.

"Get some rest, angel." Wyatt brushes his fingers down my cheek carefully before resting his face on the pillow beside mine. "We'll be here when you wake up."

SEVENTY-ONE

LEIGHTON

"**I** can walk, you know." I roll my eyes as Elias carries me through the house.

It's been a few days since they brought me home, and they haven't let me lift a finger for myself. If I wasn't so grateful to have them back perhaps I would find it annoying, but it's actually endearing as hell.

I thought they were over the top after I showed up here the night Jason beat me, but this is a whole new level. They can't let me out of their direct line of sight, to the point I've had to get used to peeing with the door open for their peace of mind.

But honestly I don't really like being away from them either, especially with everything going on outside this house at the moment.

The day after I woke up I made a public statement from my hospital bed. I shared what happened the night with Jack and the deal my father made with Jason's. I explained how my relationship with my ex-fiancé turned violent and how I fled from him because I was afraid for my life. And then I spoke about how I was kidnapped and forced to walk down the aisle to a man I knew would hurt me.

I outed my father for his plans for the city, and all the things I overheard while living with Jason. And the only false part of the whole story is how I escaped. How I broke my own wrist and made a break for it when they were distracted after they received word the cops were onto them.

And for the first time in my life, I'm free.

My mother is dragging me through the mud in the press, calling me every name under the sun, accusing me of lying about it all, but the evidence the Legion were able to drag up makes any claim she makes meaningless.

The police came to talk to me the day after I came home, and I gave them my full statement, complete with all the details Crew and Elias made sure I had a handle on before their visit.

Elias places me down on the edge of the bed and walks into the closet they cleared out for me before I was taken. I told them I didn't need that much space, but it fell on deaf ears, and if I'm honest, after so many years of being ignored and undervalued, it's kind of nice having them do things like this for me. "We've talked about this, pretty girl."

I sigh and lean back on my elbows. A few days ago this would have made me go through the roof, but a lot of the pain has started to settle now, and mostly it's just a dull ache that fades a little more each day.

He comes back with a black garment bag and lays it out beside me with a look in his eyes that seems completely out of place for him.

Is he nervous?

"What's in the bag?" I ask.

"A dress." He shoves his hair from his eyes in an anxious gesture. What the heck has gotten into him?

"Can I see it?"

He nods and takes a breath. "Close your eyes."

I do as I'm told, and although it's tempting to take a peek, I keep them closed.

Elias drags the zipper of the bag down, and the rustle of fabric makes it harder to stay put, but this is obviously important to him, and I don't want to ruin it.

"Open," he says, and when I do as I'm told, he's not standing alone anymore.

Wyatt's standing beside him with a huge smile on his handsome face and a small jewelry box in his hand while Elias holds a stunning white dress.

A wedding dress.

The bodice isn't completely dissimilar from the one I wore just a week ago, the delicate lace weaving around into a strapless sweetheart neckline. But it's the rest of the dress that takes my breath away. Soft satin falls to the floor and into a sweeping train. So simple. But so me.

This is the dress I would have picked for myself.

This is what I always imagined I would walk down the aisle in.

And this is the moment I dreamed of as a child...well apart from marrying two men, that part I never could have expected.

I open my mouth, but nothing comes out, and that just makes Wyatt's smile grow larger.

He flicks the box open and drops to one knee while Elias carefully lays the dress down beside me and helps me sit up before joining his best friend.

"There's no version of my life where I thought I would deserve a woman like you, but then you walked into our lives, and I knew there was nothing we wouldn't do to keep you. You brought a light to our darkness, and every second we've spent with you has been more than I ever thought I would have. I love you with all of me, my angel." Wyatt's words are so beautiful tears spring to my eyes.

"Before I met you, I thought I was happy. I thought I was okay with living the bachelor life with my best friend. I thought I'd loved before and decided it wasn't worth the hassle. But as soon as I saw you, it was all over for me. You are the most beautiful woman I've ever met, both inside and out. Your heart is so big, big enough for the two of us." He chuckles and takes my hand. "And we want nothing more than to spend the rest of our lives with you. We want to give you the life you deserve, full of love and joy. We want to be the ones to put that beautiful smile on your face every single day for the rest of forever."

"Will you marry us, Leighton?" Wyatt flicks the box open, and the ring staring back at me takes my breath away. The ring Jason gave me was expensive, but it was also excessively big. The damn thing would get caught on everything, I'd scratch myself on it at least twice a day, and it got in the way constantly.

The ring nestled in black felt is just as me as the wedding dress lying beside me. A beautiful diamond sits among a halo of smaller ones. The platinum band is simple, but beautiful, and I reach for it immediately.

Tears roll down my cheeks as I brush my fingers over the diamond, a quiet sob clawing its way up my throat. "Yes," I choke. "Yes."

Their faces light up, and they quickly rise from their knees, enveloping me between them as they kiss every part of my body they can reach without letting go.

This is what it feels like to be loved and cherished, and I wouldn't give up these men for every dollar on this earth.

"You don't have to wear the dress if you don't want to. You can choose whatever you want. You can have anything you want." Elias presses a kiss to my tear-stained cheek.

"I love the dress. And I love you both so much. Thank you for loving me."

I might not be able to see the future, but I know ours will be everything I ever dreamed of as a child. I never thought my happily ever after would involve two dark princes, but there's no one who could love me more than the two men holding me like their very own precious angel.

EPILOGUE

LEIGHTON

ONE YEAR LATER

I pop a grape between my lips and savor the sweet burst of flavor. I don't know what it is in the last week, but I can't get enough fruit.

Poor Wyatt has already had to make two trips to the supermarket this week to stock up on berries, the main craving that I haven't been able to get rid of.

But I've always been like this, I've always had weird cravings that last for a couple of weeks and then it passes, and the next one takes its place. It's just normally Cheetos or something, never typically so healthy.

And this is the first time in a long time the people in my life have actively allowed and encouraged me to eat what I want when I want, so I'm running with it.

The last year can't even be described as the best of my life, because I'm not living the same life I was for the first twenty-two years. The one I lead now is full of love and happiness, just like Wyatt and Elias promised me it would be in their vows ten months ago.

Our wedding was small and intimate, with just us and a couple of their friends. We extended the invitation to my mother out of courtesy, but in her own words, she didn't want to be a part of a sham marriage.

Nothing about it is a sham, though, I legally married Wyatt so I could rid myself of my family name, and so my mother would never have any right over my life and the choices that were made if the worst were to happen. But I'm just as committed to both of them.

Almost as if I've summoned them with my thoughts, they track into the room and drop into the couch across from me. We've talked about moving, maybe buying a house for the three of us, but I love it here in the brownstone where I spent my first night of true freedom, and I don't think I'll ever want to give this place up.

It's the first place I ever truly felt safe and loved.

The two of them have been acting a little cagey the last few days, but every time I've asked them what's wrong, they assure me they're fine. Are they finally going to tell me what the heck they've been up to?

I slip another grape between my lips and don't miss the way the two of them can't tear their eyes off my mouth. I thought the sex would have calmed down after a few months, that maybe we would be less desperate for one another, but I still can't change with them in the room without ending up bent over the edge of the bed or on my knees.

Not that I'm complaining. I spend my days being worshipped and encouraged to follow my dreams, and I'll never take that for granted.

If I'm really honest with myself, data science was never a passion for me, and so when it came time to find a job, although my men insisted I didn't need to work at all, I decided to do something different. All my years at my mother's side have finally come in handy for something.

After all I went through went public, a charity reached out to me to ask if I was interested in working for them, and I was more than happy to take any role they wanted to give me. I didn't expect it to be to run the whole damn thing, but it's been the most rewarding experience of my life, and the New York Shelter for Battered Women is thriving.

The Legion even helped put me in touch with one of their contacts in Chicago who runs a similar center, and Emerson Saint James has truly been a godsend every time I don't know what I'm doing, which is pretty often.

"Angel, we were wondering if we could have a talk with you about something?" Wyatt broaches carefully.

My brows tug together in confusion. "What's wrong?"

"Nothing's wrong as such." Elias looks to his best friend like neither of them are sure which one should be the one to say whatever they've come in here to say.

"Okay…"

"You're pregnant," Wyatt blurts out.

I stare at him for long seconds processing the words that just

453

came out of his mouth before a giggle rises up in my throat at how ridiculous that notion is. "No, I'm not. Don't be silly."

Elias runs a hand down his face before taking one of my hands in his much larger ones. "Pretty girl, you are. Your period is more than a month late, you've been having weird cravings, you're more emotional than normal, and that flu that won't go away…"

I open my mouth again to tell him how stupid they're being, but then I think about what he's just said.

No, it's impossible. I have an IUD. It still has another year before it needs to be replaced. And it's not like my periods have ever really been that consistent. Although I don't tend to skip them all together. Usually they're just a little late, but a month is a little concerning.

But the rest is just purely circumstantial.

"She's panicking," Wyatt whisper shouts at his best friend, his eyes wide and worried as he stares at me.

Elias drops from the couch onto the floor and kneels in front of me. His strong hands wrap around my cheeks as he forces me to look at him. "Leighton, breathe for me." His stern voice gives me no choice but to do exactly as I'm told, and I drag in an unsteady breath. "That's my good girl," he praises, and warmth washes over me. I don't know how after a year together those words still have the power to render me speechless.

Wyatt appears beside him, his calloused hands resting on my bare thighs.

"I'm sorry. I don't know how this could have happened." I swallow the sob lodged at the back of my throat. This wasn't the plan. We've never really discussed kids. We've been too busy enjoying each other.

They look at one another, confusion tugging at each of their brows. "Angel, you have nothing to be sorry for. This is the best fucking gift you could ever give us." Wyatt squeezes my thigh.

"We're not upset, pretty girl. We're fucking ecstatic." Elias drops one hand to my belly. "You're carrying our baby."

A sob of relief escapes as a few rogue tears fall against my cheeks. "I should do a test. To be sure." I've never done one before, but I guess there's a first time for everything.

"You don't need to." Wyatt smirks. "We had your pee tested a few days ago."

"You did what?" I shout, turning my glare on his beautiful face. "You stole my pee?"

Elias nods, his smile more than a little smug. "It wasn't exactly hard. Wyatt just distracted you while I grabbed it."

"That's disgusting."

He shrugs and tugs me down onto the floor between them. They each wrap their arms around me until I'm enveloped by them.

Reality starts to crash down on me, but the panic never comes. If I'd found out I was pregnant by Jason, I would have been devastated, but this isn't the same.

This child will come into the world surrounded by so much love, with two daddies who will do anything for them, and a mother who will love and encourage them every step of the way.

"Thank you for giving us the entire world, angel," Wyatt whispers against the shell of my ear.

But don't they realize they're the ones that have given me everything?

I drop a hand to my belly and smile.

We're going to be so happy, little one.

Thank you for reading Trust in the Fallen. I hope you loved my first, but certainly not last, why choose type book.

If you're wondering where the Forbidden Pleasures series is going to go from here, your guess is as good as mine! My favorite part of writing this book was all the twists and turns it took that not even I was expecting, so I think I'll be along for the ride just like you will be!

What I can promise you though is more forbidden relationships, more angst, and all the spice The Scarlet Lounge can throw at you!

If you enjoyed Trust in the Fallen, it would mean the world to me if you could review it on Amazon, Goodreads, Social Media, carrier pigeon, I'm not fussy.

You can follow me on socials for sneak peaks of future projects, including release dates and secret snippets!

ALSO BY MONTANA FYRE

Forest Falls (College Hockey Romance)

Wager

Flight

Fight

Betray

Frost Industries (Dark Mafia Romance)

When it Raynes

Dead of Wynter

Fall of Snow

Before the Storm

Tainted Love (Dark Romance)

Severed Ties

Forbidden Pleasures (Dark Romance)

Trust in the Fallen